The Zahir

ALSO BY PAULO COELHO

The Alchemist

The Pilgrimage

The Valkyries

By the River Piedra, I Sat Down and Wept

The Fifth Mountain

Veronika Decides to Die

The Devil and Miss Prym

Manual of the Warrior of Light

Eleven Minutes

The Zahir

PAULO COELHO

Translated from the Portuguese

by Margaret Jull Costa

HarperCollinsPublishers

Paulo Coelho's website address is **www.paulocoelho.com**

HarperCollinsPublishers

First published in English in the UK in 2005
by HarperCollinsPublishers
First published in Australia in 2005
This edition published in Austrlaia in 2006
by HarperCollinsPublishers Australia Pty Limited
ABN 36 009 913 517
www.harpercollins.com.au

This edition published by arrangement with Sant Jordi Asociados,
Barcelona, Spain. All rights reserved.

HarperCollinsPublishers
25 Ryde Road, Pymble, Sydney, NSW 2073, Australia
31 View Road, Glenfield, Auckland 10, New Zealand
77–85 Fulham Palace Road, London, W6 8JB, United Kingdom
2 Bloor Street East, 20th floor, Toronto, Ontario M4W 1A8, Canada
10 East 53rd Street, New York NY 10022, USA

ISBN 978 0 7322 8449 7
ISBN 0 7322 8449 X

Cover photograph © Jack Ambrose, Getty Images
Cover design James Annal
Typeset in 10.5 on 16 Sabon by Kirby Jones
Printed and bound in Australia by Griffin Press.

50gsm Bulky News used by HarperCollinsPublishers is a natural,
recyclable product made from wood grown in sustainable plantation
forests. The manufacturing processes conform to the environmental
regulations in the country of origin, New Zealand.

O Mary, conceived without sin,

pray for us who turn to you.

Amen

What man of you, having an hundred sheep,

if he lose one of them, doth not leave the ninety

and nine in the wilderness, and go after that

which is lost, until he find it?

Luke 15:4

Ithaca

When you set out on your journey to Ithaca,
pray that the road is long,
full of adventure, full of knowledge.
The Lestrygonians and the Cyclops,
the angry Poseidon – do not fear them:
You will never find such as these on your path
if your thoughts remain lofty, if a fine
emotion touches your spirit and your body.
The Lestrygonians and the Cyclops,
the fierce Poseidon you will never encounter,
if you do not carry them within your soul,
if your heart does not set them up before you.

Pray that the road is long.
That the summer mornings are many, when,
with such pleasure, with such joy
you will enter ports seen for the first time;
stop at Phoenician markets,
and purchase fine merchandise,
mother-of-pearl and coral, amber and ebony,

and sensual perfumes of all kinds,
as many sensual perfumes as you can;
visit many Egyptian cities,
to learn and learn from scholars.
Always keep Ithaca in your mind.
To arrive there is your ultimate goal.
But do not hurry the voyage at all.
It is better to let it last for many years;
and to anchor at the island when you are old,
rich with all you have gained on the way,
not expecting that Ithaca will offer you riches.
Ithaca has given you the beautiful voyage.
Without her you would never have set out on the road.
She has nothing more to give you.

And if you find her poor, Ithaca has not deceived you.
Wise as you have become, with so much experience,
you must already have understood what Ithacas mean.

Constantine Cavafy (1863–1933),
translated by Rae Dalven

Dedication

In the car, I mentioned that I had finished the first draft of my book. Later, as we set out together to climb a mountain in the Pyrenees which we both consider to be sacred and where we have already shared some extraordinary moments, I asked if she wanted to know the main theme of the book or its title; she would love to, she said, but, out of respect for my work, she had, until then, asked nothing, she had simply felt glad – very glad.

So I told her the title and the main theme. We continued walking in silence and, on the way back, we heard a noise; the wind was getting up, passing above the leafless trees and coming down towards us, causing the mountain once more to reveal its magic and its power.

Suddenly the snow began to fall. I stopped and stood contemplating that moment: the snowflakes falling, the grey sky, the forest, the woman by my side. The woman who has always been by my side.

I felt like telling her then, but decided to let her find out when she read these pages for the first time. This book is dedicated to you, Christina, my wife.

The author

According to the writer Jorge Luis Borges, the idea of the Zahir comes from Islamic tradition and is thought to have arisen at some point in the eighteenth century. *Zahir*, in Arabic, means visible, present, incapable of going unnoticed. It is someone or something which, once we have come into contact with them or it, gradually occupies our every thought, until we can think of nothing else. This can be considered either a state of holiness or of madness.

Faubourg Saint-Pères,
Encyclopaedia of the Fantastic (1953)

I AM A

FREE MAN

Her name is Esther; she is a war correspondent who has just returned from Iraq because of the imminent invasion of that country; she is thirty years old, married, without children. He is an unidentified male, between twenty-three and twenty-five years old, with dark, Mongolian features. The two were last seen in a café in Rue Faubourg St-Honoré.

The police were told that they had met before, although no one knew how often: Esther had always said that the man – who concealed his true identity behind the name Mikhail – was someone very important, although she had never explained whether he was important for her career as a journalist or for her as a woman.

The police began a formal investigation. Various theories were put forward – kidnapping, blackmail, a kidnapping that had ended in murder – none of which were beyond the bounds of possibility given that, in her search for information, her work brought her into frequent contact with people who had links with terrorist cells. They discovered that, in the weeks prior to her disappearance, regular sums of money had been withdrawn from her bank account: those in charge of the investigation felt that these could have been payments

3

made for information. She had taken no change of clothes with her, but, oddly enough, her passport was nowhere to be found.

He is a stranger, very young, with no police record, with no clue as to his identity.

She is Esther, thirty years old, the winner of two international prizes for journalism, and married.

My wife.

I immediately come under suspicion and am detained because I refuse to say where I was on the day she disappeared. However, a prison officer has just opened the door of my cell, saying that I'm a free man.

And why am I a free man? Because nowadays, everyone knows everything about everyone; you just have to ask and the information is there: where you've used your credit card, where you spend your time, who you've slept with. In my case, it was even easier: a woman, another journalist, a friend of my wife, and divorced – which is why she doesn't mind revealing that she slept with me – came forward as a witness in my favour when she heard that I had been detained. She provided concrete proof that I was with her on the day and the night of Esther's disappearance.

I talk to the chief inspector, who returns my belongings and offers his apologies, adding that my rapid detention was entirely within the law, and that I have no grounds on which to accuse or sue the State. I say that I haven't the slightest intention of doing either of those things, that I am perfectly aware that we are all under constant suspicion and under twenty-four-hour surveillance, even when we have committed no crime.

'You're free to go,' he says, echoing the words of the prison officer.

I ask: Isn't it possible that something really has happened to my wife? She had said to me once that – understandably given her vast network of contacts in the terrorist underworld – she occasionally got the feeling she was being followed.

The inspector changes the subject. I insist, but he says nothing.

I ask if she would be able to travel on her passport, and he says, of course, since she has committed no crime. Why shouldn't she leave and enter the country freely?

'So she may no longer be in France?'

'Do you think she left you because of that woman you've been sleeping with?'

That's none of your business, I reply. The inspector pauses for a second and grows serious; he says that I was arrested as part of routine procedure, but that he is nevertheless very sorry about my wife's disappearance: He is married himself and although he doesn't like my books (So he isn't as ignorant as he looks! He knows who I am!), he can put himself in my shoes and imagine what I must be going through.

I ask him what I should do next. He gives me his card and asks me to get in touch if I hear anything. I've watched this scene in dozens of films, and I'm not convinced; inspectors always know more than they say they do.

He asks me if I have ever met the person who was with Esther the last time she was seen alive. I say that I knew his code name, but didn't know him personally.

He asks if we have any domestic problems. I say that we've been together for ten years and have the same problems most married couples have – nothing more.

He asks, delicately, if we have discussed divorce recently, or if my wife was considering leaving me. I tell him we have never even considered the possibility, and say again that 'like all couples' we have our occasional disagreements.

Frequent or only occasional?

Occasional, I say.

He asks still more delicately if she suspected that I was having an affair with her friend. I tell him that it was the first – and last – time that her friend and I had slept together. It wasn't an affair; it came about simply because we had nothing else to do. It had been a bit of a dull day, neither of us had any pressing engagements after lunch, and the game of seduction always adds a little zest to life, which is why we ended up in bed together.

'You go to bed with someone just because it's a bit of a dull day?'

I consider telling him that such matters hardly form part of his investigations, but I need his help, or might need it later on – there is, after all, that invisible institution called the Favour Bank, which I have always found so very useful.

'Sometimes, yes. There's nothing else very interesting to do, the woman is looking for excitement, I'm looking for adventure, and that's that. The next day, you both pretend that nothing happened, and life goes on.'

He thanks me, holds out his hand and says that in his world, things aren't quite like that. Naturally, boredom and tedium exist, as does the desire to go to bed with someone, but everything is much more controlled, and no one ever acts on their thoughts or desires.

'Perhaps artists have more freedom,' he remarks.

I say that I'm familiar with his world, but have no wish to enter into a comparison between our different views of society and people. I remain silent, awaiting his next move.

'Speaking of freedom,' he says, slightly disappointed at this writer's refusal to enter into a debate with a police officer, 'you're free to go. Now that I've met you, I'll read your books. I know I said I didn't like them, but the fact is I've never actually read one.'

This is not the first or the last time that I will hear these words. At least this whole episode has gained me another reader. I shake his hand and leave.

I'm free. I'm out of prison, my wife has disappeared in mysterious circumstances, I have no fixed timetable for work, I have no problem meeting new people, I'm rich, famous, and if Esther really has left me, I'll soon find someone to replace her. I'm free, independent.

But what is freedom?

I've spent a large part of my life enslaved to one thing or another, so I should know the meaning of the word. Ever since I was a child, I have fought to make freedom my most precious commodity. I fought with my parents, who wanted me to be an engineer, not a writer. I fought with the other boys at school, who immediately homed in on me as the butt of their cruel jokes, and only after much blood had flowed from my nose and from theirs, only after many afternoons when I had to hide my scars from my mother – because it was up to me not her to solve my problems – did I manage to show them that I could take a thrashing without bursting into tears. I fought to get a job to support myself, and went to work as a delivery man for a hardware store, so as to be free from that old line in family blackmail: 'We'll give you money, but you'll have to do this, this and this.'

I fought – although without success – for the girl I was in love with when I was an adolescent, and who loved me too; she left me in the end because her parents convinced her that I had no future.

I fought against the hostile world of journalism – my next job – where my first boss kept me hanging around for three whole hours and only deigned to take any notice of me when I started tearing up the book he was reading: he looked at me in surprise and saw that here was someone capable of persevering and confronting the enemy, essential qualities for a good reporter. I fought for the socialist ideal, went to prison, came out and went on fighting, feeling like a working-class hero – until, that is, I heard the Beatles and decided that rock music was much more fun than Marx. I fought for the love of my first, second, and third wives. I fought to find the courage to leave my first, second, and third wives, because the love I felt for them hadn't lasted, and I needed to move on, until I found the person who had been put in this world to find me – and she was none of those three.

I fought for the courage to leave my job on the newspaper and launch myself into the adventure of writing a book, knowing full well that no one in my country could make a living as a writer. I gave up after a year, after writing more than a thousand pages – pages of such genius that even I couldn't understand them.

While I was fighting, I heard other people speaking in the name of freedom, and the more they defended this unique right, the more enslaved they seemed to be to their parents' wishes, to a marriage in which they had promised to stay with the other person 'for the rest of their lives', to the bathroom scales, to their diet, to half-finished projects, to lovers to whom they were incapable of saying 'No' or 'It's over', to weekends when they were obliged to have lunch with people they didn't even like. Slaves to luxury, to the appearance of luxury, to the appearance of the appearance of luxury. Slaves to a life they had not chosen, but which they had decided to live because someone had managed to convince them that it was all for the best. And so their identical days and nights passed, days and nights in which adventure was just a word in a book or an image on the television that was always on, and whenever a door opened, they would say:

'I'm not interested. I'm not in the mood.'

How could they possibly know if they were in the mood or not if they had never tried? But there was no point in asking; the truth was they were afraid of any change that would upset the world they had grown used to.

The inspector says I'm free. I'm free now and I was free in prison too, because freedom continues to be the thing I prize most in the world. Of course, this has led me to drink wines I did not like, to do things I should not have done and which I will not do again; it has left scars on my body and on my soul, it has meant hurting certain people, although I have since asked their forgiveness, when I realised that I could do absolutely anything except force another person to follow me in my madness, in my lust for life. I don't regret the painful times; I bear my scars as if they were medals. I know that freedom has a high price, as high as that of slavery; the only difference is that you pay with pleasure and a smile, even when that smile is dimmed by tears.

I leave the police station, and it's a beautiful day outside, a sunny Sunday that does not reflect my state of mind at all. My lawyer is waiting for me with a few consoling words and a bunch of flowers. He says that he's phoned round all the hospitals and morgues (the kind of thing you do when someone fails to return home), but has not as yet found Esther. He says that he managed to prevent journalists from finding out where I was being held. He says he needs to talk to me in order to draw up a legal strategy that will help me defend myself against any future accusation. I thank him for all his trouble; I know he's not really interested in drawing up a legal strategy, he just doesn't want to leave me alone, because he's not sure how I'll react (Will I get drunk and be arrested again? Will I cause a scandal? Will I try to kill myself?). I tell him I have some important business to sort out and that we both know perfectly well that I have no problem with the law. He insists, but I give him no choice – after all, I'm a free man.

Freedom. The freedom to be wretchedly alone.

I take a taxi to the centre of Paris and ask to be dropped near the Arc de Triomphe. I set off down the Champs-Elysées towards the Hotel Bristol, where Esther and I always used to meet for hot chocolate whenever one of us came back from some trip abroad. It was our coming-home ritual, a plunge back into the love that bound us together, even though life kept sending us off along ever more diverging paths.

I keep walking. People smile, children are pleased to have been given these few hours of spring in the middle of winter, the traffic flows freely, everything seems to be in order – except that none of them knows that I have just lost my wife; they don't even pretend not to know, they don't even care. Don't they realise the pain I'm in? They should all be feeling sad, sympathetic, supportive of a man whose soul is losing love as if it were losing blood; but they continue laughing, immersed in their miserable little lives that only happen at weekends.

What a ridiculous thought! Many of the people I pass must also have their souls in tatters, and I have no idea how or why they are suffering.

I go into a bar and buy some cigarettes; the person answers me in English. I go into a chemist's to buy a mint I particularly like, and the assistant speaks to me in English (both times I asked for the products in French). Before I reach the hotel, I am stopped by two boys just arrived from Toulouse who are looking for a particular shop; they have asked several other people, but no one understands what they say. What's going on? Have they changed languages on the Champs-Elysées in the twenty-four hours since I was arrested?

Tourism and money can perform miracles, but how come I haven't noticed this before? It has obviously been a long time since Esther and I met here to drink hot chocolate, even though we have each been away and come back several times during that period. There is always something more important. There is always some unpostponable appointment. Yes, my love, we'll have that hot chocolate next time, come back soon; I've got a really important interview today and won't be able to pick you up at the airport, take a taxi; my mobile's on, call me if there's anything urgent; otherwise, I'll see you tonight.

My mobile! I take it out of my pocket and immediately turn it on; it rings several times, and each time my heart turns over. On the tiny screen I see the names of the people who have been trying to get in touch with me, but reply to none of them. I hope for someone 'unidentified' to appear, because that would be her, since only about twenty people know my number and have sworn not to pass it on. It doesn't appear, only the numbers of friends or trusted colleagues. They must be eager to know what happened, they want to help (but how?), to ask if I need anything.

The telephone keeps ringing. Should I answer it? Should I arrange to meet up with some of these people?

I decide to remain alone until I've managed to work out what is going on.

I reach the Hotel Bristol, which Esther always described as one of the few hotels in Paris where customers are treated like guests rather than homeless people in search of shelter. I am greeted as if I were a friend of the family; I choose a table next to an exquisite clock; I listen to the piano and look out at the garden.

I need to be practical, to study the options; after all, life goes on. I am not the first nor will I be the last man whose wife has left him, but did it have to happen on a sunny day, with everyone in the street smiling and children singing, with the first signs of spring just beginning to show, the sun shining, and drivers stopping at pedestrian crossings?

I pick up a napkin. I'm going to get these ideas out of my head and put them down on paper. Let's leave sentiment to one side and see what I should do: .

Consider the possibility that she really has been kidnapped and that her life is in danger at this very moment, and that I, as her husband and constant companion, must, therefore, move heaven and earth to find her.

Response to this possibility: she took her passport with her. The police don't know this, but she also took several other personal items with her, amongst them a wallet containing images of various patron saints which she always carries with her whenever she goes abroad. She also withdrew money from her bank.

Conclusion: she was clearly preparing to leave.

Consider the possibility that she believed a promise someone gave her and it turned out to be a trap.

Response: she had often put herself in dangerous situations before; it was part of her job, but she always warned me when she did so, because I was the only person she could trust completely. She would tell me where she was going to be, who she was going to see (although, so as not to put me at risk, she usually used the person's *nom de guerre*), and what I should do if she did not return by a certain time.

Conclusion: she was not planning a meeting with one of her informants.

Consider the possibility that she has met another man.

Response: there is no response. Of all the hypotheses, this is the only one that makes any sense. And yet I can't accept it, I can't accept that she would leave like that, without giving me a reason. Both Esther and I have always prided ourselves on confronting all life's difficulties together. We suffered, but we never lied to each other, although it was part of the rules of the game not to mention any extramarital affairs. I was aware that she had changed a lot since meeting this fellow Mikhail, but did that justify ending a marriage that has lasted ten years?

Even if she had slept with him and fallen in love, wouldn't she weigh in the balance all the time that we had spent together and everything we had conquered before setting off on an adventure from which there was no turning back? She was free to travel whenever she wanted to, she lived surrounded by men, soldiers who hadn't seen a woman in ages, but I never asked any questions, and she never told me anything. We were both free, and we were proud of that.

But Esther had disappeared and left clues that were visible only to me, as if it were a secret message: I'm leaving.

Why?

Is that question worth answering?

No. Because hidden in the answer is my own inability to keep the woman I love by my side. Is it worth finding her and persuading her to come back? Begging and imploring her to give our marriage another chance?

That seems ridiculous: it would be better merely to suffer as I had in the past, when other people I loved had left me. It would be better just to lick my wounds, as I had also done in the past. For a while, I'll think obsessively about her, I'll become embittered, I'll bore my friends because all I ever talk about is my wife leaving me. I'll try to justify what happened, spend days and nights reviewing every moment spent by her side, I'll conclude that she was too hard on me, even though I always tried to do my best. I'll find other women. When I walk down the street, I'll keep seeing women who could be her. I'll suffer day and night, night and day. This could take weeks, months, possibly a year or more.

Until one morning, I'll wake up and find I'm thinking about something else, and then I'll know the worst is over. My heart might be bruised, but it will recover, and become capable of seeing the beauty of life once more. It's happened before, it will happen again, I'm sure. When someone leaves, it's because someone else is about to arrive – I'll find love again.

For a moment, I savour the idea of my new state: single and a millionaire. I can go out in broad daylight with whomever I want. I can behave at parties in a way I haven't behaved in years. The news will travel fast, and soon all kinds of women, the young and the not so young, the rich and the not as rich as they would like to be, the intelligent and those trained to say only what they think I would like to hear, will all come knocking at my door.

I want to believe that it is wonderful to be free. Free again. Ready to find my one true love, who is waiting for me and who will never allow me to experience such humiliation again.

I finish my hot chocolate and look at the clock; I know it is still too soon for me to be able to enjoy the agreeable feeling that I am once more part of humanity. For a few moments, I imagine that Esther is about to come in through that door, walk across the beautiful Persian carpets, sit down beside me and say nothing, just smoke a cigarette, look out at the courtyard garden and hold my hand. Half an hour passes, and for half an hour I believe in the story I have just created, until I realise that it is pure fantasy.

I decide not to go home. I go over to reception, ask for a room, a toothbrush and some deodorant. The hotel is full, but the manager fixes things for me: I end up with a lovely suite looking out at the Eiffel Tower, a terrace, the rooftops of Paris, the lights coming on one by one, the families getting together to have Sunday supper. And the feeling I had in the Champs-Elysées returns: the more beautiful everything is around me, the more wretched I feel.

No television. No supper. I sit on the terrace and look back over my life, a young man who dreamed of becoming a famous writer, and who suddenly saw that the reality was completely different – he writes in a language almost no one reads, in a country which is said to have almost no reading public. His family forces him to go to university (any university will do, my boy, just as long as you get a degree, otherwise you'll never be anyone). He rebels, travels the world during the hippie era, meets a singer, writes a few song lyrics, and is suddenly earning more money than his sister, who listened to what her parents said and decided to become a chemical engineer …

I write more songs, the singer goes from strength to strength; I buy a few apartments and fall out with the singer, but still have enough capital not to have to work for the next few years. I get married for the first time to an older woman, I learn a lot – how to make love, how to drive, how to speak English, how to lie in bed until late – but we split up because she considers me to be 'emotionally immature, and too ready to chase after any girl with big enough breasts'. I get married for a second and a third time to women I think will give me emotional stability: I get what I want, but discover that the stability I wanted is inseparable from a deep sense of tedium.

Two more divorces. Free again, but it's just a feeling; freedom is not the absence of commitments, but the ability to choose – and commit myself to – what is best for me.

I continue my search for love, I continue writing songs. When people ask me what I do, I say I'm a writer. When they say they only know my song lyrics, I say that's just part of my work. When they apologise and say they've never read any of my books, I explain that I'm working on a project – which is a lie. The truth is that I have money, I have contacts, but what I don't have is the courage to write a book. My dream is now realisable, but if I try and fail, I don't know what the rest of my life will be like; that's why it's better to live cherishing a dream than face the possibility that it might all come to nothing.

One day, a journalist comes to interview me. She wants to know what it's like to have my work known all over the country, but to be entirely unknown myself, since normally it's only the singer who appears in the media. She's pretty, intelligent, quiet. We meet again at a party, where there's no pressure of work, and I manage to get her into bed that same night. I fall in love, but she's not remotely interested. When I phone, she always says she's busy. The more she rejects me, the more interested I become, until, at last, I manage to persuade her to spend a weekend at my house in the country (I may have been the black sheep of the family, but sometimes rebellion pays off – I was the only one of my friends at that stage in our lives to have bought a house in the country).

We spend three days alone, contemplating the sea. I cook for her, and she tells me stories about her work and ends up falling in love with me. We come back to the city, she starts sleeping at my apartment on a regular basis. One morning, she leaves earlier than usual and returns with her typewriter; from then on, without anything being said, my home becomes her home too.

The same conflicts I had with my previous wives begin to surface: women are always looking for stability and fidelity, while I'm looking for adventure and the unknown. This time, though, the relationship lasts longer. Nevertheless, two years on, I decide it's time for Esther to take her typewriter back to her own apartment, along with everything else she brought with her.

'It's not going to work.'

'But you love me and I love you, isn't that right?'

'I don't know. If you're asking me if I like your company, the answer is yes. If, on the other hand, you're asking me if I could live without you, the answer is also yes.'

'I'm glad I wasn't born a man. I'm very content with my female condition. All you expect of us women is that we can cook well. Men on the other hand are expected to be able to do everything – they've got to be able to keep a home afloat, make love, take care of the children, bring in the money and be successful.'

'That's not it either: I'm very happy with myself. I enjoy your company, but I just don't think it's going to work.'

'You enjoy my company, but hate being by yourself. You're always looking for adventure in order to forget more important things. You always want to feel the adrenaline flowing in your veins and you forget that the only thing that should be flowing through them is blood.'

'I'm not running away from important things. Give me an example of something important.'

'Writing a book.'

'I can do that any time.'

'Go on then, do it. Then, if you like, we can go our separate ways.'

I find her comment absurd; I can write a book whenever I want to; I know publishers, journalists, all of whom owe me favours. Esther is just a woman who's afraid of losing me, she's inventing things. I tell her it's over, our relationship is at an end, it isn't a matter of what she thinks would make me happy, it's about love.

What is love? she asks. I spend half an hour explaining and realise that I can't come up with a good definition.

She says that, since I don't know how to define love, I should try and write a book.

I say that the two things are completely unrelated. I'm going to leave the apartment that very day; she can stay there for as long as she likes. I'll go and stay in a hotel until she has found somewhere else to live. She says that's fine by her, I can leave now, the apartment will be free within the month – she'll start looking for a new place tomorrow. I pack my bags, and she goes and reads a book. I say it's getting late, I'll leave tomorrow. She says I should leave at once because, tomorrow, I won't feel as strong or as determined. I ask her if she's trying to get rid of me. She laughs and says I was the one who wanted to end the relationship. We go to bed, and the following day, the desire to leave is not as urgent, and I decide I need to think things through. Esther, however, says the matter isn't over yet: this scenario will simply keep recurring as long as I refuse to risk everything for what I believe to be my real reason for living; in the end, she'll become unhappy and will leave me. Except that, if *she* left, she would do so immediately and burn any bridges that would allow her to come back. I ask her what she means. She'd get another boyfriend, she says, fall in love.

She goes off to her work at the newspaper, and I decide to take a day's leave (apart from writing lyrics, I'm also working for a recording company). I sit down at the typewriter. I get up again, read the papers, reply to some urgent letters and, when I've done that, start replying to non-urgent letters. I make a list of things I need to do, I listen to music, I take a walk around the block, chat to the baker, come home, and suddenly the whole day has gone and I still haven't managed to type a single sentence. I decide that I hate Esther, that she's forcing me to do things I don't want to do.

When she gets home, she doesn't ask me anything, but I admit that I haven't managed to do any writing. She says that I have the same look in my eye as I did yesterday.

The following day I go to work, but that evening I again go over to the desk on which the typewriter is sitting. I read, watch television, listen to music, go back to the machine, and so two months pass, with me accumulating pages and more pages of 'first sentences', but never managing to finish a paragraph.

I come up with every possible excuse – no one reads in this country, I haven't worked out a plot, or I've got a fantastic plot, but I'm still looking for the right way to develop it. Besides, I'm really busy writing an article or a song lyric. Another two months pass, and one day, she comes home bearing a plane ticket.

'Enough,' she says. 'Stop pretending that you're busy, that you're weighed down by responsibilities, that the world needs you to do what you're doing, and just go travelling for a while.' I can always become the editor of the newspaper where I publish a few articles, I can always become the president of the recording company for whom I write lyrics, and where I work simply because they don't want me to write lyrics for their competitors. I can always come back to do what I'm doing now, but my dream can't wait. Either I accept it or I forget it.

Where is the ticket for?

Spain.

I'm shocked. Air tickets are expensive; besides, I can't go away now, I've got a career ahead of me, and I need to look after it. I'll lose out on a lot of potential music partnerships; the problem isn't me, it's our marriage. If I really wanted to write a book, no one would be able to stop me.

'You can, you want to, but you don't,' she says. 'Your problem isn't me, but you, so it would be best if you spent some time alone.'

She shows me a map. I must go to Madrid, where I'll catch a bus up to the Pyrenees, on the border with France. That's where a medieval pilgrimage route begins: the road to Santiago. I have to walk the whole way. She'll be waiting for me at the other end and then she'll accept anything I say: that I don't love her any more, that I still

23

haven't lived enough to create a literary work, that I don't even want to think about being a writer, that it was nothing but an adolescent dream.

This is madness! The woman I've been living with for two long years – a real eternity in relationship terms – is making decisions about my life, forcing me to give up my work and expecting me to walk across an entire country! It's so crazy that I decide to take it seriously. I get drunk several nights running, with her beside me getting equally drunk – even though she hates drinking. I get aggressive; I say she's jealous of my independence, that the only reason this whole mad idea was born is because I said I wanted to leave her. She says that it all started when I was still at school and dreaming of becoming a writer – no more putting things off; if I don't confront myself now, I'll spend the rest of my life getting married and divorced, telling cute anecdotes about my past and going steadily downhill.

Obviously, I can't admit she's right, but I know she's telling the truth. And the more aware I am of this, the more aggressive I become. She accepts my aggression without complaint; she merely reminds me that the departure date is getting closer.

One night, shortly before that date, she refuses to make love. I smoke a whole joint of marihuana, drink two bottles of wine and pass out in the middle of the living room. When I come to, I realise that I have reached the bottom of the pit, and now all that remains is for me to clamber back up to the top. And I, who so pride myself on my courage, see how cowardly, mean and unadventurous I am being with my own life. That morning, I wake her with a kiss and tell her that I'll do as she suggests.

I set off and for thirty-eight days I follow the road to Santiago. When I arrive, I understand that my real journey only starts there. I decide to settle in Madrid and live off my royalties, to allow an ocean to separate me from Esther's body, even though we are still officially together and often talk on the phone. It's very comfortable being married and knowing that I can always return to her arms, meanwhile enjoying all the independence in the world.

I fall in love with a Catalan scientist, with an Argentine woman who makes jewellery, and with a young woman who sings in the metro. The royalties from my lyrics keep rolling in and are enough for me to live comfortably without having to work and with plenty of time to do everything, even … write a book.

The book can always wait until tomorrow, though, because the mayor of Madrid has decreed that the city should be one long party and has come up with an interesting slogan – 'Madrid is killing me' – and urges us all to visit several bars each night, coining the phrase *la movida madrileña* ('the Madrid scene'), which is something I cannot possibly put off until tomorrow; everything is such fun; the days are short and the nights are long.

One day, Esther phones to say that she's coming to see me: according to her, we need to sort out our situation once and for all. She has booked her ticket for the following week, which gives me just enough time to organise a series of excuses. ('I'm going to Portugal, but I'll be back in a month,' I tell the blonde girl who used to sing in the metro and who now sleeps in the rented apartment where I live and with whom I go out every night to enjoy *la movida madrileña*.) I tidy the apartment, expunge any trace of a female presence, and ask my friends not to breathe a word, because my wife is coming to stay for a month.

Esther gets off the plane sporting a hideous, unrecognisable haircut. We travel to the interior of Spain, discover little towns that mean a great deal for one night, but which, if I went back there today, I wouldn't even be able to find. We go to bullfights, flamenco shows, and I am the best husband in the world, because I want her to go home feeling that I still love her. I don't know why I want to give this impression, perhaps because, deep down, I know that the Madrid dream will eventually end.

I complain about her haircut and she changes it and is pretty again. There are only ten days left of her holiday and I want her to go home feeling happy and to leave me alone to enjoy this Madrid that is killing me, the discotheques that open at ten in the morning, the bullfights, the endless conversations about the same old topics, the alcohol, the women, more bullfights, more alcohol, more women, and absolutely no timetable.

One Sunday, while we are walking to a bar that serves food all night, she brings up the forbidden topic: the book I said I was writing. I drink a whole bottle of sherry, kick any metal doors we pass on the way back, verbally abuse other people in the street, ask why she bothered travelling all this way if her one aim was to make my life a hell and to destroy my happiness. She says nothing, but we both know that our relationship has reached its limits. I have a dreamless night's sleep, and the following morning, having complained to the building manager about the phone that doesn't work, having told off the cleaning woman because she hasn't changed the bedclothes for a week, having taken a long, long bath to get rid of the hangover from the night before, I sit down at my typewriter, just to show Esther that I am trying, honestly trying, to work.

And suddenly, the miracle happens. I look across at the woman who has just made some coffee and is now reading the newspaper, whose eyes look tired and desperate, who is her usual silent self, who does not always show her affection in gestures, the woman who made me say 'yes' when I wanted to say 'no', who forced me to fight for what she, quite rightly, believed was my reason for living, who let me set off alone because her love for me was greater even than her love for herself, who made me go in search of my dream; and, suddenly, seeing that small, quiet woman, whose eyes said more than any words, who was often terrified inside, but always courageous in her actions, who could love someone without humbling herself and who never ever apologised for fighting for her man, suddenly, my fingers press down on the keys.

The first sentence emerges. Then the second.

I spend two days without eating, I sleep the bare minimum, the words seem to spring from some unknown place, as they did when I used to write lyrics, in the days when, after much arguing and much meaningless conversation, my musical partner and I would know that 'it' was there, ready, and it was time to set 'it' down in words and notes. This time, I know that 'it' comes from Esther's heart; my love is reborn, I write the book because she exists, because she has survived all the difficult times without complaint, without ever once seeing herself as victim. I start by describing the experience that has affected me most profoundly in those last few years – the road to Santiago.

As I write, I realise that the way I see the world is going through a series of major changes. For many years, I studied and practised magic, alchemy and the occult; I was fascinated by the idea of a small group of people being in possession of an immense power that could in no way be shared with the rest of humanity, because it would be far too dangerous to allow such vast potential to fall into inexperienced hands. I was a member of secret societies, I became involved in exotic sects, I bought obscure, extremely expensive books, spent an enormous amount of time performing rituals and invocations. I was always joining and leaving different groups and fraternities, always thinking that I had finally met the person who could reveal to me the mysteries of the invisible world, but, in the end, was always disappointed to discover that most of these people – however well-intentioned – were merely following this or that dogma and tended to be fanatics, because fanaticism is the only way to put an end to the doubts that constantly trouble the human soul.

I discovered that many of the rituals did actually work, but I discovered, too, that those who declared themselves to be the masters and holders of the secrets of life, who claimed to know techniques that gave them the ability to achieve their every desire, had completely lost touch with the teachings of the ancients. Following the road to Santiago, coming into contact with ordinary people, discovering that the Universe spoke its own language of 'signs' and that, in order to understand this language, we had only to look with an open mind at what was going on around us – all this made me wonder if the occult really was the one doorway into those mysteries. In my book about the road to Santiago, I discuss other possible ways of growing and end with this thought: 'All you have to do is to pay attention; lessons always arrive when you are ready, and if you can read the signs, you will learn everything you need to know in order to take the next step.'

We humans have two great problems: the first is knowing when to begin, the second is knowing when to stop.

A week later, I begin the first, second and third draft. Madrid is no longer killing me, it is time to go back home. I feel that one cycle has ended and that I urgently need to begin another. I say goodbye to the city as I have always said goodbye in life: thinking that I might change my mind and come back one day.

I return to my own country with Esther, convinced that it might be time to get another job, but until I do (and I don't because I don't need to) I continue revising the book. I can't believe that anyone will have much interest in the experiences of one man following a romantic but difficult route across Spain.

Four months later, when I am busy on my tenth draft, I discover that both the typescript and Esther have gone. Just as I'm about to go mad with anxiety, she returns with a receipt from the post office – she has sent it off to an old boyfriend of hers, who now runs a small publishing house.

The ex-boyfriend publishes the book. There is not a word about it in the press, but a few people buy it. They recommend it to other people, who also buy it and recommend it to others. Six months later, the first edition has sold out. A year later, there have been three more print runs and I am beginning to earn money from the one thing I never dreamed I would – from literature.

I don't know how long this dream will continue, but I decide to live each moment as if it were the last. And I see that this success opens the door I have so long wanted to open: other publishers are keen to publish my next book.

Obviously, I can't follow the road to Santiago every year, so what am I going to write about next? Will I have to endure the same rigmarole of sitting down in front of the typewriter and then finding myself doing everything but write sentences and paragraphs? It's important that I continue to share my vision of the world and to describe my experiences of life. I try for a few days and for many nights, and decide that it's impossible. Then, one evening, I happen upon (happen upon?) an interesting story in *The Thousand and One Nights*; in it I find the symbol of my own path, something that helps me to understand who I am and why I took so long to make the decision that was always there waiting for me. I use that story as the basis for another story about a shepherd who goes in search of his dream, a treasure hidden in the pyramids of Egypt. I speak of the love that lies waiting for him there, as Esther had waited for me while I walked round and round in circles.

I am no longer someone dreaming of becoming something: I am. I am the shepherd crossing the desert, but where is the alchemist who helps him to carry on? When I finish this novel, I don't entirely understand what I have written: it is like a fairy tale for grown-ups, and grown-ups are more interested in war, sex, or stories about power. Nevertheless, the publisher accepts it, the book is published, and my readers once again take it into the bestseller lists.

Three years later, my marriage is in excellent shape; I am doing what I always wanted to do; the first translation appears, then the second, and success – slowly but surely – takes my work to the four corners of the earth.

I decide to move to Paris because of its cafés, its writers and its cultural life. I discover that none of this exists any more: the cafés are full of tourists and photographs of the people who made those places famous. Most of the writers there are more concerned with style than content; they strive to be original, but succeed only in being dull. They are locked in their own little world, and I learn an interesting French expression: *renvoyer l'ascenseur*, meaning literally 'to send the lift back up', but used metaphorically to mean 'to return a favour'. In practice, this means that I say nice things about your book, you say nice things about mine, and thus we create a whole new cultural life, a revolution, an apparently new philosophy; we suffer because no one understands us, but then that's what happened with all the geniuses of the past: being misunderstood by one's contemporaries is surely just part and parcel of being a great artist.

'They send the lift back up', and, at first, such writers have some success: people don't want to run the risk of openly criticising something they don't understand, but they soon realise they are being conned and stop believing what the critics say.

The Internet and its simple language are all that it takes to change the world. A parallel world emerges in Paris: new writers struggle to make their words and their souls understood. I join these new writers in cafés that no one has heard of, because neither the writers nor the cafés are as yet famous. I develop my style alone and I learn from a publisher all I need to know about mutual support.

'What is this Favour Bank?'

'You know. Everyone knows.'

'Possibly, but I still haven't quite grasped what you're saying.'

'It was an American writer who first mentioned it. It's the most powerful bank in the world, and you'll find it in every sphere of life.'

'Yes, but I come from a country without a literary tradition. What favours could I do for anyone?'

'That doesn't matter in the least. Let me give you an example: I know that you're an up-and-coming writer and that, one day, you'll be very influential. I know this because, like you, I too was once ambitious, independent, honest. I no longer have the energy I once had, but I want to help you because I can't or don't want to grind to a halt just yet. I'm not dreaming about retirement, I'm still dreaming about the fascinating struggle that is life, power, and glory.

'I start making deposits in your account – not cash deposits, you understand, but contacts. I introduce you to such and such a person, I arrange certain deals, as long as they're legal. You know that you owe me something, but I never ask you for anything.'

'And then one day …'

'Exactly. One day, I'll ask you for a favour and you could, of course, say "No", but you're conscious of being in my debt. You do what I ask, I continue to help you, and other people see that you're a decent, loyal sort of person and so they too make deposits in your account – always in the form of contacts, because this world is made up of contacts and nothing else. They too will one day ask you for a favour, and you will respect and help the people who have helped you, and, in time, you'll have spread your net worldwide, you'll know everyone you need to know and your influence will keep on growing.'

'I could refuse to do what you ask me to do.'

'You could. The Favour Bank is a risky investment, just like any other bank. You refuse to grant the favour I asked you, in the belief that I helped you because you deserved to be helped, because you're the best and everyone should automatically recognise your talent. Fine, I say thank you very much and ask someone else into whose account I've also made various deposits; but from then on, everyone knows, without me having to say a word, that you are not to be trusted.

'You'll grow only half as much as you could have grown, and certainly not as much as you would have liked to. At a certain point, your life will begin to decline, you got halfway, but not all the way, you are half-happy and half-sad, neither frustrated nor fulfilled. You're neither cold nor hot, you're lukewarm, and as an evangelist in some holy book says: "Lukewarm things are not pleasing to the palate."'

The publisher places a lot of deposits – or contacts – into my account at the Favour Bank. I learn, I suffer, my books are translated into French, and, in the tradition of that country, the stranger is welcomed. Not only that, the stranger is an enormous success! Ten years on, I have a large apartment with a view over the Seine, I am loved by my readers and loathed by the critics (who adored me until I sold my first 100,000 copies, but, from that moment on, I ceased to be 'a misunderstood genius'). I always repay promptly any deposits made and soon I too am a lender – of contacts. My influence grows. I learn to ask for favours and to do the favours others ask of me.

Esther gets permission to work as a journalist. Apart from the normal conflicts in any marriage, I am contented. I understand for the first time that all the frustrations I felt about previous love affairs and marriages had nothing to do with the women involved, but with my own bitterness. Esther, however, was the only woman who understood one very simple thing: in order to be able to find her, I first had to find myself. We have been together for eight years; I believe she is the love of my life, and although I do occasionally (or, to be honest, frequently) fall in love with other women who cross my path, I never consider the possibility of divorce. I never ask her if she knows about my extramarital affairs. She never makes any comment on the subject.

That is why I am astonished when, as we are leaving a cinema, she tells me that she has asked her magazine if she can file a report on a civil war in Africa.

'What are you saying?'

'That I want to be a war correspondent.'

'You're mad. You don't need to do that. You're already doing the work you want to do now. You earn good money – not that you need that money to live on. You have all the contacts you need in the Favour Bank. You have talent and you've earned your colleagues' respect.'

'All right then, let's just say I need to be alone.'

'Because of me?'

'We've built our lives together. I love my man and he loves me, even though he's not always the most faithful of husbands.'

'You've never said anything about that before.'

'Because it doesn't matter to me. I mean, what is fidelity? The feeling that I possess a body and a soul that aren't mine? Do you imagine I haven't been to bed with other men during all these years we've been together?'

'I don't care and I don't want to know.'

'Well, neither do I.'

'So, what's all this about wanting to write about a war in some godforsaken part of the world?'

'Like I said, I need to.'

'Haven't you got everything you need?'

'I have everything a woman could want.'

'What's wrong with your life then?'

'Precisely that. I have everything, but I'm not happy. And I'm not the only one either; over the years, I've met and interviewed all kinds of people: the rich, the poor, the powerful, and those who just make do. I've seen the same infinite bitterness in everyone's eyes, a sadness which people weren't always prepared to acknowledge, but which, regardless of what they were telling me, was nevertheless there. Are you listening?'

'Yes, I'm listening. I was just thinking. So, according to you, no one is happy?'

'Some people appear to be happy, but they simply don't give the matter much thought. Others make plans: I'm going to have a husband, a home, two children, a house in the country. As long as they're busy doing that, they're like bulls looking for the bullfighter: they react instinctively, they blunder on, with no idea where the target is. They get their car, sometimes they even get a Ferrari, and they think that's the meaning of life, and they never question it. Yet their eyes betray the sadness that even they don't know they carry in their soul. Are you happy?'

'I don't know.'

'I don't know if everyone is unhappy. I know they're all busy: working overtime, worrying about their children, their husband, their career, their degree, what they're going to do tomorrow, what they need to buy, what they need to have in order not to feel inferior, etc. Very few people actually say to me: "I'm unhappy." Most say: "I'm fine, I've got everything I ever wanted." Then I ask: "What makes you happy?" Answer: "I've got everything a person could possibly want – a family, a home, work, good health." I ask again: "Have you ever stopped to wonder if that's all there is to life?" Answer: "Yes, that's all there is." I insist: "So the meaning of life is work, family, children who will grow up and leave you, a wife or husband who will become more like a friend than a real lover. And, of course, one day your work will end too. What will you do when that happens?" Answer: there is no answer. They change the subject.'

'No, what they say is: "When the children have grown up, when my husband – or my wife – has become more my friend than my passionate lover, when I retire, then I'll have time to do what I always wanted to do: travel." Question: "But didn't you say you were happy now? Aren't you already doing what you always wanted to do?" Then they say they're very busy and change the subject.'

'If I insist, they always do come up with something they're lacking. The businessman hasn't yet closed the deal he wanted, the housewife would like to have more independence and more money, the boy who's in love is afraid of losing his girlfriend, the new graduate wonders if he chose his career or if it was chosen for him, the dentist wanted to be a singer, the singer wanted to be a politician, the politician wanted to be a writer, the writer wanted to be a farmer. And even when I did meet someone who was doing what he had chosen to do, that person's soul was still in torment. He hadn't found peace yet either. So I'll ask you again: "Are you happy?"'

'No. I have the woman I love, the career I always dreamed of having, the kind of freedom that is the envy of all my friends, the travel, the honours, the praise. But there's something ...'

'What?'

'I have the idea that, if I stopped, life would become meaningless.'

'You can't just relax, look at Paris, take my hand and say: I've got what I wanted, now let's enjoy what life remains to us.'

'I can look at Paris, take your hand, but I can't say those words.'

'I bet you everyone walking along this street now is feeling the same thing. The elegant woman who just passed us spends her days trying to hold back time, always checking the scales, because she thinks that is what love depends on. Look across the road: a couple with two children. They feel intensely happy when they're out with their children, but, at the same time, their subconscious keeps them in a constant state of terror: they think of the job they might lose, the disease they might catch, the health insurance that might not come up with the goods, one of the children getting run over. And in trying to distract themselves, they try as well to find a way of getting free of those tragedies, of protecting themselves from the world.'

'And the beggar on the corner?'

'I don't know about him. I've never spoken to a beggar. He's certainly the picture of misery, but his eyes, like the eyes of any beggar, seem to be hiding something. His sadness is so obvious that I can't quite believe in it.'

'What's missing?'

'I haven't a clue. I look at the celebrity magazines with everyone smiling and contented, but since I am myself married to a celebrity, I know that it isn't quite like that: everyone is laughing and having fun at that moment, in that photo, but later that night, or in the morning, the story is always quite different. "What do I have to do in order to continue appearing in this magazine?" "How can I disguise the fact that I no longer have enough money to support my luxurious lifestyle?" "How can I best manipulate my luxurious lifestyle to make it seem even more luxurious than anyone else's?" "The actress in the photo with me and with whom I'm smiling and celebrating could steal a part from me tomorrow!" "Am I better dressed than she is? Why are we smiling when we loathe each other?" "Why do we sell happiness to the readers of this magazine when we are profoundly unhappy ourselves, the slaves of fame.'''

'We're not the slaves of fame.'

'Don't get paranoid. I'm not talking about us.'

'What do you think is going on, then?'

'Years ago, I read a book that told an interesting story. Just suppose that Hitler had won the war, wiped out all the Jews and convinced his people that there really was such a thing as a master race. The history books start to be changed, and, a hundred years later, his successors manage to wipe out all the Indians. Three hundred years later and the Blacks have been eliminated too. It takes five hundred years, but, finally, the all-powerful war machine succeeds in erasing the oriental race from the face of the earth as well. The history books speak of remote battles waged against barbarians, but no one reads too closely, because it's of no importance.

Two thousand years after the birth of Nazism, in a bar in Tokyo, a city that has been inhabited for five centuries now by tall, blue-eyed people, Hans and Fritz are enjoying a beer. At one point, Hans looks at Fritz and asks: "Fritz, do you think it was always like this?"

"What?" asks Fritz.

"The world."

"Of course the world was always like this, isn't that what we were taught?"

"Of course, I don't know what made me ask such a stupid question," says Hans. They finish their beer, talk about other things and forget the question entirely.'

'You don't even need to go that far into the future, you just have to go back two thousand years. Can you see yourself worshipping a guillotine, a scaffold or an electric chair?'

'I know where you're heading – to that worst of all human tortures, the cross. I remember that Cicero referred to it as "an abominable punishment" that inflicted terrible suffering on the crucified person before he or she died. And yet, nowadays people wear it around their neck, hang it on their bedroom wall and have come to identify it as a religious symbol, forgetting that they are looking at an instrument of torture.'

'Two hundred and fifty years passed before someone decided that it was time to abolish the pagan festivals surrounding the winter solstice, the time when the sun is farthest from the earth. The apostles, and those who came after them, were too busy spreading Jesus' message to worry about the *natalis invict Solis*, the Mithraic festival of the birth of the sun, which occurred on 25 December. Then a bishop decided that these solstice festivals were a threat to the faith and that was that! Now we have masses, Nativity scenes, presents, sermons, plastic babies in wooden mangers, and the cast-iron conviction that Christ was born on that very day!'

'And then there's the Christmas tree. Do you know where that comes from?'

'No idea.'

'St Boniface decided to "christianise" a ritual intended to honour the god Odin when he was a child. Once a year, the Germanic tribes would place presents around an oak tree for the children to find. They thought this would bring joy to the pagan deity.'

'Going back to the story of Hans and Fritz: do you think that civilisation, human relations, our hopes, our conquests, are all just the product of some other garbled story?'

'When you wrote about the road to Santiago, you came to the same conclusion, didn't you? You used to believe that only a select few knew the meaning of magic symbols, but now you realise that we all know the meaning, it's just that we've forgotten it.'

'Knowing that doesn't make any difference. People do their best not to remember and not to accept the immense magical potential they possess, because that would upset their neat little universes.'

'But we all have the ability, don't we?'

'Absolutely, we just don't all have the courage to follow our dreams and to follow the signs. Perhaps that's where the sadness comes from.'

'I don't know. And I'm not saying that I'm unhappy all the time. I have fun, I love you, I adore my work. Yet now and then, I feel this profound sadness, occasionally mingled with feelings of guilt or fear; the feeling passes, but always comes back later on, and then passes off again. Like Hans, I ask that same question; when I can't answer it, I simply forget. I could go and help starving children, set up a foundation for street children, start trying to save people in the name of Jesus, do something that would give me the feeling I was being useful, but I don't want to.'

'So why do you want to go and cover this war?'

'Because I think that in time of war, men live life at the limit; after all, they could die the next day. Anyone living like that must act differently.'

'So you want to find an answer to Hans's question?'

'Yes, I do.'

Today, in this beautiful suite in the Hotel Bristol, with the Eiffel Tower glittering for five minutes every time the clock strikes the hour, with an empty bottle of wine beside me and my cigarettes fast running out, with people greeting me as if nothing very serious had happened, I ask myself: was it then, coming out of the cinema, that it all began? Should I have let her go off in search of that garbled story or should I have put my foot down and told her to forget the whole idea because she was my wife and I needed her with me, needed her support?

Nonsense. At the time, I knew, as I know now, that I had no option but to accept what she wanted. If I had said: 'Choose between me and becoming a war correspondent', I would have been betraying everything that Esther had done for me. I wasn't convinced by her declared aim – to go in search of 'a garbled story' – but I concluded that she needed a bit of freedom, to get out and about, to experience strong emotions. And what was wrong with that?

I accepted, not without first making it clear that this constituted a very large withdrawal from the Favour Bank (which, when I think about it now, seems a ludicrous thing to say). For two years, Esther followed various conflicts at close quarters, changing continents more often than she changed her shoes. Whenever she came back, I thought that this time she would give it up – it's just not possible to live for very long in a place where there's no decent food, no daily bath, and no cinemas or theatres. I asked her if she had found the answer to Hans's question, and she always told me that she was on the right track, and I had to be satisfied with that. Sometimes, she was away from home for months at a time; contrary to what it says in the 'official history of marriage' (I was starting to use her terminology), that distance only made our love grow stronger, and showed us how important we were to each other. Our relationship, which I thought had reached its ideal point when we moved to Paris, was getting better and better.

As I understand it, she first met Mikhail when she needed a translator to accompany her to some country in Central Asia. At first, she talked about him with great enthusiasm – he was a very sensitive person, someone who saw the world as it really was and not as we had been told it should be. He was five years younger than her, but had a quality that Esther described as 'magical'. I listened patiently and politely, as if I were really interested in that boy and his ideas, but the truth is I was far away, going over in my mind all the things I had to do, ideas for articles, answers to questions from journalists and publishers, strategies for how to seduce a particular woman who appeared to be interested in me, plans for future book promotions.

I don't know if Esther noticed this. I certainly failed to notice that Mikhail gradually disappeared from our conversations, then vanished completely. Esther's behaviour became increasingly eccentric: even when she was in Paris, she started going out several nights a week, telling me that she was researching an article on beggars.

I thought she must be having an affair. I agonised for a whole week and asked myself: should I tell her my doubts or just pretend that nothing is happening? I decided to ignore it, on the principle that 'what the eye doesn't see, the heart doesn't grieve over'. I was utterly convinced that there wasn't the slightest possibility of her leaving me; she had worked so hard to help me become the person I am, and it would be illogical to let all that go for some ephemeral affair.

If I had really been interested in Esther's world, I should at least have asked what had happened to her translator and his 'magical' sensibility. I should have been suspicious of that silence, that lack of information. I should have asked to go with her on one of those 'research trips' to visit beggars.

When she occasionally asked if I was interested in her work, my answer was always the same: 'Yes, I'm interested, but I don't want to interfere, I want you to be free to follow your dream in your chosen way, just as you helped me to do the same.'

This, of course, was tantamount to saying that I wasn't the slightest bit interested. But because people always believe what they want to believe, Esther seemed satisfied with my response.

The words spoken by the inspector when I was released from the police cell come back to me again: *You're a free man*. But what is freedom? Is it seeing that your husband isn't interested in what you are doing? Is it feeling alone and having no one with whom to share your innermost feelings, because the person you married is entirely focused on his own work, on his important, magnificent, difficult career?

I look at the Eiffel Tower: another hour has passed, and it is glittering again as if it were made of diamonds. I have no idea how often this has happened since I have been at the window.

I know that, in the name of the freedom of our marriage, I did not notice that Mikhail had disappeared from my wife's conversations, only to reappear in a bar and disappear again, this time taking her with him and leaving behind the famous, successful writer as prime suspect.

Or, worse still, as a man abandoned.

HAN'S

QUESTION

In Buenos Aires, the Zahir is a common 20-centavo coin; the letters N and T and the number 2 bear the marks of a knife or a letter-opener; 1929 is the date engraved on the reverse. (In Gujarat, at the end of the eighteenth century, the Zahir was a tiger; in Java, it was a blind man from the Surakarta mosque who was stoned by the faithful; in Persia, an astrolabe that Nadir Shah ordered to be thrown into the sea; in Mahdi's prisons, in around 1892, a small compass that had been touched by Rudolf Karl von Slatin ...)

A year later, I wake thinking about the story by Jorge Luis Borges, about something which, once touched or seen, can never be forgotten, and which gradually so fills our thoughts that we are driven to madness. My Zahir is not a romantic metaphor – a blind man, a compass, a tiger, or a coin.

It has a name, and her name is Esther.

Immediately after leaving prison, I appeared on the covers of various scandal sheets: they began by alleging a possible crime, but, in order to avoid ending up in court, they always concluded with the statement that I had been cleared (cleared? I hadn't even been accused!). They allowed a week to pass; they checked to see if the sales had been good (they had, because I was the kind of writer who was normally above suspicion, and everyone wanted to find out how it was possible for a man who writes about spirituality to have such a dark side). Then they returned to the attack, alleging that my wife had run away because of my many extramarital affairs: a German magazine even hinted at a possible relationship with a singer, twenty years my junior, who said she had met me in Oslo, in Norway (this was true, but the meeting had only taken place because of the Favour Bank – a friend of mine had asked me to go and had been with us throughout the only supper we had together). The singer said that there was nothing between us (so why put a photo of us on the cover?) and took the opportunity to announce that she was releasing a new album: she had used both the magazine and me, and I still don't know whether the failure of the album was a consequence of this kind of cheap publicity (the album wasn't bad, by the way – what ruined everything were the press releases).

The scandal over the famous writer did not last long; in Europe, and especially in France, infidelity is not only accepted, it is even secretly admired. And no one likes to read about the sort of thing that could so easily happen to them.

The topic disappeared from the front covers, but the hypotheses continued: she had been kidnapped, she had left home because of physical abuse (photo of a waiter saying that we often argued: I remember that I did, in fact, have an argument with Esther in a restaurant about her views on a South American writer, which were completely opposed to mine). A British tabloid alleged –

and luckily this had no serious repercussions – that my wife had gone into hiding with an Islamist terrorist organisation.

This world is so full of betrayals, divorces, murders, assassination attempts, that a month later the subject had been forgotten by the ordinary public. Years of experience had taught me that this kind of thing would never affect my faithful readership (it had happened before, when a journalist on an Argentinian television programme claimed that he had 'proof' that I had had a secret meeting in Chile with the future first lady of the country – but my books remained on the bestseller lists). As an American artist almost said: Sensationalism was only made to last fifteen minutes. My main concern was quite different: to reorganise my life, to find a new love, to go back to writing books, and to put away any memories of my wife in the little drawer that exists on the frontier between love and hate.

Or should I say memories of my ex-wife (I needed to get used to the term).

Part of what I had foreseen in that hotel room did come to pass. For a while, I barely left the apartment: I didn't know how to face my friends, how to look them in the eye and say simply: 'My wife has left me for a younger man.' When I did go out, no one asked me anything, but after a few glasses of wine I felt obliged to bring the subject up – as if I could read everyone's mind, as if I really believed that they had nothing more to occupy them than what was happening in my life, but that they were too polite or smug to say anything. Depending on my mood, Esther was either a saint who deserved better, or a treacherous, perfidious woman who had embroiled me in such a complicated situation that I had even been thought a criminal.

Friends, acquaintances, publishers, people I sat next to at the many gala dinners I was obliged to attend, listened with some curiosity at first. Gradually, though, I noticed that they tended to change the subject; they had been interested in the subject at some point, but it was no longer part of their current curiosities: they were more interested in talking about the actress who had been murdered by a singer or about the adolescent girl who had written a book about her affairs with well-known politicians. One day, in Madrid, I noticed that the number of guests at events and suppers was beginning to fall off. Although it may have been good for my soul to unburden myself of my feelings, to blame or to bless Esther, I began to realise that I was becoming something even worse than a betrayed husband: I was becoming the kind of boring person no one wants to be around.

I decided, from then on, to suffer in silence, and the invitations once more flooded in through my letter box.

But the Zahir, about which I initially used to think with either irritation or affection, continued to grow in my soul. I started looking for Esther in every woman I met. I would see her in every bar, every cinema, at bus stops. More than once I ordered a taxi driver to stop in the middle of the street or to follow someone, until I could persuade myself that the person was not the person I was looking for.

With the Zahir beginning to occupy my every thought, I needed an antidote, something that would not take me to the brink of despair.

There was only one possible solution: a girlfriend.

I encountered three or four women I felt drawn to, but then I met Marie, a 35-year-old French actress. She was the only one who did not spout such nonsense as: 'I like you as a man, not as the celebrity everyone wants to meet' or 'I wish you weren't quite so famous', or worse still: 'I'm not interested in money.' She was the only one who was genuinely pleased at my success, because she too was famous and knew that celebrity counts. Celebrity is an aphrodisiac. It was good for a woman's ego to be with a man and know that he had chosen her even though he had had the pick of many others.

We were often seen together at parties and receptions; there was speculation about our relationship, but neither she nor I confirmed or denied anything, and the matter was left hanging, and all that remained for the magazines was to wait for the photo of the famous kiss – which never came, because both she and I considered such public exhibitionism vulgar. She got on with her filming and I with my work; when I could, I would travel to Milan, and when she could, she would meet me in Paris; we were close, but not dependent on each other.

Marie pretended not to know what was going on in my soul, and I pretended not to know what was going on in hers (an impossible love for a married neighbour, even though she could have had any man she wanted). We were friends, companions, we enjoyed the same things; I would even go so far as to say that there was between us a kind of love, but different from the love I felt for Esther or that Marie felt for her neighbour.

I started taking part in book-signings again, I accepted invitations to give lectures, write articles, attend charity dinners, appear on television programmes, help out with projects for up-and-coming young artists. I did everything except what I should have been doing, i.e. writing a book.

This didn't matter to me, however, for in my heart of hearts I believed that my career as a writer was over, because the woman who had made me begin was no longer there. I had lived my dream intensely while it lasted, I had got farther than most people are lucky enough to get, I could spend the rest of my life having fun.

I thought this every morning. In the afternoon, I realised that the only thing I really liked doing was writing. By nightfall, there I was once more trying to persuade myself that I had fulfilled my dream and should try something new.

The following year was a Holy Year in Spain, the *Año Santo Compostelano*, which occurs whenever the day of St James of Compostela, 25 July, falls on a Sunday. A special door to the Cathedral in Santiago stands open for 365 days, and, according to tradition, anyone who goes through that door receives a series of special blessings.

There were various commemorative events throughout Spain, and since I was extremely grateful for the pilgrimage I had made, I decided to take part in at least one event: a talk, in January, in the Basque country. In order to get out of my routine – trying to write a book/going to a party/to the airport/visiting Marie in Milan/going out to supper/to a hotel/to the airport/surfing the Internet/going to the airport/to an interview/to another airport – I chose to drive the 1,400 kilometres there alone.

Everywhere – even those places I have never visited before – reminds me of my private Zahir. I think how Esther would love to see this, how much she would enjoy eating in this restaurant or walking by this river. I spend the night in Bayonne and, before I go to sleep, I turn on the television and learn that there are about 5,000 trucks stuck on the frontier between France and Spain, due to a violent and entirely unexpected snowstorm.

I wake up thinking that I should simply drive back to Paris: I have an excellent excuse for cancelling the engagement, and the organisers will understand perfectly – the traffic is in chaos, there is ice on the roads, both the French and Spanish governments are advising people not to leave home this weekend because the risk of accidents is so high. The situation is worse than it was last night: the morning paper reports that on one stretch of road alone there are 17,000 people trapped; civil defence teams have been mobilised to provide them with food and temporary shelters, since many people have already run out of fuel and cannot use their car heaters.

The hotel staff tell me that if I really have to travel, if it's a matter of life or death, there is a minor road I can take, which, while it will avoid the blockages, will add about two hours to my journey time, and no one can guarantee what state the road will be in. Instinctively, I decide to go ahead; something is forcing me on, out onto the icy asphalt and to the hours spent patiently waiting in bottlenecks.

Perhaps it is the name of the city: Vitória – Victory. Perhaps it is the feeling that I have grown too used to comfort and have lost my ability to improvise in crisis situations. Perhaps it is the enthusiasm of the people who are, at this moment, trying to restore a cathedral built many centuries ago and who, in order to draw attention to their efforts, have invited a few writers to give talks. Or perhaps it is the old saying of the conquistadors of the Americas: 'it is not life that matters, but the journey'.

And so I keep on journeying. After many long, tense hours, I reach Vitória, where some even tenser people are waiting for me. They say that there hasn't been a snowstorm like it for more than thirty years, they thank me for making the effort, and continue with the official programme, which includes a visit to the Cathedral of Santa María.

A young woman with shining eyes starts telling me the story. To begin with there was the city wall. The wall remained, but one part of it was used to build a chapel. Many years passed, and the chapel became a church. Another century passed, and the church became a Gothic cathedral. The cathedral had had its moments of glory, there had been structural problems, for a time it had been abandoned, then restoration work had distorted the whole shape of the building, but each generation thought it had solved the problem and would rework the original plans. Thus, in the centuries that followed, they raised a wall here, took down a beam there, added a buttress over there, created or bricked up stained-glass windows.

And the cathedral withstood it all.

I walk through the skeleton of the cathedral, studying the restoration work currently being carried out: this time the architects guarantee that they have found the perfect solution. Everywhere there are metal supports, scaffolding, grand theories about what to do next and some criticism about what was done in the past.

And suddenly, in the middle of the central nave, I realise something very important: the cathedral is me, it is all of us. We are all growing and changing shape, we notice certain weaknesses that need to be corrected, we don't always choose the best solution, but we carry on regardless, trying to remain upright and decent, in order to do honour not to the walls or the doors or the windows, but to the empty space inside, the space where we worship and venerate what is dearest and most important to us.

Yes, we are all cathedrals, there is no doubt about it; but what lies in the empty space of my inner cathedral?

Esther, the Zahir.

She fills everything. She is the only reason I am alive. I look around, I prepare myself for the talk I am to give, and I understand why I braved the snow, the traffic jams and the ice on the roads: in order to be reminded that every day I need to rebuild myself and to accept – for the first time in my entire existence – that I love another human being more than I love myself.

On the way back to Paris – in far more favourable weather conditions – I am in a kind of trance: I do not think, I merely concentrate on the traffic. When I get home, I ask the maid not to let anyone in, and ask her if she can sleep over for the next few nights and make me breakfast, lunch and supper. I stamp on the small apparatus that connects me to the Internet, destroying it completely. I unplug the telephone. I put my mobile in a box and send it to my publisher, saying that he should only give it back to me when I come round personally to pick it up.

For a week, I walk by the Seine each morning and, when I get back, I lock myself in my study. As if I were listening to the voice of an angel, I write a book, or, rather, a letter, a long letter to the woman of my dreams, to the woman I love and will always love. This book might one day reach her hands and even if it doesn't, I am now a man at peace with his spirit. I no longer wrestle with my wounded pride, I no longer look for Esther on every corner, in every bar and cinema, at every supper, I no longer look for her in Marie or in the newspapers.

On the contrary, I am pleased that she exists; she has shown me that I am capable of a love of which I myself knew nothing, and this leaves me in a state of grace.

I accept the Zahir, and will let it lead me into a state of either holiness or madness.

A Time to Rend and a Time to Sew – the title is from a verse in Ecclesiastes – was published at the end of April. By the second week of May, it was already number one in the bestseller lists.

The literary supplements, which have never been kind to me, redoubled their attacks. I cut out some of the key phrases and stuck them in a notebook along with reviews from previous years; they said basically the same thing, merely changing the title of the book:

'... once again, despite the troubled times we live in, the author offers us an escape from reality with a story about love ...' (as if people could live without love)

'... short sentences, superficial style ...' (as if long sentences equalled profundity)

'... the author has discovered the secret of success – marketing ...' (as if I had been born in a country with a long literary tradition and had had millions to invest in my first book)

'... it will sell as well as all his other books, which just proves how unprepared human beings are not to face up to the encircling tragedy ...' (as if they knew what it meant to be prepared).

Some reviews, however, were different, adding that I was profiting from last year's scandal in order to make even more money. As always, these negative reviews only served to sell more of my books: my faithful readers bought the book anyway, and those who had forgotten about the whole sorry business were reminded of it again and so also bought copies, because they wanted to hear my version of Esther's disappearance (since the book was not about that, but was, rather, a hymn to love, they must have been sorely disappointed and would doubtless have decided that the critics were spot on). The rights were immediately sold to all the countries where my books were usually published.

Marie, who read the typescript before I sent it to the publisher, showed herself to be the woman I had hoped she was: instead of being jealous, or saying that I shouldn't bare my soul like that, she encouraged me to go ahead with it and was thrilled when it was a success. At the time, she was reading the teachings of a little-known mystic, whom she quoted in all our conversations.

'When people praise us, we should always keep a close eye on how we behave.'

'The critics never praise me.'

'I mean your readers: you've received more letters than ever. You'll end up believing that you're better than you are, and allow yourself to slip into a false sense of security, which could be very dangerous.'

'Ever since my visit to the cathedral in Vitória, I do think I'm better than I thought I was, but that has nothing to do with readers' letters. Absurd though it may seem, I discovered love.'

'Great. What I like about the book is the fact that, at no point, do you blame your ex-wife. And you don't blame yourself either.'

'I've learned not to waste my time doing that.'

'Good. The universe takes care of correcting our mistakes.'

'Do you think Esther's disappearance was some kind of "correction", then?'

'I don't believe in the curative powers of suffering and tragedy; they happen because they're part of life and shouldn't be seen as a punishment. Generally speaking, the universe tells us when we're wrong by taking away what is most important to us: our friends. And that, I think I'm right in saying, is what was happening with you.'

'I learned something recently: our true friends are those who are with us when the good things happen. They cheer us on and are pleased by our triumphs. False friends only appear at difficult times, with their sad, supportive faces, when, in fact, our suffering is serving to console them for their miserable lives. When things were bad last year, various people I had never even seen before turned up to "console" me. I hate that.'

'I've had the same thing happen to me.'

'But I'm very grateful that you came into my life, Marie.'

'Don't be too grateful too soon, our relationship isn't strong enough. As a matter of fact, I've been thinking of moving to Paris or asking you to come and live in Milan: it wouldn't make any difference to either of us in terms of work. You always work at home and I always work away. Would you like to change the subject now or shall we continue discussing it as a possibility?'

'I'd like to change the subject.'

'Let's talk about something else then. It took a lot of courage to write that book. What surprises me, though, is that you don't once mention the young man.'

'I'm not interested in him.'

'You must be. Every now and again you must ask yourself: why did she choose him?'

'I never ask myself that.'

'You're lying. I'd certainly like to know why my neighbour didn't divorce his boring, smiling wife, always busy with the housework, the cooking, the children and the bills. If I ask myself that, you must too.'

'Are you saying that I hate him because he stole my wife?'

'No, I want to hear you say that you forgive him.'

'I can't do that.'

'It's hard I know, but you've no option. If you don't do it, you'll always be thinking of the pain he caused you and that pain will never pass. I'm not saying you've got to like him. I'm not saying you should seek him out. I'm not suggesting you should start thinking of him as an angel. What was his name now? Something Russian wasn't it?'

'It doesn't matter what his name was.'

'You see? You don't even want to say his name. Are you superstitious?'

'Mikhail. There you are, that's his name.'

'The energy of hatred won't get you anywhere; but the energy of forgiveness, which reveals itself through love, will transform your life in a positive way.'

'Now you're sounding like some Tibetan sage, spouting stuff that is all very nice in theory, but impossible in practice. Don't forget, I've been hurt before.'

'Exactly, and you're still carrying inside you the little boy, the school weakling, who had to hide his tears from his parents. You still bear the marks of the skinny little boy who couldn't get a girlfriend and who was never any good at sport. You still haven't managed to heal the scars left by some of the injustices committed against you in your life. But what good does that do?'

'Who told you about that?'

'I just know. I can see it in your eyes, and it doesn't do you any good. All it does is feed a constant desire to feel sorry for yourself, because you were the victim of people stronger than you. Or else it makes you go to the other extreme and disguise yourself as an avenger ready to hit out at the people who hurt you. Isn't that a waste of time?'

'It's just human.'

'Oh, it is, but it's not intelligent or reasonable. Show some respect for your time on this earth, and know that God has always forgiven you and always will.'

Looking around at the crowd gathered for my book-signing at a megastore in the Champs-Elysées, I thought: how many of these people will have had the same experience I had with my wife?

Very few. Perhaps one or two. Even so, most of them would identify with what was in my new book.

Writing is one of the most solitary activities in the world. Once every two years, I sit down in front of the computer, gaze out on the unknown sea of my soul, and see a few islands – ideas that have developed and which are ripe to be explored. Then I climb into my boat – called The Word – and set out for the nearest island. On the way, I meet strong currents, winds and storms, but I keep rowing, exhausted, knowing that I have drifted away from my chosen course and that the island I was trying to reach is no longer on my horizon.

I can't turn back, though, I have to continue somehow or else I'll be lost in the middle of the ocean; at that point, a series of terrifying scenarios flash through my mind, such as spending the rest of my life talking about past successes, or bitterly criticising new writers, simply because I no longer have the courage to publish new books. Wasn't my dream to be a writer? Then I must continue creating sentences, paragraphs, chapters, and go on writing until I die, and not allow myself to get caught in such traps as success or failure. Otherwise, what meaning does my life have? Being able to buy an old mill in the south of France and tending my garden? Giving lectures instead, because it's easier to talk than to write? Withdrawing from the world in a calculated, mysterious way, in order to create a legend that will deprive me of many pleasures?

Shaken by these alarming thoughts, I find a strength and a courage I didn't know I had: they help me to venture into an unknown part of my soul. I let myself be swept along by the current, and finally anchor my boat at the island I was being carried towards. I spend days and nights describing what I see, wondering why I'm doing this, telling myself that it's really not worth the pain and the effort, that I don't need to prove anything to anyone, that I've got what I wanted and far more than I ever dreamed of having.

I notice that I go through the same process as I did when writing my first book: I wake up at nine o'clock in the morning, ready to sit down at my computer immediately after breakfast; then I read the newspapers, go for a walk, visit the nearest bar for a chat, come home, look at the computer, discover that I need to make several phone calls, look at the computer again, by which time lunch is ready, and I sit eating and thinking that I really ought to have started writing at eleven o'clock, but now I need a nap, I wake at five in the afternoon, finally turn on the computer, go to check my e-mails, then remember that I've destroyed my Internet connection; I could go to a place ten minutes away where I can get online, but couldn't I, just to free my conscience from these feelings of guilt, couldn't I at least write for half an hour?

I begin out of a feeling of duty, but suddenly 'the thing' takes hold of me and I can't stop. The maid calls me for supper and I ask her not to interrupt me; an hour later, she calls me again; I'm hungry, but I must write just one more line, one more sentence, one more page. By the time I sit down at the table, the food is cold, I gobble it down and go back to the computer – I am no longer in control of where I place my feet, the island is being revealed to me, I am being propelled along its paths, finding things I have never even thought or dreamed of. I drink a cup of coffee, and another, and at two o'clock in the morning I finally stop writing, because my eyes are tired.

I go to bed, spend another hour making notes of things to use in the next paragraph and which always prove completely useless – they serve only to empty my mind so that sleep can come. I promise myself that the next morning, I'll start at eleven o'clock prompt. And the following day, the same thing happens – the walk, the conversations, lunch, a nap, the feelings of guilt, then irritation at myself for destroying the Internet connection, until I, at last, make myself sit down and write the first page …

Suddenly, two, three, four, eleven weeks have passed, and I know that I'm near the end; I'm gripped by a feeling of emptiness, the feeling of someone who has set down in words things he should have kept to himself. Now, though, I have to reach the final sentence – and I do.

When I used to read biographies of writers, I always thought they were simply trying to make their profession seem more interesting when they said that 'the book writes itself, the writer is just the typist'. Now I know that this is absolutely true, no one knows why the current took them to that particular island and not to the one they wanted to reach. The obsessive re-drafting and editing begins, and when I can no longer bear to re-read the same words one more time, I send it to my publisher, where it is edited again, and then published.

And it is a constant source of surprise to me to discover that other people were also in search of that very island and that they find it in my book. One person tells another person about it, the mysterious chain grows, and what the writer thought of as a solitary exercise becomes a bridge, a boat, a means by which souls can travel and communicate.

From then on, I am no longer the man lost in the storm: I find myself through my readers, I understand what I wrote when I see that others understand it too, but never before. On a few rare occasions, like the one that is just about to happen, I manage to look those people in the eye and then I understand that my soul is not alone.

At the appointed time, I start signing books. There is brief eye-to-eye contact and a feeling of solidarity, joy and mutual respect. There are handshakes, a few letters, gifts, comments. Ninety minutes later, I ask for a ten-minute rest, no one complains, and my publisher (as has become traditional at my book-signings in France) orders champagne to be served to everyone still in the line (I have tried to get this tradition adopted in other countries, but they always say that French champagne is too expensive and end up serving mineral water instead, but that, too, shows respect for those still waiting).

I return to the table. Two hours later, contrary to what anyone observing the event might think, I am not tired, but full of energy; I could carry on all night. The shop, however, has closed its doors and the queue is dwindling. There are forty people left inside, they become thirty, twenty, eleven, five, four, three, two ... and suddenly our eyes meet.

'I waited until the end. I wanted to be the last because I have a message for you.'

I don't know what to say. I glance to one side, at the publishers, sales people and booksellers, who are all talking enthusiastically; soon we will go out to eat and drink and share the excitement of the day, and describe some of the strange things that happened while I was signing books.

I have never seen him before, but I know who he is. I take the book from him and write: 'For Mikhail, with best wishes.'

I say nothing. I must not lose him – a word, a sentence, a sudden movement might cause him to leave and never come back. In a fraction of a second, I understand that he and only he can save me from the blessing – or the curse – of the Zahir, because he is the only one who knows where to find it, and I will finally be able to ask the questions I have been repeating to myself for so long.

'I wanted you to know that she's all right, that she may even have read your book.'

The publishers, sales people and booksellers come over. They all embrace me and say it's been a great afternoon. Let's go and relax and drink and talk about it all.

'I'd like to invite this young man to supper,' I say. 'He was the last in the queue and he can be the representative of all the other readers who were here with us today.'

'I can't, I'm afraid. I have another engagement.'

And turning to me, rather startled, he adds:

'I only came to give you that message.'

'What message?' asks one of the sales people.

'He never usually invites anyone!' says my publisher. 'Come on, let's all go and have supper!'

'It's very kind of you, but I have a meeting I go to every Thursday.'

'When does it start?'

'In two hours' time.'

'And where is it?'

'In an Armenian restaurant.'

My driver, who is himself Armenian, asks which one and says that it's only fifteen minutes from the place where we are going to eat. Everyone is doing their best to please me: they think that the person I'm inviting to supper should be happy and pleased to be so honoured, that anything else can surely wait.

'What's your name?' asks Marie.

'Mikhail.'

'Well, Mikhail,' and I see that Marie has understood everything, 'why don't you come with us for an hour or so; the restaurant we're going to is just around the corner.

Then the driver will take you wherever you want to go. If you prefer, though, we can cancel our reservation and all go and have supper at the Armenian restaurant instead – that way, you'd feel less anxious.'

I can't stop looking at him. He isn't particularly handsome or particularly ugly. He's neither tall nor short. He's dressed in black, simple and elegant – and by elegance I mean a complete absence of brand names or designer labels.

Marie links arms with Mikhail and heads for the exit. The bookseller still has a pile of books waiting to be signed for readers who could not come to the signing, but I promise that I will drop by the following day. My legs are trembling, my heart pounding, and yet I have to pretend that everything is fine, that I'm glad the book-signing was a success, that I'm interested in what other people are saying. We cross the Champs-Elysées, the sun is setting behind the Arc de Triomphe, and, for some reason, I know that this is a sign, a good sign.

As long as I can keep control of the situation.

Why do I want to speak to him? The people from the publishing house keep talking to me and I respond automatically; no one notices that I am far away, struggling to understand why I have invited to supper someone whom I should, by rights, hate. Do I want to find out where Esther is? Do I want to have my revenge on this young man, so lost, so insecure, and yet who was capable of luring away the person I love? Do I want to prove to myself that I am better, much better than him? Do I want to bribe him, seduce him, make him persuade my wife to come back?

I can't answer any of these questions, and that doesn't matter. The only thing I have said up until now is: 'I'd like to invite this young man to supper.' I had imagined the scene so often before: we meet, I grab him by the throat, punch him, humiliate him in front of Esther; or I get a thrashing and make her see how hard I'm fighting for her, suffering for her. I had imagined scenes of aggression or feigned indifference or public scandal, but the words 'I'd like to invite this young man to supper' had never once entered my head.

No need to ask what I will do next, all I have to do now is to keep an eye on Marie, who is walking along a few paces ahead of me, holding on to Mikhail's arm, as if she were his girlfriend. She won't let him go and yet I wonder, at the same time, why she's helping me, when she knows that a meeting with this young man could also mean that I'll find out where my wife is living.

We arrive. Mikhail makes a point of sitting far away from me; perhaps he wants to avoid getting caught up in a conversation with me. Laughter, champagne, vodka and caviar – I glance at the menu and am horrified to see that the bookseller is spending about a thousand dollars on the entrées alone. There is general chatter; Mikhail is asked what he thought of the afternoon's event; he says he enjoyed it; he is asked about the book; he says he enjoyed it very much. Then he is forgotten, and attention turns to me – was I happy with how things had gone, was the queue organised to my liking, had the security team been up to scratch? My heart is still pounding, but I present a calm front, I thank them for everything, for the efficient way in which the event was run.

Half an hour of conversation and a lot of vodka later, I can see that Mikhail is beginning to relax. He isn't the centre of attention any more, he doesn't need to say very much, he just has to endure it for a little while longer and then he can go. I know he wasn't lying about the Armenian restaurant, so at least now I have a clue. My wife must still be in Paris! I must pretend to be friendly, try to win his confidence, the initial tensions have all disappeared.

An hour passes. Mikhail looks at his watch and I can see that he is about to leave. I must do something – now. Every time I look at him, I feel more and more insignificant and understand less and less how Esther could have exchanged me for someone who seems so unworldly (she mentioned that he had 'magical' powers). However difficult it might be to pretend that I feel perfectly at ease talking to someone who is my enemy, I must do something.

'Let's find out a bit more about our reader,' I say, and there is an immediate silence. 'Here he is, about to leave at any moment, and he's hardly said a word about his life. What do you do?'

Despite the number of vodkas he has drunk, Mikhail seems suddenly to recover his sobriety.

'I organise meetings at the Armenian restaurant.'

'What does that involve?'

'I stand on stage and tell stories. And I let the people in the audience tell their stories too.'

'I do the same thing in my books.'

'I know, that's how I first met … '

He's going to say who he is!

'Were you born here?' asks Marie, thus preventing him from finishing his sentence ('... how I first met your wife').

'I was born in the Kazakhstan steppes.'

Kazakhstan. Who's going to be brave enough to ask where Kazakhstan is?

'Where's Kazakhstan?' asks the sales representative.

Blessed are those who are not afraid to admit that they don't know something.

'I was waiting for someone to ask that,' and there is an almost gleeful look in Mikhail's eyes now. 'Whenever I say where I was born, about ten minutes later people are saying that I'm from Pakistan or Afghanistan ... My country is in Central Asia. It has barely 14 million inhabitants in an area far larger than France with its population of 60 million.'

'So it's a place where no one can complain about the lack of space, then,' says my publisher, laughing.

'It's a place where, during the last century, no one had the right to complain about anything, even if they wanted to. When the Communist regime abolished private ownership, the livestock were simply abandoned and 48.6 per cent of the population died. Do you understand what that means? Nearly half the population of my country died of hunger between 1932 and 1933.'

Silence falls. After all, tragedies get in the way of celebrations, and one of the people present tries to change the subject. However, I insist that my 'reader' tells us more about his country.

'What are the steppes like?' I ask.

'They're vast plains with barely any vegetation, as I'm sure you know.'

I do know, but it had been my turn to ask a question, to keep the conversation going.

'I've just remembered something about Kazakhstan,' says my publisher. 'Some time ago, I was sent a typescript by a writer who lives there, describing the atomic tests that were carried out on the steppes.'

'Our country has blood in its soil and in its soul. Those tests changed what cannot be changed, and we will be paying the price for many generations to come. We even made an entire sea disappear.'

It is Marie's turn to speak.

'No one can make a sea disappear.'

'I'm twenty-five years old, and that is all the time it took, just one generation, for the water that had been there for millennia to be transformed into dust. Those in charge of the Communist regime decided to divert two rivers, Amu-Darya and Syr-Darya, so that they could irrigate some cotton plantations. They failed, but, by then, it was too late – the sea had ceased to exist, and the cultivated land became a desert.

The lack of water affected the whole climate. Nowadays, vast sandstorms scatter 150,000 tons of salt and dust every year. Fifty million people in five countries were affected by the Soviet bureaucrats' irresponsible – and irreversible – decision. The little water that was left is polluted and is the source of all kinds of diseases.'

I made a mental note of what he was saying. It could be useful in one of my lectures. Mikhail went on, and his tone of voice was no longer ecological, but tragic.

'My grandfather says that the Aral Sea was once known as the Blue Sea, because of the colour of its waters. It no longer exists, and yet the people there refuse to leave their houses and move somewhere else: they still dream of waves and fishes, they still have their fishing rods and talk about boats and bait.'

'Is it true about the atomic tests, though?' asks my publisher.

'I think that everyone born in my country feels what the land felt, because every Kazakh carries his land in his blood. For forty years, the plains were shaken by nuclear or thermonuclear bombs, a total of 456 in 1989. Of those tests, 116 were carried out in the open, which amounts to a bomb 2,500 times more powerful than the one that was dropped on Hiroshima during the Second World War. As a result, thousands of people were contaminated by radioactivity and subsequently contracted lung cancer, whilst thousands of children were born with motor deficiencies, missing limbs or mental problems.'

Mikhail looks at his watch.

'Now, if you don't mind, I have to go.'

Half of those around the table are sorry, the conversation was just getting interesting. The other half are glad: it's absurd to talk about such tragic events on such a happy occasion.

Mikhail says goodbye to everyone with a nod of his head and gives me a hug, not because he feels a particular affection for me, but so that he can whisper:

'As I said before, she's fine. Don't worry.'

'"Don't worry," he says. Why should I worry about a woman who left me? It was because of her that I was questioned by the police, splashed all over the front pages of the scandal sheets; it was because of her that I spent all those painful days and nights, nearly lost all my friends and ... '

' ... and wrote *A Time to Rend and a Time to Sew*. Come on, we're both adults, with plenty of experience of life. Let's not deceive ourselves. Of course, you'd like to know how she is. In fact, I'd go further: you'd like to see her.'

'If you're so sure about that, why did you help persuade him to come to supper with us? Now I have a clue: he appears every Thursday at that Armenian restaurant.'

'I know. You'd better follow that up.'

'Don't you love me?'

'More than yesterday and less than tomorrow, as it says on those postcards you can buy in stationery shops. Yes, of course, I love you. I'm hopelessly in love, if you must know. I'm even considering changing my address and coming to live in this huge, empty apartment of yours, but whenever I suggest it, you always change the subject. Nevertheless, I forget my pride and try to explain what a big step it would be for us to live together, and hear you say that it's too soon for that; perhaps you're afraid you'll lose me the way you lost Esther, or perhaps you're still waiting for her to come back, or perhaps you don't want to lose your freedom, or are simultaneously afraid of being alone and afraid of living with someone – in short, our relationship's a complete disaster. But, now that you ask, there's my answer: I love you very much.'

'So why did you help?'

'Because I can't live for ever with the ghost of a woman who left without a word of explanation. I've read your book. I believe that only by finding her and resolving the matter will your heart ever truly be mine. That's what happened with the neighbour I was in love with. I was close enough to him to be able to see what a coward he was when it came to our relationship, how he could never commit himself to the thing he wanted with all his heart, but which he always felt was too dangerous to actually have. You've often said that absolute freedom doesn't exist; what does exist is the freedom to choose anything you like and then commit yourself to that decision. The closer I was to my neighbour, the more I admired you: a man who decided to go on loving the wife who had abandoned him and who wanted nothing more to do with him. You not only decided to do that, you made your decision public. This is what you say in your book; it's a passage I know by heart:

"When I had nothing more to lose, I was given everything. When I ceased to be who I am, I found myseif. When I experienced humiliation and yet kept on walking, I understood that I was free to choose my destiny. Perhaps there's something wrong with me, I don't know, perhaps my marriage was a dream I couldn't understand while it lasted. All I know is that even though I can live without her, I would still like to see her again, to say what I never said when we were together: I love you more than I love myself. If I could say that, then I could go on living, at peace with myself, because that love has redeemed me."'

'Mikhail told me that Esther had probably read my book. That's enough.'

'Maybe, but for you to be able to love her fully, you need to find her and tell her that to her face. It might not be possible, she might not want to see you, but you would, at least, have tried. I would be free from the "ideal woman" and you would be free from the absolute presence of what you call the Zahir.'

'You're very brave.'

'No, I'm not, I'm afraid. But I have no choice.'

The following morning, I swore to myself that I would not try to find out where Esther was living. For two years, I had unconsciously preferred to believe that she had been forced to leave, that she had been kidnapped or was being blackmailed by some terrorist group. Now that I knew she was alive and well (that was what the young man had told me), why try to see her again? My ex-wife had the right to look for happiness, and I should respect her decision.

This idea lasted a little more than four hours; later in the afternoon, I went to a church, lit a candle and made another promise, this time a sacred, ritual promise: to try and find her. Marie was right. I was too old to continue deceiving myself by pretending I didn't care. I respected her decision to leave, but the very person who had helped me build my life had very nearly destroyed me. She had always been so brave: why, this time, had she fled like a thief in the night, without looking her husband in the eye and explaining why? We were both old enough to act and face the consequences of our actions: my wife's (or, rather, my ex-wife's) behaviour was completely out of character, and I needed to know why.

It was another week – an eternity – before the 'performance' at the restaurant. In the next few days, I agreed to do interviews that I would never normally accept; I wrote various newspaper articles, practised yoga and meditation, read a book about a Russian painter, another about a crime committed in Nepal, wrote prefaces for two books and recommendations for another four, something which publishers were always asking me to do, and which I usually refused.

There was still an awful lot of time to kill, and so I decided to pay off a few debts at the Favour Bank – accepting supper invitations, giving brief talks at schools where the children of friends were studying, visiting a golf club, doing an improvised book-signing at a bookshop in Avenue de Suffren owned by a friend (he put an advertisement in the window three days before and all of twenty people turned up). My secretary remarked that I was obviously very happy, because she hadn't seen me so active in ages; I said that having a book in the bestseller list encouraged me to work even harder than I usually did.

There were two things I didn't do that week. First, I didn't read any unsolicited typescripts – according to my lawyers, these should always be returned immediately to the sender, otherwise, sooner or later, I would run the risk of someone claiming that I had plagiarised one of their stories (I've never understood why people send me their typescripts anyway – after all, I'm not a publisher).

Second, I didn't look in an atlas to find out where Kazakhstan was, even though I knew that, in order to gain Mikhail's trust, I should try to find out a bit more about where he came from.

People are waiting patiently for someone to open the door that leads to the room at the back of the restaurant. The place has none of the charm of bars in St-Germain-des-Prés, no cups of coffee served with a small glass of water, no well-dressed, well-spoken people. It has none of the elegance of theatre foyers, none of the magic of other shows being put on all over the city in small bistros, with the actors always trying their hardest, in the hope that some famous impresario will be in the audience and will introduce himself at the end of the show, tell them they're wonderful and invite them to appear at some important arts centre.

To be honest, I can't understand why the place is so full: I've never seen it mentioned in the listings magazines that specialise in entertainment and the arts in Paris.

While I'm waiting, I talk to the owner and learn that he is planning to turn the whole restaurant area into a theatre.

'More and more people come every week,' he says. 'I agreed initially because a journalist asked me as a favour and said that, in return, he'd publish a review of my restaurant in his magazine. Besides, the room is rarely used on Thursdays, and while people are waiting, they have a meal; in fact, I probably take more money on a Thursday than I do on any other night of the week. The only thing that concerned me was that the actors might belong to a sect. As you probably know, the laws here are very strict.'

Yes, I did know; certain people had even suggested that my books were linked to some dangerous philosophical trend, to a strand of religious teaching that was out of step with commonly accepted values. France, normally so liberal, was slightly paranoid about the subject. There had been a recent long report about the 'brainwashing' practised on certain unwary people. As if those same people were able to make all kinds of other choices about school, university, toothpaste, cars, films, husbands, wives, lovers, but, when it came to matters of faith, were easily manipulated.

'How do they advertise these events?' I ask.

'I've no idea. If I did, I'd use the same person to promote my restaurant.'

And just to clear up any doubts, since he doesn't know who I am, he adds:

'By the way, it isn't a sect. They really are just actors.'

The door to the room is opened, the people flock in, depositing five euros in a small basket. Inside, standing impassive on the improvised stage, are two young men and two young women, all wearing full, white skirts, stiffly starched to make them stand out. As well as these four, there is an older man carrying a conga drum and a woman with a huge bronze cymbal covered in small, tinkling attachments; every time she inadvertently brushes against this instrument, it emits a sound like metallic rain.

Mikhail is one of the young men, although he looks completely different from the person I met at the book-signing: his eyes, fixed on some point in space, shine with a special light.

The audience sit down on the chairs scattered around the room. Young men and women dressed in such a way that if you met them in the street, you would think they were into hard drugs. Middle-aged executives or civil servants with their wives. A few nine- or ten-year-old children, possibly brought by their parents. A few older people, who must have made a great effort to get here, since the nearest metro station is five blocks away.

They drink, smoke, talk loudly, as if the people on the stage did not exist. The volume of conversation gradually increases; there is much laughter, it's a real party atmosphere. A sect? Only if it's a confraternity of smokers. I glance anxiously about, thinking I can see Esther in all the women there, sometimes even when they bear no physical resemblance at all to my wife (why can't I get used to saying 'my ex-wife'?).

I ask a well-dressed woman what this is all about. She doesn't seem to have the patience to respond; she looks at me as if I were a novice, a person who needs to be educated in the mysteries of life.

'Love stories,' she says. 'Stories and energy.'

Stories and energy. Perhaps I had better not pursue the subject, although the woman appears to be perfectly normal. I consider asking someone else, but decide that it's best to say nothing. I'll find out soon enough for myself. A gentleman sitting by my side looks at me and smiles:

'I've read your books and so, of course, I know why you're here.'

I'm shocked. Does he know about the relationship between Mikhail and my wife – I must again correct myself – the relationship between one of the people on stage and my ex-wife?

'An author like you would be bound to know about the Tengri. They're intimately connected with what you call "warriors of light".'

'Of course,' I say, relieved.

And I think: I've never even heard of the Tengri.

Twenty minutes later, by which time the air in the room is thick with cigarette smoke, we hear the sound of that cymbal. Miraculously, the conversations stop, the anarchic atmosphere seems to take on a religious aura; audience and stage are equally silent; the only sounds one can hear come from the restaurant next door.

Mikhail, who appears to be in a trance and is still gazing at some point in the distance, begins:

'In the words of the Mongolian creation myth: "There came a wild dog who was blue and grey and whose destiny was imposed on him by the heavens. His mate was a roe deer."'

His voice sounds different, more feminine, more confident.

'Thus begins another love story. The wild dog with his courage and strength, the doe with her gentleness, intuition and elegance. Hunter and hunted meet and love each other. According to the laws of nature, one should destroy the other, but in love there is neither good nor evil, there is neither construction nor destruction, there is merely movement. And love changes the laws of nature.'

He gestures with his hand and the four people on stage turn on the spot.

'In the steppes where I come from, the wild dog is seen as a feminine creature. Sensitive, capable of hunting because he has honed his instincts, but timid too. He does not use brute force, but strategy. Courageous, cautious, quick. He can change in a second from a state of complete relaxation to the tension he needs to pounce on his prey.'

Accustomed as I am to writing stories, I think: 'And what about the doe?' Mikhail is equally used to telling stories and answers the question hanging in the air:

'The roe deer has the male attributes of speed and an understanding of the earth. The two travel along together in their symbolic worlds, two impossibilities who have found each other, and because they overcome their own natures and their barriers, they make the world possible too. That is the Mongolian creation myth: out of two different natures love is born. In contradiction, love grows in strength. In confrontation and transformation, love is preserved.'

We have our life. It took the world a long time and much effort to get where it is, and we organise ourselves as best we can; it isn't ideal, but we rub along. And yet there is something missing, there is always something missing, and that is why we are gathered here tonight, so that we can help each other to think a little about the reason for our existence. Telling stories that make no sense, looking for facts that do not fit our usual way of perceiving reality, so that, perhaps in one or two generations, we can discover another way of living.

As Dante wrote in *The Divine Comedy*: "The day that man allows true love to appear, those things which are well made will fall into confusion and will overturn everything we believe to be right and true." The world will become real when man learns how to love; until then we will live in the belief that we know what love is, but we will always lack the courage to confront it as it truly is.

Love is an untamed force. When we try to control it, it destroys us. When we try to imprison it, it enslaves us. When we try to understand it, it leaves us feeling lost and confused.

This force is on earth to make us happy, to bring us closer to God and to our neighbour, and yet, given the way that we love now, we enjoy one hour of anxiety for every minute of peace.'

Mikhail paused. The strange cymbal sounded again.

'As on every Thursday, we are not going to tell stories about love. We are going to tell stories about the lack of love. We will see what lies on the surface – the layer where we find all our customs and values – in order to understand what lies beneath. When we penetrate beneath that layer we will find ourselves. Who would like to begin?'

Several people raised their hand. Mikhail pointed to a young woman of Arab appearance. She turned to a man on his own, on the other side of the room.

'Have you ever failed to get an erection when you've been to bed with a woman?'

Everyone laughed. The man, however, avoided giving a direct answer.

'Are you asking that because your boyfriend is impotent?'

Again everyone laughed. While Mikhail had been speaking, I had once more begun to suspect that this was indeed some new sect, but when sects hold meetings, I can't imagine that they smoke and drink and ask embarrassing questions about each other's sex lives.

'No, he's not,' said the girl firmly. 'But it has occasionally happened to him. And I know that if you had taken my question seriously, your answer would have been "Yes, I have." All men, in all cultures and countries, independent of any feelings of love or sexual attraction, have all experienced impotence at one time or another, often when they're with the person they most desire. It's normal.'

Yes, it was normal, and the person who had told me this was a psychiatrist, to whom I went when I thought I had a problem.

The girl went on:

'But the story we're told is that all men can always get an erection. When he can't, the man feels useless, and the woman is convinced she isn't attractive enough to arouse him. Since it's a taboo subject, he can't talk to his friends about it. He tells the woman the old lie: "It's never happened to me before." He feels ashamed of himself and often runs away from someone with whom he could have had a really good relationship, if only he had allowed himself a second, third or fourth chance. If he had trusted more in the love of his friends, if he had told the truth, he would have found out that he wasn't the only one. If he had trusted more in the love of the woman, he would not have felt humiliated.'

Applause. Cigarettes are lit, as if a lot of the people there – men and women – feel a great sense of relief.

Mikhail points to a man who looks like an executive in some big multinational.

'I'm a lawyer and I specialise in contested divorces.'

'What does that mean?' asks someone in the audience.

'It's when one of the parties won't agree to the separation,' replies the lawyer, irritated at being interrupted and as if he found it absurd that anyone should not know the meaning of such a straightforward legal term.

'Go on,' says Mikhail, with an authority that I would never have imagined in the young man I had met at the book-signing.

The lawyer continues:

'Today I received a report from the London-based firm Human and Legal Resources. This is what it says:

a) two-thirds of all employees in a company have some kind of love relationship. Imagine! That means that in any office of three people, two will end up having some form of intimate contact.

b) 10 per cent leave their job because of this, 40 per cent have relationships that last more than three months, and in the case of certain professions that require people to spend long periods away from home, at least eight out of ten end up having an affair.

Isn't that unbelievable?'

'Well, of course, we have to bow down to statistics!' remarks one of a group of young men who are all dressed as if they were members of some dangerous band of robbers. 'We all believe in statistics! That means that my mother must be being unfaithful to my father, but it's not her fault, it's the fault of the statistics!'

More laughter, more cigarettes, more relief, as if the people in the audience were hearing things they had always been afraid to hear and that hearing them freed them from some kind of anxiety. I think about Esther and about Mikhail – ' … professions that require people to spend long periods away from home, eight out of ten … '.

I think about myself and the many times this has happened to me. They are, after all, statistics. We are not alone.

Other stories are told of jealousy, abandonment, depression, but I am no longer listening. My Zahir has returned in its full intensity – even though, for a few moments, I had believed I was merely engaging in a little group therapy, I am, in fact, in the same room as the man who stole my wife. My neighbour, the one who recognised me, asks if I'm enjoying myself. He distracts me for a moment from my Zahir, and I am happy to respond.

'I still can't quite see the point. It's like a self-help group, like Alcoholics Anonymous or marriage guidance.'

'But doesn't what you hear strike you as genuine?'

'Possibly, but again, I can't see the point.'

'This isn't the most important part of the evening; it's just a way of not feeling so alone. By talking about our lives, we come to realise that most people have experienced the same thing.'

'And what's the practical result?'

'If we're not alone, then we have more strength to find out where we went wrong and to change direction. But, as I said, this is just an interval between what the young man says at the beginning and the moment when we invoke the energy.'

'Who is the young man?'

Our conversation is interrupted by the sound of the cymbal. This time, it is the older man with the conga drum who speaks.

'The time for reasoning is over. Let us move on now to the ritual, to the emotion that crowns and transforms everything. For those of you who are here for the first time tonight, this dance develops our capacity to accept Love. Love is the only thing that activates our intelligence and our creativity, that purifies and liberates us.'

The cigarettes are extinguished, the clink of glasses stops. That same strange silence descends upon the room; one of the young women says a prayer:

'We will dance, Lady, in homage to you. May our dancing make us fly up to heaven.'

Did I hear right? Did she say 'Lady'? She did.

The other young woman lights the candles in four candelabra; the other lights are switched off. The four figures in white, with their starched white skirts, come down from the stage and mingle with the audience. For nearly half an hour, the second young man, with a voice that seems to emerge from his belly, intones a monotonous, repetitive song, which, curiously, makes me forget the Zahir a little and slip into a kind of somnolence. Even one of the children, who had kept running up and down during the 'talking about love' session, is now quiet and still, her eyes fixed on the stage. Some of those present have their eyes closed, others are staring at the floor or at some invisible point in space, as I had seen Mikhail do.

When he stops singing, the percussion – the cymbal and the drum – strike up a rhythm familiar to me from religious ceremonies originating in Africa.

The white-clothed figures start to spin, and in that packed space, the audience makes room so that the wide skirts can trace movements in the air. The instruments play faster, the four spin ever faster too, emitting sounds that belong to no known language, as if they were speaking directly with angels or with 'the Lady'.

My neighbour gets to his feet and begins to dance too and to utter incomprehensible words. Ten or twelve other people in the audience do the same, while the rest watch with a mixture of reverence and amazement.

I don't know how long the dance went on for, but the sound of the instruments seemed to keep time with the beating of my heart, and I felt an enormous desire to surrender myself, to say strange things, to move my body; it took a mixture of self-control and a sense of the absurd to stop myself from spinning like a mad thing on the spot. Meanwhile, as never before, the figure of Esther, my Zahir, seemed to hover before me, smiling, calling on me to praise 'the Lady'.

I struggled not to enter into that unknown ritual, wanting it all to end as quickly as possible. I tried to concentrate on my main reason for being there that night

– to talk to Mikhail, to have him take me to my Zahir – but I found it impossible to remain still. I got up from my chair and just as I was cautiously, shyly taking my first steps, the music abruptly stopped.

In the room lit only by the candles, all I could hear was the laboured breathing of those who had danced. Gradually, the sound faded, the lights were switched back on, and everything seemed to have returned to normal. Glasses were again filled with beer, wine, water, soft drinks, the children started running about and talking loudly, and soon everyone was chatting, as if nothing, absolutely nothing, had happened.

'It's nearly time to close the meeting,' said the young woman who had lit the candles. 'Alma has one final story.'

Alma was the woman playing the cymbal. She spoke with the accent of someone who has lived in the East.

'The master had a buffalo. The animal's widespread horns made him think that if he could manage to sit between them, it would be like sitting on a throne. One day, when the animal was distracted, he climbed up between the horns and did just that. The buffalo, however, immediately lumbered to its feet and threw him off. When his wife saw this, she began to cry.

"Don't cry," said the master, once he had recovered. "I may have suffered, but I also realised my dream."'

People started leaving. I asked my neighbour what he had felt.

'You should know. You write about it in your books.'

I didn't know, but I had to pretend that I did.

'Maybe I do know, but I want to be sure.'

He looked at me, unconvinced, and clearly began to doubt that I really was the author he thought he knew.

'I was in touch with the energy of the Universe,' he replied. 'God passed through my soul.'

And he left, so as not to have to explain what he had said.

In the empty room there were now only the four actors, the two musicians and myself. The women went off to the ladies' toilet, presumably to change their clothes. The men took off their white costumes right there in the room and donned their ordinary clothes. They immediately began putting away the candelabra and the musical instruments in two large cases.

The older man, who had played the drum during the ceremony, started counting the money and putting it into six equal piles. I think it was only then that Mikhail noticed my presence.

'I thought I'd see you here.'

'And I imagine you know the reason.'

'After I've let the divine energy pass through my body, I know the reason for everything. I know the reason for love and for war. I know why a man searches for the woman he loves.'

I again felt as if I were walking along a knife-edge. If he knew that I was here because of my Zahir, then he also knew that this was a threat to his relationship with Esther.

'Can we talk, like two men of honour fighting for something worthwhile?'

Mikhail seemed to hesitate slightly. I went on:

'I know that I'll emerge bruised and battered, like the master who wanted to sit between the buffalo's horns, but

I deserve it. I deserve it because of the pain I inflicted, however unconsciously. I don't believe Esther would have left me if I had respected her love.'

'You understand nothing,' said Mikhail.

These words irritated me. How could a 25-year-old tell an experienced man who had suffered and been tested by life that he understood nothing? I had to control myself, to humble myself, to do whatever was necessary. I could not go on living with ghosts, I could not allow my whole universe to continue being dominated by the Zahir.

'Maybe I really don't understand, but that's precisely why I'm here – in order to understand. To free myself by understanding what happened.'

'You understood everything quite clearly, and then suddenly stopped understanding; at least that's what Esther told me. As happens with all husbands, there came a point when you started to treat your wife as if she were just part of the goods and chattels.'

I was tempted to say: 'Why didn't she tell me that herself? Why didn't she give me a chance to correct my mistakes and not leave me for a 25-year-old who will only end up treating her just as I did.' Some more cautious words emerged from my mouth however.

'I don't think that's true. You've read my book, you came to my book-signing because you knew what I felt and wanted to reassure me. My heart is still in pieces: have you ever heard of the Zahir?'

'I was brought up in the Islamic religion, so, yes, I'm familiar with the idea.'

'Well, Esther fills up every space in my life. I thought that by writing about my feelings, I would free myself

100

from her presence. Now I love her in a more silent way, but I can't think about anything else. I beg you, please, I'll do anything you want, but I need you to explain to me why she disappeared like that. As you yourself said, I understand nothing.'

It was very hard to stand there pleading with my wife's lover to help me understand what had happened. If Mikhail had not come to the book-signing, perhaps that moment in the cathedral in Vitória, where I acknowledged my love for her and out of which I wrote *A Time to Rend and a Time to Sew*, would have been enough. Fate, however, had other plans, and the mere possibility of being able to see my wife again had upset everything.

'Let's have lunch together,' said Mikhail, after a long pause. 'You really don't understand anything. But the divine energy that today passed through my body is generous with you.'

We arranged to meet the next day. On the way home, I remembered a conversation I had had with Esther three months before she disappeared.

A conversation about divine energy passing through the body.

'Their eyes really are different. There's the fear of death in them, of course, but beyond that, there's the idea of sacrifice. Their lives are meaningful because they are ready to offer them up for a cause.'

'You're talking about soldiers, are you?'

'Yes, and I'm talking as well about something I find terribly hard to accept, but which I can't pretend I don't see. War is a ritual. A blood ritual, but also a love ritual.'

'You're mad.'

'Maybe I am. But I've met other war correspondents, too, who go from one country to the next, as if the routine of death were part of their lives. They're not afraid of anything, they face danger the way a soldier does. And all for a news report? I don't think so. They can no longer live without the danger, the adventure, the adrenaline in their blood. One of them, a married man with three children, told me that the place where he feels most at ease is in a war zone, even though he adores his family and talks all the time about his wife and kids.'

'I just can't understand it at all. Look, Esther, I don't want to interfere in your life, but I think this experience will end up doing you real harm.'

'It would harm me more to be living a life without meaning. In a war, everyone knows they're experiencing something important.'

'A historic moment, you mean?'

'No, that isn't enough of a reason for risking your life. No, I mean that they're experiencing the true essence of man.'

'War?'

'No, love.'

'You're becoming like them.'

'I think I am.'

'Tell your news agency you've had enough.'

'I can't. It's like a drug. As long as I'm in a war zone, my life has meaning. I go for days without having a bath, I eat whatever the soldiers eat, I sleep three hours a night and wake up to the sound of gunfire. I know that at any moment someone could lob a grenade into the place where we're sitting, and that makes me live, do you see? Really live, I mean, loving every minute, every second. There's no room for sadness, doubts, nothing; there's just a great love for life. Are you listening?'

'Absolutely.'

'It's as if there was a divine light shining in the midst of every battle, in the midst of that worst of all possible situations. Fear exists before and after, but not while the shots are being fired, because, at that moment, you see men at their very limit, capable of the most heroic of actions and the most inhumane. They run out under a hail of bullets to rescue a comrade, and at the same time shoot anything that moves – children, women – anyone who comes within their line of fire will die. People from small, provincial towns where nothing ever happened and where they were always decent citizens find themselves invading museums, destroying centuries-old works of art and stealing things they don't need. They take photos of atrocities that they themselves committed and, rather than trying to conceal these, they feel proud. And people who, before, were always disloyal and treacherous feel a kind of camaraderie and solidarity and become incapable of doing wrong. It's a mad world, completely topsy-turvy.'

'Has it helped you answer the question that Hans asked Fritz in that bar in Tokyo in the story you told me?'

'Yes, the answer lies in some words written by the Jesuit Teilhard de Chardin, the same man who said that our world is surrounded by a layer of love. He said: "We can harness the energy of the winds, the seas, the sun. But the day man learns to harness the energy of love, that will be as important as the discovery of fire."'

'And you could only learn that by going to a war zone?'

'I'm not sure, but it did allow me to see that, paradoxical though it may seem, people are happy when they're at war. For them, the world has meaning. As I said before, total power or sacrificing themselves for a cause gives meaning to their lives. They are capable of limitless love, because they no longer have anything to lose. A fatally wounded soldier never asks the medical team: "Please save me!" His last words are usually: "Tell my wife and my son that I love them." At the last moment, they speak of love!'

'So, in your opinion, human beings only find life meaningful when they're at war.'

'But we're always at war. We're at war with death, and we know that death will win in the end. In armed conflicts, this is simply more obvious, but the same thing happens in daily life. We can't allow ourselves the luxury of being unhappy all the time.'

'What do you want me to do?'

'I need help. And that doesn't mean saying to me: "Go and hand in your notice", because that would only leave me feeling even more confused than before. We need to find a way of channelling all this, of allowing the energy of this pure, absolute love to flow through our bodies and spread around us. The only person so far who has helped me understand this is a rather otherworldly interpreter who says he's had revelations about this energy.'

'Are you talking about the love of God?'

'If someone is capable of loving his partner without restrictions, unconditionally, then he is manifesting the love of God. If the love of God becomes manifest, he will love his neighbour. If he loves his neighbour, he will love himself. If he loves himself, then everything returns to its proper place. History changes.

History will never change because of politics or conquests or theories or wars; that's mere repetition, it's been going on since the beginning of time. History will only change when we are able to use the energy of love, just as we use the energy of the wind, the seas, the atom.'

'Do you think we two could save the world?'

'I think there are more people out there who think the same way. Will you help me?'

'Yes, as long as you tell what I have to do.'

'But that's precisely what I don't know!'

I had been a regular customer at this charming pizzeria ever since my very first visit to Paris, so much so that it has become part of my history. Most recently, I had held a supper here to celebrate receiving the medal of Officer of Arts and Literature presented to me by the Ministry of Culture, even though many people felt that the commemoration of such an important event should have taken place somewhere more elegant and more expensive. But Roberto, the owner, had become a kind of good luck charm to me; whenever I went to his restaurant, something good happened in my life.

'I could start with some small talk about the success of *A Time to Rend and a Time to Sew* or the contradictory emotions I felt last night as I watched your performance.'

'It's not a performance, it's a meeting,' he said. 'We tell stories and we dance in order to feel the energy of love.'

'I could talk about anything just to put you at your ease, but we both know why we're here.'

'We're here because of your wife,' said Mikhail, who was now full of a young man's defiance and in no way resembled the shy boy at the book-signing or the spiritual leader of that 'meeting'.

PAULO COELHO

'You mean my ex-wife. And I would like to ask you a favour: take me to her. I want her to look me in the eye and tell me why she left. Only then will I be free of the Zahir. Otherwise, I'll go on thinking about her day and night, night and day, going over and over our story, our history, again and again, trying to pinpoint the moment when I went wrong and our paths began to diverge.'

He laughed.

'Reviewing history's a great idea, that's the only way you can make things change.'

'Very clever, but I'd prefer to leave philosophical discussions to one side for the moment. I'm sure that, like all young men, you hold in your hands the precise formula for putting the world to rights. However, like all young men, you will one day be as old as me and then you'll see that it's not so easy to change things. But there's no point talking about that now. Can you grant me that favour?'

'I must first ask you something: did she say goodbye?'

'No.'

'Did she say she was going away?'

'No, she didn't. You know that.'

'Do you think that, given the kind of person Esther is, she would be capable of leaving a man she had lived with for more than ten years without first confronting him and explaining her reasons?'

'That's precisely what I find most troubling. But what are you getting at?'

The conversation was interrupted by Roberto, who wanted to know if we were ready to order. Mikhail asked for a Napolitana and I told Roberto to choose for me – this was hardly the moment to be worrying about what I should eat. The only thing we needed urgently was a bottle of red wine, as quickly as possible. When Roberto asked me what sort of wine and I muttered an inaudible reply, he understood that he should simply leave us alone and not ask me anything else during lunch, but take all the necessary decisions himself, thus leaving me free to concentrate on my conversation with the young man before me.

The wine arrived within thirty seconds. I filled our glasses.

'What's she doing?'

'Do you really want to know?'

It irritated me to receive a question in response to mine.

'Yes, I do.'

'She's making carpets and giving French lessons.'

Carpets! My wife (ex-wife, please, do try and get used to it), who had all the money she could possibly need, had a degree in journalism, spoke four languages, was now obliged to making a living weaving carpets and giving French lessons to foreigners? I must get a grip on myself. I couldn't risk wounding the young man's male pride, even though I thought it shameful that he couldn't give Esther everything she deserved.

'Please, you must understand what I've been going through for the last year or more. I'm no threat to your relationship with Esther. I just need a couple of hours with her, or one hour, it doesn't matter.'

Mikhail appeared to be savouring my words.

'You haven't answered my question,' he said, with a smile. 'Do you think that, given the kind of person Esther is, she would leave the man of her life without at least saying goodbye and without explaining why?'

'No, I don't.'

'Then why all this stuff about "she left me"? Why do you say: "I'm no threat to your relationship with Esther"?'

I was confused. I felt something like hope stirring inside me – not that I knew what I was hoping for or where that hope had come from.

'Are you telling me that ...'

'Exactly. I'm telling you that she hasn't left you or me. She has just disappeared for a while, possibly for ever, but we must both respect that.'

It was as if a bright light were suddenly shining in that pizzeria, a place that had always brought me good memories and good stories. I desperately wanted to believe what the young man was saying; the Zahir was now pulsating all around me.

'Do you know where she is?'

'Yes, I do. But even though I miss her as much as you do, I must respect her silence. I find this whole situation as confusing as you do. Esther may have found satisfaction in the Love that Devours, she might be waiting for one of us to go and find her, she may have met a new man, or she may have withdrawn from the world altogether. Whatever the truth, if you do decide to go and find her, I can't stop you. But, if you do, you must know one thing: you must find not only her body, but also her soul.'

I felt like laughing. I felt like hugging him, or possibly killing him – my emotions changed with startling speed.

'Did you and she ...'

'Did we sleep together? That's none of your business. I found in Esther the partner I was looking for, the person who helped me set out on the mission I was entrusted with, the angel who opened the doors, the roads, the paths that will allow us – if our Lady is willing – to restore the energy of love to the earth. We share the same mission. And just to put your mind at rest: I have a girlfriend, the blonde girl who was on stage with me last night. Her name's Lucrecia; she's Italian.'

'Are you telling me the truth?'

'Yes, in the name of the Divine Energy, I am.'

He took a scrap of dark fabric out of his pocket.

'Do you see this? The cloth is actually green; it looks black because it's caked with dried blood. A soldier somewhere in the world asked her before he died to remove his shirt, then cut it into tiny pieces and distribute those pieces to anyone capable of understanding the message of his death. Do you have a piece?'

'No, Esther has never even mentioned it to me.'

'Whenever she meets someone whom she feels should receive the message, she also gives them a little of the soldier's blood.'

'And what is the message?'

'If she didn't give you a piece of the shirt, I don't think I can tell you; not, of course, that she swore me to secrecy.'

'Do you know anyone else who has a piece of that cloth?'

'All the people who appear with me at the restaurant do. We're only there because Esther brought us together.'

I needed to tread carefully, to build up a relationship, to make a deposit in the Favour Bank. I mustn't frighten him or seem over-eager; I should ask him about himself and his work, about his country, of which he had spoken with such pride; I needed to find out if what he was telling me was true or if he had some ulterior motive; I needed to be absolutely sure that he was still in touch with Esther or if he had lost track of her as well. He may have come from a remote country, where the values are different, but I knew that the Favour Bank operated everywhere: it was an institution that knew no frontiers.

On the one hand, I wanted to believe everything he was saying. On the other, my heart had suffered and bled enough during the thousand and one nights I had lain awake, waiting for the sound of the key in the door, for Esther to come in and lie down beside me, without saying a word. I had promised myself that if this ever happened, I would ask her no questions. I would just kiss her and say 'sleep well, my love' and we would wake the next day, hand in hand, as if this whole nightmare had never happened.

Roberto arrived with the pizzas. He seemed to be endowed with some kind of sixth sense that told him when I needed time to think.

I looked at Mikhail again. Keep calm; if you don't get your pulse rate under control, you'll have a heart attack. I drank a whole glass of wine and noticed that he had done the same.

Why was *he* so nervous?

'Oh, I believe what you say. But we've got plenty of time to talk.'

'You're going to ask me to take you to her.'

He had spoiled my game. I would have to start again.

'Yes, I am. I'm going to try to persuade you. I'm going to do everything in my power to do just that. I'm in no hurry though; we've got a whole pizza to eat first. Besides, I want to know more about you.'

I noticed that he was trying to keep his hands from trembling.

'I'm a person with a mission. I haven't yet managed to fulfil it, but I think I still have time to do so.'

'Perhaps I can help you.'

'Oh, you can. Anyone can; you just have to help spread the energy of love throughout the world.'

'I can do more than that.'

I didn't want to go any further; I didn't want it to look as if I were trying to buy his loyalty. Careful. I had to be very careful. He could be telling the truth, but he could also be lying, trying to take advantage of my suffering.

'I only know of one kind of loving energy,' I went on. 'The one I feel for the woman who left, or, rather, went away and who is waiting for me. If I could see her again, I would be a happy man. And the world would be a better place because one soul would be content.'

He glanced up at the ceiling and back down at the table, and I allowed the silence to last as long as possible.

'I can hear a voice,' he said at last, unable to look at me.

The great advantage of writing about spirituality is that I know I'm bound to keep encountering people with some kind of gift. Some of those gifts are real, others are fraudulent, some of those people are trying to use me, others are merely testing me out. I have seen so many amazing things that I no longer have the slightest doubt that miracles can happen, that everything is possible, and that people are beginning to re-learn the inner powers they long ago forgot.

However, this was not the ideal moment to speak of such matters. I was only interested in the Zahir. I needed the Zahir to become Esther again.

'Mikhail ...'

'Mikhail isn't my real name. My real name is Oleg.'

'Oleg then ...'

'Mikhail is the name I chose when I decided to be reborn to life. Like the warrior archangel, with his fiery sword, opening up a path so that – what is it you call them? – so that the "warriors of light" can find each other. That is my mission.'

'It's my mission too.'

'Wouldn't you rather talk about Esther?'

What? Was he changing the subject again back to the very thing that interested me?

'I'm not feeling very well.' His gaze was starting to wander; he kept glancing around the restaurant as if I were not there. 'I don't want to talk about that. The voice ...'

Something strange, something very strange, was happening. How far was he prepared to go in order to impress me? Would he end up asking me to write a book about his life and powers, like so many others had before him?

Whenever I have a clear objective, I will do anything to achieve it; that, after all, was what I said in my books and I could hardly betray my own words. I had an objective now: to gaze once more into the eyes of the Zahir. Mikhail had given me a lot of new information: he wasn't her lover, Esther hadn't left me, it was just a matter of time before I could bring her back. There was also the possibility that this meeting in the pizzeria was all a farce, that he was just someone with no other means of earning a living than by exploiting someone else's pain in order to achieve his own ends.

I drank another glass of wine; Mikhail did the same.

Take care, my instinct was telling me.

'Yes, I do want to talk about Esther, but I want to know more about you too.'

'That's not true. You're just trying to seduce me, to persuade me to do things I was perfectly prepared to do anyway. Your pain is preventing you from seeing things clearly; you think I could be lying, that I'm trying to take advantage of the situation.'

Mikhail might know exactly what I was thinking, but he was speaking more loudly than good manners permit. People were starting to turn round to see what was going on.

'You're just trying to impress me; you don't realise what an impact your books had on my life or how much I learned from them. Your pain has made you blind, mean-spirited and obsessed with the Zahir. It isn't your love for her that made me accept your invitation to have lunch; in fact, I'm not sure I'm entirely convinced of your love; it might just be wounded pride. The reason I'm here ...'

His voice was growing louder; he was still glancing wildly around, as if he were losing control.

'The lights ...'

'What's wrong?'

'The reason I'm here is her love for you!'

'Are you all right?'

Roberto had noticed that something was wrong. He came over to the table, smiling, and put his hand casually on Mikhail's shoulder.

'Well, the pizza was obviously pretty terrible. No need to pay, you can leave when you like.'

That was the way out we needed. We could simply get up and go, thus avoiding the depressing spectacle of someone in a pizzeria pretending to be communing with the spirit world just to impress or embarrass me, although I did feel that this was more than a theatrical performance.

'Can you feel the wind blowing?'

At that moment, I was sure he wasn't acting; on the contrary, he was making an enormous effort to control himself and was more frightened by what was happening than I was.

'The lights, the lights are starting to appear! Please, get me out of here!'

His body began to be shaken by tremors. There was now no hiding what was going on; the people at the other tables had got up.

'In Kazakh ...'

He did not manage to finish the sentence. He pushed the table away from him; pizzas, glasses and cutlery went flying, hitting the diners on the next table. His expression had changed completely, his whole body was shaking and only the whites of his eyes were now visible. His head was thrown violently back and I heard the sound of bones cracking. A gentleman from one of the other tables leapt to his feet. Roberto caught Mikhail before he fell, while the other man picked up a spoon from the floor and placed it in Mikhail's mouth.

The whole thing can only have lasted a matter of seconds, but to me it seemed like an eternity. I could imagine the scandal sheets describing how a famous writer –and, despite all the adverse reviews, a possible candidate for a major literary prize – had concocted some sort of séance in a pizzeria just to get publicity for his new book. My paranoia was racing out of control; they would find out that the medium in question was the same man who had run off with my wife; it would all start again, and this time I wouldn't have the necessary courage or energy to face the same test.

I knew a few of the other diners, but which of them were really my friends? Who would be capable of remaining silent about what they were seeing?

Mikhail's body stopped shaking and relaxed; Roberto was holding him upright in his chair. The other man took Mikhail's pulse, examined his eyes and then turned to me:

'It's obviously not the first time this has happened. How long have you known him?'

'Oh, they're regular customers,' replied Roberto, seeing that I had become incapable of speech. 'But this is the first time it's happened in public, although, of course, I've had other such cases in my restaurant before.'

'Yes,' said the man. 'I noticed that you didn't panic.'

The remark was clearly aimed at me, for I must have looked deathly pale. The man went back to his table and Roberto tried to reassure me:

'He's the personal physician of a very famous actress,' he said. 'Although it looks to me as if you're more in need of medical attention than your guest here.'

Mikhail – or Oleg or whatever the name was of the young man sitting opposite me – was beginning to come to. He looked around him and, far from seeming embarrassed, he merely smiled rather shyly.

'I'm sorry,' he said. 'I did try to control it.'

I was doing my best to remain calm. Roberto again came to my rescue.

'Don't worry. Our writer here has enough money to pay for the broken plates.'

Then he turned to me:

'Epilepsy. It was just an epileptic fit, that's all.'

I left the restaurant with Mikhail, who immediately hailed a taxi.

'But we haven't talked yet! Where are you going?'

'I'm in no state to talk now. And you know where to find me.'

There are two kinds of world: the one we dream about and the real one.

In my dream world, Mikhail had told the truth: I was just going through a difficult patch, experiencing the kind of misunderstanding that can occur in any love relationship. Esther was somewhere, waiting patiently for me to discover what had gone wrong in our marriage and for me then to go to her and ask her forgiveness so that we could resume our life together.

In that dream world, Mikhail and I talked calmly, left the pizzeria, took a taxi, rang the doorbell of a house where my ex-wife (or my wife? The question now formulated itself the other way round) wove carpets in the morning, gave French lessons in the afternoon and slept alone at night, waiting, like me, for the bell to ring, for her husband to enter bearing a large bouquet of flowers and to carry her off to drink hot chocolate in a hotel near the Champs-Elysées.

In the real world, any meeting with Mikhail would always be tense, because I feared a recurrence of what had happened at the pizzeria. Everything he had said was just the product of his imagination; he had no more idea where Esther was than I did. In the real world, I was at the Gare de l'Est at 11.45 in the morning, waiting for the Strasbourg train to arrive, bringing with it an important American actor and director who very much wanted to produce a film based on one of my books.

Up until then, whenever anyone had mentioned the possibility of making a film adaptation, my answer had always been 'No, I'm not interested.' I believe that each reader creates his own film inside his head, gives faces to the characters, constructs every scene, hears the voices, smells the smells. And that is why, whenever a reader goes to see a film based on a novel that he likes, he leaves feeling disappointed, saying: 'The book is so much better than the film.'

This time, my agent had been more insistent. She told me that this actor and producer was very much 'on our side', and was hoping to do something entirely different from any of the other proposals we had received. The meeting had been arranged two months earlier, and we were to have supper that night to discuss details and see if we really were thinking along the same lines.

In the last two weeks, however, my diary had changed completely: it was Thursday, and I needed to go to the Armenian restaurant, to try to re-establish contact with the young epileptic who swore that he could hear voices, but who was nevertheless the only person who knew where to find the Zahir. I interpreted this as a sign not to sell the film rights of the book and so tried to cancel the meeting with the actor; he insisted and said that it didn't matter in the least; we could have lunch instead the following day: 'No one could possibly feel sad about having to spend a night in Paris alone,' he said, leaving me with no possible comeback.

In the world of my imagination, Esther was still my companion, and her love gave me the strength to go forward and explore all my frontiers.

In the real world, she was pure obsession, sapping my energy, taking up all the available space, and obliging me to make an enormous effort just to continue with my life, my work, my meetings with film producers, my interviews.

How was it possible that, even after two years, I had still not managed to forget her? I could not bear having to think about it any more, analysing all the possibilities, and trying various ways out: deciding simply to accept the situation, writing a book, practising yoga, doing some charity work, seeing friends, seducing women, going out to supper, to the cinema (always avoiding adaptations of books, of course, and seeking out films that had been specially written for the screen), to the theatre, the ballet, to soccer games. The Zahir always won, though; it was always there, making me think: 'I wish she was here with me.'

I looked at the station clock – fifteen minutes to go. In the world of my imagination, Mikhail was an ally. In the real world, I had no concrete proof of this, apart from my great desire to believe what he was saying; he could well be an enemy in disguise.

I returned to the usual questions: Why had she said nothing to me? Or had she been trying to do just that when she asked me the question that Hans had asked? Had Esther decided to save the world, as she had hinted in our conversation about love and war, and was she 'preparing' me to join her on this mission?

My eyes were fixed on the railway tracks. Me and Esther, walking along parallel to each other, never touching. Two destinies that ...

Railway tracks.

How far apart were they?

In order to forget about the Zahir, I tried asking one of the platform staff.

'They're 143.5 centimetres or 4 feet 8½ inches apart,' he replied.

He seemed to be a man at peace with life, proud of his job; he didn't fit Esther's stereotype at all, that we all harbour a great sadness in our soul.

But his answer didn't make any sense at all: 143.5 centimetres or 4 feet 8½ inches?

Absurd. Logically, it should be either 150 centimetres or 5 feet. A round number, easy for builders of carriages and railway employees to remember.

'But why?' I asked the man.

'Because that's the width between the wheels on the carriages.'

'But surely the wheels are that distance apart because the tracks are.'

'Look, just because I work in a railway station doesn't mean I know everything about trains. That's just the way things are.'

He was no longer a happy person, at peace with his work; he could answer one question, but could go no further. I apologised and spent what remained of the fifteen minutes staring at the tracks, feeling intuitively that they were trying to tell me something.

Strange though it may seem, the tracks seemed to be saying something about my marriage, and about all marriages.

The actor arrived, and he was far nicer than I expected, despite being so famous. I left him at my favourite hotel and went home. To my surprise, Marie was there waiting for me, saying that, due to adverse weather conditions, filming had been put off until the following week.

'I assume that, since today is Thursday, you'll be going to the restaurant.'

'Do you want to come too?'

'Yes, I do. Why? Would you prefer to go alone?'

'Yes, I would.'

'Well, I've decided to come anyway. The man hasn't yet been born who can tell me where I can and cannot go.'

'Do you know why all railway tracks are 143.5 centimetres apart?'

'I can try and find out on the Internet. Is it important?'

'Very.'

'Leaving railway tracks to one side for the moment, I was talking to some friends of mine who are fans of your books. They think that anyone who can write books like *A Time to Rend and a Time to Sew*, or the one about the shepherd or the pilgimage to Santiago, must be some kind of sage who has an answer for everything.'

'Which is not quite true, as you know.'

'What is the truth then? How is it that you can pass on to your readers things that are beyond your own knowledge?'

'They're not beyond my knowledge. Everything that's written in my books is part of my soul, part of the lessons I've learned throughout my life, and which I try to apply to myself. I'm a reader of my own books. They show me things that I already knew, even if only unconsciously.'

'What about the reader?'

'I think it's the same for the reader. A book – and we could be talking about anything here, a film, a piece of music, a garden, the view of a mountain – reveals something. "Reveal" means both to un-veil and to re-veil. Removing the veil from something that already exists is different from me trying to teach others the secret of how to live a better life.

Love is giving me a pretty hard time at the moment, as you know. Now this could be seen as a descent into hell or it could be seen as a revelation. It was only when I wrote *A Time to Rend and a Time to Sew* that I understood my own capacity for love. And I learned this while I was actually typing the words and sentences.'

'But what about the spiritual side? What about the spirituality that appears to be present on every page of your books?'

'I'm beginning to like the idea of you coming with me to the Armenian restaurant, because you'll learn – or, rather, become conscious of – three important things. First, that as soon as people decide to confront a problem, they realise that they are far more capable than they thought they were. Second, that all energy and all knowledge come from the same unknown source, which we usually call God. What I've tried to do in my life, ever since I first started out on what I believe to be my path, is to honour that energy, to connect up with it every day, to allow myself to be guided by the signs, to learn by doing and not by thinking about doing.

Third, that no one is alone in their troubles; there is always someone else thinking, rejoicing or suffering in the same way, and that gives us the strength to confront the challenge before us.'

'Does that include suffering for love?'

'It includes everything. If there is suffering, then it's best to accept it, because it won't go away just because you pretend it's not there. If there is joy, then it's best to accept that too, even though you're afraid it might end one day. Some people can only relate to life through sacrifice and renunciation. Some people can only feel part of humanity when they think they are "happy". But why all these questions?'

'Because I'm in love and I'm afraid of suffering.'

'Don't be afraid; the only way to avoid that suffering would be to refuse to love.'

'I can feel Esther's presence. Apart from the young man's epileptic fit, you haven't told me anything else about what happened at the pizzeria. That's a bad sign for me, although it might be a good sign for you.'

'It might be a bad sign for me too.'

'Do you know what I would like to know? I'd like to know if you love me as much as I love you. But I don't have the courage to ask. Why do I have such frustrating relationships with men? I always feel like I have to be in a relationship and that means I have to be this fantastic, intelligent, sensitive, exceptional person. The effort of seduction forces me to give of my best and that helps me. Besides, it's really hard living on your own, and I don't know if that's the best option either.'

'So you want to know if I'm still capable of loving a woman, even though she left me without a word of explanation.'

'I read your book. I know you are.'

'You want to know whether, despite loving Esther, I'm still capable of loving you?'

'I wouldn't dare ask that question because the answer could ruin my life.'

'You want to know if the heart of a man or a woman can contain enough love for more than one person?'

'Since that's a less direct question than the previous one, yes, I'd like an answer.'

'I think it's perfectly possible as long as one of those people doesn't turn into ...'

'... a Zahir. Well, I'm going to fight for you anyway, because I think you're worth it. Any man capable of loving a woman as much as you loved – or love – Esther deserves all my respect and all my efforts. And to show that I want to keep you by my side, to show how important you are in my life, I'm going to do as you ask, however absurd it might be: I'm going to find out why railway tracks are always 4 feet 8½ inches apart.'

The owner of the Armenian restaurant had done exactly what he had told me he was planning to do: the whole restaurant, and not just the room at the back, was now full of people who had come for the 'meeting'. Marie eyed them with some curiosity and occasionally commented on what a very varied crowd they were.

'Why bring children to something like this? It's absurd.'

'Perhaps they haven't got anyone they can leave them with.'

At nine o'clock on the dot, the six 'performers' – the two musicians in oriental dress and the four young people in their white shirts and full skirts – walked onto the stage. Service at the tables came to an immediate halt, and the people in the audience fell silent.

'In the Mongolian creation myth, doe and wild dog come together,' said Mikhail in that voice which was not his own. 'Two beings with very different natures: in the wild, the dog would normally kill the deer for food. In the Mongolian myth, they both understand that they each need the qualities of the other if they are to survive in a hostile world and that they should, therefore, join forces.

To do this, they must first learn to love. And in order to love, they must cease to be who they are, otherwise they will never be able to live together. With the passing of time, the wild dog comes to accept that his instinct, always focused on the struggle to survive, now serves a greater purpose: finding someone with whom he can rebuild the world.'

He paused.

'When we dance, we spin around that same Energy, which rises up to our Lady and returns to us imbued with all her strength, just as the water in rivers evaporates, is transformed into clouds and returns in the form of rain. My story today is about the circle of love.

One morning, a farmer knocked loudly on the door of a monastery. When Brother Porter opened the door, the farmer held out to him a magnificent bunch of grapes.

"Dear Brother Porter, these are the finest grapes from my vineyard. Please accept them as a gift from me."

"Why, thank you! I'll take them straight to the Abbot, who will be thrilled with such a gift."

"No, no. I brought them for you."

"For me? But I don't deserve such a beautiful gift from nature."

"Whenever I knocked on the door, you opened it. When the harvest had been ruined by drought, you gave me a piece of bread and a glass of wine every day. I want this bunch of grapes to bring you a little of the sun's love, the rain's beauty and God's miraculous power."

Brother Porter put the grapes down where he could see them and spent the whole morning admiring them: they really were lovely. Because of this, he decided to give the present to the Abbot, whose words of wisdom had always been such a boon to him.

The Abbot was very pleased with the grapes, but then he remembered that one of the other monks was ill and thought: "I'll give him the grapes. Who knows, they might bring a little joy into his life."

But the grapes did not remain for very long in the room of the ailing monk, for he in turn thought: "Brother Cook has taken such good care of me, giving me only the very best food to eat. I'm sure these grapes will bring him great happiness." And when Brother Cook brought him his lunch, the monk gave him the grapes.

"These are for you. You are in close touch with the gifts Nature gives us and will know what to do with this, God's produce."

Brother Cook was amazed at the beauty of the grapes and drew his assistant's attention to their perfection. They were so perfect that no one could possibly appreciate them more than Brother Sacristan, who had charge of the Holy Sacrament, and whom many in the monastery considered to be a truly saintly man.

Brother Sacristan, in turn, gave the grapes to the youngest of the novices in order to help him understand that God's work is to be found in the smallest details of the Creation. When the novice received them, his heart was filled with the Glory of God, because he had never before seen such a beautiful bunch of grapes. At the same time, he remembered the day he had arrived at the monastery and the person who had opened the door to him; that gesture of opening the door had allowed him to be there now in that community of people who knew the value of miracles.

Shortly before dark, he took the bunch of grapes to Brother Porter.

"Eat and enjoy. You spend most of your time here all alone, and these grapes will do you good."

Brother Porter understood then that the gift really was intended for him; he savoured every grape and went to sleep a happy man. In this way, the circle was closed; the circle of happiness and joy which always wraps around those who are in contact with the energy of love.'

The woman called Alma sounded the cymbal.

'As we do every Thursday, we listen to a story of love and tell stories about the lack of love. Let us look at what is on the surface and then, little by little, we will understand what lies beneath: our habits, our values. And when we can penetrate that layer, we will be able to find ourselves. Who would like to begin?'

Several hands went up, including – to Marie's surprise – mine. The noise started up again; people shifted in their seats. Mikhail pointed to a tall, pretty woman with blue eyes.

'Last week, I went to see a male friend of mine who lives alone in the mountains, near the border with Spain; he loves the good things in life and has often said that any wisdom he may have acquired comes from the fact that he lives each moment to the full. Now, right from the start, my husband was against my going to see this friend. He knows what he's like, that his favourite pastimes are shooting birds and seducing women. But I needed to talk to this friend; I was going through a difficult time and only he could help me. My husband suggested I see a psychiatrist or go on a trip; we even had a row about it, but despite all these domestic pressures, I set off. My friend came to meet me at the airport and we spent the afternoon talking; we ate supper, drank some wine, talked a bit more and then I went to bed. When I woke up the next morning, we went for a walk near where he lives and he dropped me back at the airport.

As soon as I got home, the questions began. Was he alone? Yes. You mean he didn't have a girlfriend with him? No, he didn't. Did you have anything to drink? Yes, I did. Why don't you want to talk about it? But I am talking about it! Alone together in a house in the mountains, eh? Very romantic. So? And all you did was talk, you say? Yes, that's all. And you expect me to believe that? Why shouldn't you believe it? Because it goes against human nature – if a man and a woman get together, have a bit to drink and talk about personal things, they're bound to end up in bed!

I agree with my husband. It does go against everything we're taught. He'll never believe the story I've just told, but it's absolutely true. Since then, our life has become a little hell. It will pass, but going through all this pain is pointless, and all because we've been told that if a man and a woman like each other and circumstances allow, they're bound to end up in bed together.'

Applause. Cigarettes were lit. The clink of glasses and bottles.

'What's going on?' whispered Marie. 'Group therapy for couples?'

'It's all part of the "meeting". No one says whether it's right or wrong, they just tell stories.'

'But why do they do it in public, in this irreverent way, with people drinking and smoking?'

'Perhaps it's to stop things getting too heavy. That way it's easier. And if it helps to make things easier, what's wrong with that?'

'Easier? Talking to a load of strangers who might go and repeat this story to her husband tomorrow?'

Someone else had started talking, and so I wasn't able to tell Marie that it didn't matter: everyone was there to talk about the lack of love disguised as love.

'I'm the husband of the woman who just told that story,' said a man, who must have been at least twenty years older than the pretty, young blonde woman. 'Everything she said is true, but there's something she doesn't know and which I haven't had the courage to tell her. I'll do so now.

When she went off to the mountains, I couldn't sleep all night, and I started imagining, in detail, what was going on. When she arrives, the fire is already lit; she takes off her coat, takes off her sweater; she's not wearing a bra under her thin T-shirt. He can clearly see the shape of her breasts.

She pretends not to notice him looking at her. She says she's going to the kitchen to get another bottle of champagne. She's wearing very tight jeans, she walks slowly, and she doesn't need to turn round to know that he's watching her every move. She comes back, they talk about very personal things, which makes them feel even closer.

They finish talking about the problem that took her there. Her mobile phone rings; it's me, wanting to know if she's all right. She goes over to him, puts the phone to his ear and they both listen to what I have to say; it's an awkward conversation, because I know it's too late to put any kind of pressure on her, it's best just to pretend that everything's fine and tell her to enjoy her time in the mountains, because the following day she'll be back in Paris, taking care of the kids and doing the shopping.

I hang up, knowing that he has heard the whole conversation. The two of them – because, before, they were sitting on separate sofas – are now very close indeed.

At that point, I stopped thinking about what was happening in the mountains. I got up, went into my children's bedroom, walked over to the window and looked out over Paris, and do you know what I felt? I felt excited, very, very excited; the thought of the two of them together, knowing that my wife could, at that very moment, be kissing another man, making love with him, had aroused me sexually.

I felt awful. How could I possibly get excited over something like that? The next day, I talked to two friends; obviously, I didn't use myself as an example, but I asked them if they had ever felt aroused when they caught another man staring at their wife's cleavage. They didn't really answer the question because it's such a taboo. But they both agreed that it's always nice to know that your wife is desired by another man, although they wouldn't go any further than that. Is this a secret fantasy hidden in the hearts of all men? I don't know. This last week has been a little hell for both of us simply because

I didn't understand my own feelings. And because I can't understand them, I blame her for provoking in me feelings that make my world seem suddenly unsafe.'

This time a lot of cigarettes were lit, but there was no applause. It was as if, even there, the subject continued to be a taboo.

I put up my hand again, and meanwhile asked myself if I agreed with what the man had just said. Yes, I did. I had imagined similar scenarios involving Esther and the soldiers she met in war zones, but I had never dared say as much, not even to myself.

Mikhail looked in my direction and nodded.

I don't know how I managed to get to my feet and look at that audience, who were still visibly shocked by the story of the man who had felt aroused by the thought of his wife having sex with another man. No one seemed to be listening, and that helped me make a start.

'I apologise for not being as direct as the two previous speakers, but I nevertheless have something to say. I went to a train station today and learned that the distance between railway tracks is always 143.5 centimetres or 4 feet 8½ inches. Why this absurd measurement? I asked my girlfriend to find out and this is what she discovered. When they built the first train carriages, they used the same tools as they had for building horse-drawn carriages. And why that distance between the wheels on carriages? Because that was the width of the old roads along which the carriages had to travel. And who decided that roads should be that width? Well, suddenly, we are plunged back into the distant past. It was the Romans, the first great road-builders, who decided to make their roads that width.

And why? Because their war chariots were pulled by two horses, and when placed side by side, the horses they used at the time took up 143.5 centimetres.

So the distance between the tracks I saw today, used by our state-of-the-art high-speed trains, was determined by the Romans. When people went to the United States and started building railways there, it didn't occur to them to change the width and so it stayed as it was. This even affected the building of space shuttles. American engineers thought the fuel tanks should be wider, but the tanks were built in Utah and had to be transported by train to the Space Center in Florida, and the tunnels couldn't take anything wider. And so they had to accept the measurement that the Romans had decided was the ideal. But what has all this to do with marriage?'

I paused. Some people were not in the slightest bit interested in railway tracks and had started talking amongst themselves. Others were listening attentively, amongst them Marie and Mikhail.

'It has everything to do with marriage and with the two stories we have just heard. At some point in history, someone turned up and said: when two people get married, they must stay frozen like that for the rest of their lives. You will move along side by side like two tracks, keeping always that same distance apart. Even if sometimes one of you needs to be a little further away or a little closer, that is against the rules. The rules say: be sensible, think of the future, think of your children. You can't change, you must be like two railway tracks that remain the same distance apart all the way from their point of departure to their destination. The rules don't allow for love to change, or to grow at the start and diminish halfway through – it's too dangerous. And so, after the enthusiasm of the first few years, they maintain the same distance, the same solidity, the same functional nature. Your purpose is to allow the train bearing the survival of the species to head off into the future: your children will only be happy if you stay just as you were – 143.5 centimetres apart. If you're not happy with something that never changes, think of them, think of the children you brought into the world.

Think of your neighbours. Show them that you're happy, eat roast beef on Sundays, watch television, help the community. Think of society: dress in such a way that everyone knows you're in perfect harmony. Never glance to the side, someone might be watching you, and that could bring temptation, it could mean divorce, crisis, depression.

Smile in all the photos. Put the photos in the living room, so that everyone can see them. Cut the grass, practise a sport – oh, yes, you must practise a sport in order to stay frozen in time. When sport isn't enough, have plastic surgery. But never forget, these rules were established long ago and must be respected. Who established these rules? That doesn't matter. Don't question them, because they will always apply, even if you don't agree with them.'

I sat down. There was a mixture of enthusiastic applause and indifference, and I wondered if I had gone too far. Marie was looking at me with a mixture of admiration and surprise.

The woman on stage sounded the cymbal.

I told Marie to stay where she was, while I went outside to smoke a cigarette:

'They'll perform a dance now in the name of love, in the name of the Lady.'

'You can smoke in here, can't you?'

'Yes, but I need to be alone.'

It may have been early Spring, but it was still very cold; nevertheless, I was in need of some fresh air. Why had I told that story? My marriage to Esther had never been the way I described: two railway tracks, always beside each other, always forming two correct, straight lines. We had had our ups and downs; one or other of us had occasionally threatened to leave for good; and yet we continued on together.

Until two years ago.

Or until the moment when she began to want to know why she was unhappy.

No one should ever ask themselves that: why am I unhappy? The question carries within it the virus that will destroy everything. If we ask that question, it means we want to find out what makes us happy. If what makes us happy is different from what we have now, then we must either change once and for all or stay as we are, feeling even more unhappy.

I now found myself in precisely that situation: I had a lively, interesting girlfriend, my work was going well, and there was every chance that, in the fullness of time, things would sort themselves out. I should resign myself to the situation. I should accept what life was offering me, not follow Esther's example, not look at anyone else, but remember Marie's words, and build a new life with her.

No, I can't think like that. If I behave in the way people expect me to behave, I will become their slave. It requires enormous self-control not to succumb, because our natural tendency is to want to please, even if the person to be pleased is us. If I do that, I will lose not only Esther, but Marie, my work, my future, as well as any respect I have for myself and for what I have said and written.

When I went back in, I found that people were starting to leave. Mikhail appeared, having already changed out of his stage clothes.

'Listen, what happened at the pizzeria …'

'Oh, don't worry about that,' I said. 'Let's go for a walk by the Seine.'

Marie got the message and said that she needed an early night. I asked her to give us a lift in her taxi as far as the bridge just opposite the Eiffel Tower; that way, I could walk home afterwards. I thought of asking where Mikhail lived, but felt that the question might be construed as an attempt to verify, with my own eyes, that Esther really wasn't living with him.

On the way, Marie kept asking him what the 'meeting' was about, and he always gave the same answer: it's a way of recovering love. He said that he had liked my story about the railway tracks.

'That's how love got lost,' he said. 'When we started laying down rules for when love should or shouldn't appear.'

'When was that?' Marie asked.

'I don't know, but I know it's possible to retrieve that Energy. I know, because when I dance, or when I hear the voice, Love speaks to me.'

Marie didn't know what he meant by 'hearing the voice', but, by then, we had reached the bridge. Mikhail and I got out and started walking in the cold Paris night.

'I know you were frightened by what you saw. The biggest danger when someone has a fit is that their tongue will roll back and they'll suffocate. The owner of the restaurant knew what to do, so it's obviously happened there before. It's not that unusual. But your diagnosis is wrong. I'm not an epileptic. It happens whenever I get in touch with the Energy.'

Of course he was an epileptic, but there was no point in contradicting him. I was trying to act normally. I needed to keep the situation under control. I was surprised how easily he had agreed to this second meeting.

'I need you. I need you to write something about the importance of love,' said Mikhail.

'Everyone knows that love is important. That's what most books are about.'

'All right, let me put my request another way. I need you to write something about the new Renaissance.'

'What's the new Renaissance?'

'It's similar to the Italian Renaissance of the fifteenth and sixteenth centuries, when geniuses like Erasmus, Leonardo and Michelangelo rejected the limitations of the present and the oppressive conventions of their own time and turned instead to the past. We're beginning to see a return to a magical language, to alchemy and the idea of the Mother Goddess, to people reclaiming the freedom to do what they believe in and not what the Church or the Government demand of them. As in fifteenth- and sixteenth-century Florence, we are discovering that the past contains the answers to the future.

Your story about the railway tracks, for example: in how many other areas of our lives are we obeying rules we don't understand? People read what you write, couldn't you introduce the subject somewhere?'

'I never make deals over what I write,' I replied, remembering once more that I needed to keep my self-respect. 'If it's an interesting subject, if it's in my soul, if the boat called "Word" carries me to that particular island, I might write about it. But none of this has anything to do with my search for Esther.'

'I know, and I'm not trying to impose any conditions, I'm just suggesting something that seems important to me.'

'Did she tell you about the Favour Bank?'

'She did. But this isn't a matter for the Favour Bank. It's to do with a mission that I can't fulfil on my own.'

'What you do in the Armenian restaurant, is that your mission?'

'That's just a tiny part of it. We do the same thing on Fridays with a group of beggars. And on Wednesdays we work with a group of new nomads.'

New nomads? It was best not to interrupt; the Mikhail who was talking to me now had none of the arrogance he had shown in the pizzeria, none of the charisma he had revealed on stage or the vulnerability he had revealed on that evening at the book-signing. He was a normal person, a colleague with whom we always end up, late at night, talking over the world's problems.

'I can only write about things that really touch my soul,' I insist.

'Would you like to come with us to talk to the beggars?'

I remembered Esther's remark about the phoney sadness in the eyes of those who should be the most wretched people in the world.

'Let me think about it first.'

We were approaching the Louvre, but he paused to lean on the parapet, and we both stood there contemplating the passing boats, which dazzled us with their spotlights.

'Look at them,' I said, because I needed to talk about something, afraid that he might get bored and go home. 'They only see what the spotlights show them. When they go home, they'll say they know Paris. Tomorrow, they'll go and see the Mona Lisa and claim they've visited the Louvre. But they don't know Paris and have never really been to the Louvre. All they did was go on a boat and look at a painting, one painting, instead of looking at a whole city and trying to find out what's happening in it, visiting the bars, going down streets that don't appear in any of the tourist guides, and getting lost in order to find themselves again. It's the difference between watching a porn movie and making love.'

'I admire your self-control. There you are talking about the boats on the Seine, all the while waiting for the right moment to ask the question that brought you to me. Feel free to talk openly about anything you like.'

There was no hint of aggression in his voice, and so I decided to come straight to the point.

'Where is Esther?'

'Physically, she's a long way away, in Central Asia. Spiritually, she's very close, accompanying me day and night with her smile and the memory of her enthusiastic words. She was the one who brought me here, a poor 21-year-old with no future, an aberration in the eyes of the people in my village, or else a madman or some sort of shaman who had made a pact with the devil, and, in the eyes of the people in the city, a mere peasant looking for work.

I'll tell you my story another day, but the long and the short of it is that I knew English and started working as her interpreter. We were near the border of a country where the Americans were building a lot of military bases, preparing for the war in Afghanistan, and it was impossible to get a visa. I helped her cross the mountains illegally. During the week we spent together, she made me realise that I was not alone, that she understood me.

I asked her what she was doing so far from home. After a few evasive answers, she finally told me what she must have told you: that she was looking for the place where love had hidden itself away. I told her about my mission to make the energy of love circulate freely in the world again. Basically, we were both looking for the same thing.

Esther went to the French embassy and arranged a visa for me, as an interpreter of the Kazakh language, even though no one in my country speaks anything but Russian.

I came to live here. We always met up when she returned from her missions abroad; we made two more trips together to Kazakhstan; she was fascinated by the Tengri culture, and by a nomad she had met and whom she believed held the key to everything.'

I would have liked to know what Tengri was, but the question could wait. Mikhail continued talking, and in his eyes I saw the same longing to be with Esther that I myself was feeling.

'We started working here in Paris. It was her idea to get people together once a week. She said: "The most important thing in all human relationships is conversation, but people don't talk any more, they don't sit down to talk and listen. They go to the theatre, the cinema, watch television, listen to the radio, read books, but they almost never talk. If we want to change the world, we have to go back to a time when warriors would gather round a fire and tell stories."'

I remember Esther saying that all the really important things in our lives had arisen out of long conversations we'd had sitting at a table in some bar or walking along a street or in a park.

'It was my idea that these meetings should be on a Thursday because that's how it is in the tradition in which I was brought up. But it was her idea to make occasional forays into the Paris streets at night. She said that beggars were the only ones who never pretend to be happy; on the contrary, they pretend to be sad.

She gave me your books to read. I sensed that you too – possibly unconsciously – imagined the same world as we did. I realised that I wasn't alone, even if I was the only one to hear the voice. Gradually, as more and more people started coming to the meetings, I began to believe that I really could fulfil my mission and help the energy of love to return, even if that meant going back into the past, back to the moment when that Energy left or went into hiding.'

'Why did Esther leave me?'

Was that all I was interested in? The question irritated Mikhail slightly.

'Out of love. Today, you used the example of the railway tracks. Well, she isn't just another track running along beside you. She doesn't follow rules, nor, I imagine, do you. I miss her too, you know.'

'So ...'

'So if you want to find her, I can tell you where she is. I've already felt the same impulse, but the voice tells me that now is not the moment, that no one should interrupt her encounter with the energy of love. I respect the voice, the voice protects us, protects me, you, Esther.'

'When will the moment be right?'

'Perhaps tomorrow, in a year's time, or never, and, if that were the case, then we would have to respect that decision. The voice is the Energy, and that is why she only brings people together when they are both truly prepared for that moment. And yet we all try and force the situation even if it means hearing the very words we don't want to hear: "Go away." Anyone who fails to obey the voice and arrives earlier or later than he should, will never get the thing he wants.'

'I'd rather hear her tell me to go away than be stuck with the Zahir day and night. If she said that, she would at least cease to be an *idée fixe* and become a woman who now has a different life and different thoughts.'

'She would no longer be the Zahir, but it would be a great loss. If a man and a woman can make the Energy manifest, then they are helping all the men and women of the world.'

'You're frightening me. I love her, you know I do, and you say that she still loves me. I don't know what you mean by being prepared; I can't live according to other people's expectations, not even Esther's.'

'As I understand it from conversations I had with her, at some point you got lost. The world started revolving exclusively around you.'

'That's not true. She was free to forge her own path. She decided to become a war correspondent, even though I didn't want her to. She felt driven to find out why people were unhappy, even though I told her this was impossible. Does she want me to go back to being a railway track running alongside another railway track, always keeping the same stupid distance apart, just because the Romans decided that was the way it should be?'

'On the contrary.'

Mikhail started walking again, and I followed him.

'Do you believe that I hear a voice?'

'To be perfectly honest, I don't know. But now that we're here, let me show you something.'

'Everyone thinks I'm just having an epileptic fit, and I let them believe that because it's easier. But the voice has been speaking to me ever since I was a child, when I first saw the Lady.'

'What lady?'

'I'll tell you later.'

'Whenever I ask you something, you say: "I'll tell you later."'

'The voice is telling me something now. I know that you're anxious and frightened. In the pizzeria, when I felt that warm wind and saw the lights, I knew that these were symptoms of my connection with the Power. I knew it was there to help us both. If you think that all the things I've been telling you are just the ravings of a young epileptic who wants to manipulate the feelings of a famous writer, I'll bring you a map tomorrow showing you where Esther is living, and you can go and find her. But the voice is telling us something.'

'Are you going to say what exactly, or will you tell me later?'

'I'll tell you in a moment. I haven't yet properly understood the message.'

'But you promise to give me the address and the map.'

'I promise. In the name of the divine energy of love, I promise. Now what was it you wanted to show me?'

I pointed to a golden statue of a young woman riding a horse.

'This. She used to hear voices. As long as people respected what she said, everything was fine. When they started to doubt her, the wind of victory changed direction.'

Joan of Arc, the Maid of Orléans, the heroine of the Hundred Years War, who, at the age of seventeen, was made commander of the French troops because she heard voices and the voices told her the best strategy for defeating the English. Two years later, she was condemned to be burned at the stake, accused of witchcraft. I had used part of the interrogation, dated 24 February 1431, in one of my books.

She was questioned by Maître Jean Beaupère. Asked how long it had been since she had heard the voice, she replied:

'I heard it three times, yesterday and today. In the morning, at Vespers, and again when the Ave Maria rang in the evening ...'

Asked if the voice was in the room, she replied that she did not know, but that she had been woken by the voice. It wasn't in the room, but it was in the castle.

She asked the voice what she should do, and the voice asked her to get out of bed and place the palms of her hands together.

Then she said to the bishop who was questioning her:

'You say you are my judge. Take care what you are doing; for in truth I am sent by God, and you place yourself in great danger. My voices have entrusted to me certain things to tell to the King, not to you. The voice comes to me from God. I have far greater fear of doing wrong in saying to you things that would displease it than I have of answering you.'

'Are you suggesting ...'

'That you're the reincarnation of Joan of Arc. No, I don't think so. She died when she was barely nineteen, and you're twenty-five. She took command of the French troops and, according to what you've told me, you can't even take command of your own life.'

We sat down on the wall by the Seine.

'I believe in signs,' I said. 'I believe in fate. I believe that every single day people are offered the chance to make the best possible decision about everything they do. I believe that I failed and that, at some point, I lost my connection with the woman I loved. And now, all I need is to put an end to that cycle. That's why I want the map, so that I can go to her.'

He looked at me and he was once more the person who appeared on stage and went into a trance-like state. I feared another epileptic fit – in the middle of the night, here, in an almost deserted place.

'The vision gave me power. That power is almost visible, palpable. I can manage it, but I can't control it.'

'It's getting a bit late for this kind of conversation. I'm tired, and so are you. Will you give me that map and the address?'

'The voice … Yes, I'll give you the map tomorrow afternoon. What's your address?'

I gave him my address and was surprised to realise that he didn't know where Esther and I had lived.

'Do you think I slept with your wife?'

'I would never even ask. It's none of my business.'

'But you did ask when we were in the pizzeria.'

I had forgotten. Of course it was my business, but I was no longer interested in his answer.

Mikhail's eyes changed. I felt in my pocket for something to place in his mouth should he have a fit, but he seemed calm and in control.

'I can hear the voice now. Tomorrow I will bring you the map, detailed directions and times of flights. I believe that she is waiting for you. I believe that the world would be happier if just two people, even two, were happier. Yet the voice is telling me that we will not see each other tomorrow.'

'I'm having lunch with an actor over from the States, and I can't possibly cancel, but I'll be home during the rest of the afternoon.'

'That's not what the voice is telling me.'

'Is the voice forbidding you to help me find Esther?'

'No, I don't think so. It was the voice that encouraged me to go to the book-signing. From then on, I knew more or less how things would turn out because I had read *A Time to Rend and a Time to Sew*.'

'Right then,' and I was terrified he might change his mind, 'let's stick to our arrangement. I'll be at home from two o'clock onwards.'

'But the voice says the moment is not right.'

'You promised.'

'All right.'

He held out his hand and said that he would come to my apartment late tomorrow afternoon. His last words to me that night were:

'The voice says that it will only allow these things to happen when the time is right.'

As I walked back home, the only voice I could hear was Esther's, speaking of love. And as I remembered that conversation, I realised that she had been talking about our marriage.

'When I was fifteen, I was desperate to find out about sex. But it was a sin, it was forbidden. I couldn't understand why it was a sin, could you? Can you tell me why all religions, all over the world, even the most primitive of religions and cultures, consider that sex is something that should be forbidden?'

'How did we get onto this subject? All right, why is sex something to be forbidden?'

'Because of food.'

'Food?'

'Thousands of years ago, tribes were constantly on the move; men could make love with as many women as they wanted and, of course, have children by them. However, the larger the tribe, the more chances there were of it disappearing. Tribes fought amongst themselves for food, killing first the children and then the women, because they were the weakest. Only the strongest survived, but they were all men. And without women men cannot continue to perpetuate the species.

Then someone, seeing what was happening in a neighbouring tribe, decided to avoid the same thing happening in his. He invented a story according to which the gods forbade men to make love indiscriminately with any of the women in a tribe. They could only make love with one or, at most, two. Some men were impotent, some women were sterile, some members of the tribe, for perfectly natural reasons, thus had no children at all, but no one was allowed to change partners.

They all believed the story because the person who told it to them was speaking in the name of the gods. He must have been different in some way: he perhaps had a deformity, an illness that caused convulsions, or some special gift, something, at any rate, that marked him out from the others, because that is how the first leaders emerged. In a few years, the tribe grew stronger, with just the right number of men needed to feed everyone, with enough women capable of reproducing and enough children to replace the hunters and reproducers. Do you know what gives a woman most pleasure within marriage?'

'Sex.'

'No, making food. Watching her man eat. That is a woman's moment of glory, because she spends all day thinking about supper. And the reason must lie in that story hidden in the past – in hunger, the threat of extinction and the path to survival.'

'Do you regret not having had any children?'

'It didn't happen, did it? How can I regret something that didn't happen?'

'Do you think that would have changed our marriage?'

'How can I possibly know? I look at my friends, both male and female: are they any happier because they have children? Some are, some aren't. And if they are happy with their children that doesn't make their relationship either better or worse. They still think they have the right to control each other. They still think that the promise "to live happily ever after" must be kept, even at the cost of daily unhappiness.'

'War isn't good for you, Esther. It brings you into contact with a very different reality from the one we experience here. I know I'll die one day, but that just makes me live each day as if it were a miracle. It doesn't make me think obsessively about love, happiness, sex, food and marriage.'

'War doesn't leave me time to think. I simply am, full stop. Whenever it occurs to me that, at any moment, I could be hit by a stray bullet, I just think: "Good, at least I don't have to worry about what will happen to my child." But I think too: "What a shame, I'm going to die and nothing will be left of me. I am only capable of losing a life, not bringing a life into the world."'

'Do you think there's something wrong with our relationship? I only ask because I get the feeling sometimes that you want to tell me something, but that you keep stopping yourself.'

'Yes, there is something wrong. We feel obliged to be happy together. You think you owe me everything that you are, and I feel privileged to have a man like you at my side.'

'I have a wife whom I love, but I don't always remember that and find myself asking: "What's wrong with me?"'

'It's good that you're able to recognise that, but I don't think there's anything wrong with you or with me, because I ask myself the same question. What's wrong is the way in which we show our love now. If we were to accept that this creates problems, we could live with those problems and be happy. It would be a constant battle, but it would at least keep us active, alive and cheerful, with many universes to conquer; the trouble is we're heading towards a point where things are becoming too comfortable, where love stops creating problems and confrontations and becomes instead merely a solution.'

'What's wrong with that?'

'Everything. I can no longer feel the energy of love, what people call passion, flowing through my flesh and through my soul.'

'But something is left.'

'Left? Does every marriage have to end like this, with passion giving way to something people call "a mature relationship"? I need you. I miss you. Sometimes I'm jealous. I like thinking about what to give you for supper, even though sometimes you don't even notice what you're eating. But there's a lack of joy.'

'No, there isn't. Whenever you're far away, I wish you were near. I imagine the conversations we'll have when you or I come back from a trip. I phone you to make sure everything's all right. I need to hear your voice every day. I'm still passionate about you, I can guarantee you that.'

'It's the same with me, but what happens when we're together? We argue, we quarrel over nothing, one of us wants to change the other, to impose his or her view of reality. You demand things of me that make no sense at all, and I do the same. Sometimes, in the silence of our hearts, we say to ourselves: "How good it would be to be free, to have no commitments."'

'You're right. And at moments like that, I feel lost, because I know that I'm with the woman I want to be with.'

'And I'm with the man I always wanted to have by my side.'

'Do you think that could change?'

'As I get older, and fewer men look at me, I find myself thinking: "Just leave things as they are." I'm sure I can happily deceive myself for the rest of my life. And yet, whenever I go off to cover a war, I see that a greater love exists, much greater than the hatred that makes men kill each other. And then, and only then, do I think I can change things.'

'But you can't be constantly covering wars.'

'Nor can I live constantly in the sort of peace that I find with you. It's destroying the one important thing I have: my relationship with you, even if the intensity of my love remains undiminished.'

'Millions of people the world over are thinking the same thing right now, they resist fiercely and allow those moments of depression to pass. They withstand one, two, three crises and, finally, find peace.'

'You know that isn't how it is. Otherwise you wouldn't have written the books you've written.'

I had arranged to meet the American actor/director for lunch at Roberto's pizzeria. I needed to go back there as soon as possible in order to dispel any bad impression I might have caused. Before I left, I told the maid and the caretaker of the apartment building that if I was not back in time and a young man with Mongolian features should deliver a package for me, they must take him up to my apartment, ask him to wait in the living room and give him anything he needed. If, for some reason, the young man could not wait, then they should ask him to leave the package with one of them.

Above all, they must not let him leave without handing over the package!

I caught a taxi and asked to be dropped on the corner of Boulevard St-Germain and Rue St-Pères. A fine rain was falling, but it was only a few yards to the restaurant, its discreet sign and Roberto's generous smile, for he sometimes stood outside, smoking a cigarette. A woman with a pushchair was coming towards me along the narrow pavement, and because there wasn't room for both of us, I stepped off the kerb to let her pass.

It was then, in slow motion, that the world gave a giant lurch: the ground became the sky, the sky became the ground; I had time to notice a few architectural details on the top of the building on the corner – I had often walked past before, but had never looked up. I remember the sensation of surprise, the feeling of a wind blowing hard in my ear and the sound of a dog barking in the distance; then everything went dark.

I was bundled abruptly down a black hole at the end of which was a light. Before I could reach it, however, invisible hands were dragging me roughly back up, and I woke to voices and shouts all around me: it could only have lasted a matter of seconds. I was aware of the taste of blood in my mouth, the smell of wet asphalt, and then I realised that I had had an accident. I was conscious and unconscious at the same time; I tried without success to move; I could make out another person lying on the ground beside me; I could smell that person's smell, their perfume; I imagined it must be the woman who had been pushing her baby along the pavement. Oh, dear God!

Someone came over and tried to help me up; I yelled at them not to touch me, any movement could be dangerous. I had learned during a trivial conversation one trivial night that were I ever to fracture my neck, any sudden movement could leave me permanently paralysed.

I struggled to remain conscious; I waited for a pain that never came; I tried to move, then thought better of it. I experienced a feeling like cramp, like torpor. I again asked not to be moved. I heard a distant siren and knew then that I could sleep, that I no longer needed to fight to save my life; whether it was won or lost, it was no longer up to me, it was up to the doctors, to the nurses, to fate, to 'the thing', to God.

I heard the voice of a child – she told me her name, but I couldn't quite grasp it – asking me to keep calm, promising me that I wouldn't die. I wanted to believe what she said, I begged her to stay by my side, but she vanished; I was aware of someone placing something plastic around my neck, putting a mask over my face, and then I went to sleep again, and this time there were no dreams.

When I regained consciousness, all I could hear was a horrible buzzing in my ears; the rest was silence and utter darkness. Suddenly, I felt everything moving, and I was sure I was being carried along in my coffin, that I was about to be buried alive!

I tried banging on the walls, but I couldn't move a muscle. For what seemed an eternity, I felt as if I were being propelled helplessly forwards; then, mustering all my remaining strength, I uttered a scream that echoed round the enclosed space and came back to my own ears, almost deafening me; but I knew that once I had screamed, I was safe, for a light immediately began to appear at my feet: they had realised I wasn't dead!

Light, blessed light – which would save me from that worst of all tortures, suffocation – was gradually illuminating my whole body: they were finally removing the coffin lid. I broke out in a cold sweat, felt the most terrible pain, but was also happy and relieved that they had realised their mistake and that joy could return to the world!

The light finally reached my eyes: a soft hand touched mine, someone with an angelic face was wiping the sweat from my brow.

'Don't worry,' said the angelic face, with its golden hair and white robes. 'I'm not an angel, you didn't die, and this isn't a coffin, it's just a body scanner, to find out if you suffered any other injuries. There doesn't appear to be anything seriously wrong, but you'll have to stay in for observation.'

'No broken bones?'

'Just general abrasions. If I brought you a mirror, you'd be horrified, but the swelling will go down in a few days.'

I tried to get up, but she very gently stopped me. Then I felt a terrible pain in my head and groaned.

'You've had an accident; it's only natural that you should be in pain.'

'I think you're lying to me,' I managed to say. 'I'm a grown man, I've had a good life, I can take bad news without panicking. Some blood vessel in my head is about to burst, isn't it?'

Two nurses appeared and put me on a stretcher. I realised that I had an orthopaedic collar around my neck.

'Someone told us that you asked not to be moved,' said the angel. 'Just as well. You'll have to wear this collar for a while, but barring any unforeseen events – because one can never tell what might happen – you'll just have had a nasty shock. You're very lucky.'

'How long? I can't stay here.'

No one said anything. Marie was waiting for me outside the radiology unit, smiling. The doctors obviously already told her that my injuries were not, in principle, very serious. She stroked my hair and carefully disguised any shock she might feel at my appearance.

Our small cortège proceeded along the corridor – Marie, the two nurses pushing the stretcher, and the angel in white. The pain in my head was getting worse all the time.

'Nurse, my head ...'

'I'm not a nurse. I'm your doctor for the moment. We're waiting for your own doctor to arrive. As for your head, don't worry. When you have an accident, your body closes down all the blood vessels as a defence mechanism, to avoid loss of blood. When it sees that the danger is over, the vessels open up again, the blood starts to flow and that feels painful, but that's all it is. Anyway, if you like, I can give you something to help you sleep.'

I refused. And as if surfacing from some dark corner of my soul, I remembered the words I had heard the day before:

'The voice says that it will only allow these things to happen when the time is right.'

He couldn't have known. It wasn't possible that everything that had happened on the corner of Boulevard St-Germain and Rue St-Pères was the result of some universal conspiracy, of something predetermined by the gods, who, despite being fully occupied in taking care of this precariously balanced planet on the verge of extinction, had all downed tools merely to prevent me from going in search of the Zahir. Mikhail could not possibly have foreseen the future, unless he really had heard a voice and there *was* a plan and this was all far more important than I imagined.

Everything was beginning to be too much for me: Marie's smiles, the possibility that someone really had heard a voice, the increasingly agonising pain in my head.

'Doctor, I've changed my mind. I want to sleep. I can't stand the pain.'

She said something to one of the nurses pushing the trolley, who went off and returned even before we had reached my room. I felt a prick in my arm and immediately fell asleep.

When I woke up, I wanted to know exactly what had happened; I wanted to know if the woman passing me on the pavement had escaped injury and what had happened to her baby. Marie said that I needed to rest, but, by then, Dr Louit, my doctor and friend, had arrived and felt that there was no reason not to tell me. I had been knocked down by a motorbike. The body I had seen lying on the ground beside me had been the young male driver. He had been taken to the same hospital and, like me, had escaped with only minor abrasions. The police investigation carried out immediately after the accident made it clear that I had been standing in the middle of the road at the time of the accident, thus putting the motorcyclist's life at risk.

It was, apparently, all my fault, but the motorcyclist had decided not to press charges. Marie had been to see him and talk to him; she had learned that he was an immigrant working illegally and was afraid of having any dealings with the police. He had been discharged twenty-four hours later, because he had been wearing a helmet, which lessened the risk of any damage to the brain.

'Did you say he left twenty-four hours later? Does that mean I've been in here more than a day?'

'You've been in here for three days. When you came out of the body scanner, the doctor here phoned me to ask if she could keep you on sedatives. It seemed to me that you'd been rather tense, irritated and depressed lately, and so I told her she could.'

'So what happens next?'

'Two more days in hospital and then three weeks with that contraption around your neck; you're through the critical 48-hour period. Of course, part of your body could still rebel against the idea of continuing to behave itself and then we'd have a problem on our hands. But let's face that emergency if and when it arises; there's no point in worrying unnecessarily.'

'So, I could still die?'

'As you well know, all of us not only can but will die.'

'Yes, but could I still die as a result of the accident?'

Dr Louit paused.

'Yes. There's always the chance that a blood clot could have formed which the machines have failed to pick up and that it could break free at any moment and cause an embolism. There's also the possibility that a cell has gone berserk and is starting to form a cancer.'

'You shouldn't say things like that,' said Marie.

'We've been friends for five years. He asked me a question and I gave him an answer. And now, if you don't mind, I have to get back to my office. Medicine isn't quite as you think. In the world we live in, if a boy goes out to buy five apples, but arrives home with only two, people would conclude that he had eaten the three missing apples. In my world, there are other possibilities: he could have eaten them, but he could also have been robbed; the money he'd been given might not have been enough to buy the five apples he'd been sent for; he could have lost them on the way home; he could have met someone who was hungry and decided to share the fruit with that person, and so on. In my world, everything is possible and everything is relative.'

'What do you know about epilepsy?'

Marie knew at once that I was talking about Mikhail and could not conceal a flicker of displeasure. She said she had to go, there was a film crew waiting.

Dr Louit, however, having picked up his things ready to leave, stopped to answer my question.

'It's an excess of electrical impulses in one specific area of the brain, which provoke convulsions of greater or lesser severity. There's no definitive study on the subject, but they think attacks may be provoked when the person is under great strain. But don't worry, while epileptic symptoms can appear at any age, epilepsy itself is unlikely to be brought on by colliding with a motorcycle.'

'So what causes it?'

'I'm not a specialist, but, if you like, I can find out.'

'Yes, if you would. And I have another question too, but please don't go thinking that my brain's been affected by the accident. Is it possible that epileptics can hear voices and have premonitions?'

'Did someone tell you this accident was going to happen?'

'Not exactly, but that's what I took it to mean.'

'Look, I can't stay any longer, I'm giving Marie a lift, but I'll see what I can find out about epilepsy for you.'

For the two days that Marie was away, and despite the shock of the accident, the Zahir took up its usual space in my life. I knew that if Mikhail had kept his word, there would be an envelope waiting for me at home containing Esther's address; now, however, the thought frightened me.

What if Mikhail was telling the truth about the voice?

I started trying to remember the details of the accident: I had stepped down from the kerb, automatically looking to see if anything was coming; I'd seen a car approaching, but it had appeared to be a safe distance away. And yet I had still been hit, possibly by a motorbike trying to overtake the car and which had been outside my field of vision.

I believe in signs. After I had walked the road to Santiago, everything had changed completely: what we need to learn is always there before us, we just have to look around us with respect and attention in order to discover where God is leading us and which step we should take next. I also learned a respect for mystery: as Einstein said, God does not play dice with the Universe; everything is interconnected and has a meaning. That meaning may remain hidden nearly all the time, but we always know we are close to our true mission on earth when what we are doing is touched with the energy of enthusiasm.

If it is, then all is well. If not, then we had better change direction.

When we are on the right path, we follow the signs, and if we occasionally stumble, Divinity comes to our aid, preventing us from making a mistake. Was the accident a sign? Had Mikhail intuited a sign that was intended for me?

I decided that the answer to these questions was 'Yes'.

And perhaps because of this, because I accepted my destiny and allowed myself to be guided by something greater than myself, I noticed that, during the day, the Zahir began to diminish in intensity. I knew that all I had to do was open the envelope, read her address, and go and knock on her door, but the signs all indicated that this was not the moment. If Esther really was as important in my life as I thought, if she still loved me (as Mikhail said she did), why force a situation that would simply lead me into making the same mistakes I had made in the past?

How to avoid repeating them?

By knowing myself better, by finding out what had changed and what had provoked this sudden break in a road that had always been marked by joy.

Was that enough?

No, I also needed to know who Esther was, what changes she had undergone during the time we were together.

And was it enough to be able to answer these two questions?

There was a third: why had fate brought us together?

I had a lot of free time in that hospital room, and so I made a general review of my life. I had always sought both adventure and security, knowing that the two things did not really mix. I was sure of my love for Esther and yet I easily fell in love with other women, merely because the game of seduction is the most interesting game in the world.

Had I shown my wife that I loved her? Perhaps for a while, but not always. Why? Because I didn't think it was necessary; she must know I loved her; she couldn't possibly doubt my feelings.

I remember that, many years ago, someone asked me if there was a common denominator amongst all the various girlfriends I had had in my life. The answer was easy: ME. And when I realised this, I saw how much time I had wasted looking for the right person – the women changed, but I remained the same and so got nothing from those shared experiences. I had lots of girlfriends, but I was always waiting for the right person. I controlled and was controlled and the relationship never went any further than that, until Esther arrived and changed everything.

I was thinking tenderly of my ex-wife; I was no longer obsessed with finding her, with finding out why she had left without a word of explanation. *A Time to Rend and a Time to Sew* had been a true account of my marriage, but it was, above all, my own testimony, declaring that I am capable of loving and needing someone else. Esther deserved more than just words, especially since I had never said those words while we were together.

It is always important to know when something has reached its end. Closing circles, shutting doors, finishing chapters, it doesn't matter what we call it; what matters is to leave in the past those moments in life that are over. Slowly, I began to realise that I could not go back and force things to be as they once were: those two years, which up until then had seemed an endless inferno, were now beginning to show me their true meaning.

And that meaning went far beyond my marriage: all men and all women are connected by an energy which many people call love, but which is, in fact, the raw material from which the universe was built. This energy cannot be manipulated, it leads us gently forwards, it contains all we have to learn in this life. If we try to make it go in the direction we want, we end up desperate, frustrated, disillusioned, because that energy is free and wild.

We could spend the rest of our life saying that we love such a person or thing, when the truth is that we are merely suffering because, instead of accepting love's strength, we are trying to diminish it so that it fits the world in which we imagine we live.

The more I thought about this, the weaker the Zahir became and the closer I moved to myself. I prepared myself mentally to do a great deal of work, work that would require much silence, meditation, and perseverance. The accident had helped me understand that I could not force something that had not yet reached its 'time to sew'.

I remembered what Dr Louit had said: after such a trauma to the body, death could come at any moment. What if that were true? What if in ten minutes' time, my heart stopped beating?

A nurse came into the room to bring me my supper and I asked him:

'Have you thought about your funeral?'

'Don't worry,' he replied. 'You'll survive; you already look much better.'

'I'm not worried. I know I'm going to survive. A voice told me I would.'

I mentioned the 'voice' deliberately, just to provoke him. He eyed me suspiciously, thinking that perhaps it was time to call for another examination and check that my brain really hadn't been affected.

'I know I'm going to survive,' I went on. 'Perhaps for a day, for a year, for thirty or forty years, but one day, despite all the scientific advances, I'll leave this world and I'll have a funeral. I was thinking about it just now and I wondered if you had ever thought about it.'

'Never. And I don't want to either; besides, that's what really terrifies me, knowing that everything will end.'

'Whether you like it or not, whether you agree or disagree, that is a reality none of us can escape. Do you fancy having a little chat about it?'

'I've got other patients to see, I'm afraid,' he said, putting the food down on the table and leaving as quickly as possible, as if running away – not from me, but from my words.

The nurse might not want to talk about it, but how about me thinking about it alone? I remembered some lines from a poem I had learned as a child:

> *When the Unwanted Guest arrives …*
> *I might be afraid.*
> *I might smile or say:*
> *My day was good, let night fall.*
> *You will find the fields ploughed, the house clean,*
> *the table set,*
> *and everything in its place.*

It would be nice if that were true – everything in its place. And what would my epitaph be? Esther and I had both made wills, in which, amongst other things, we had chosen cremation: my ashes were to be scattered to the winds in a place called Cebreiro, on the road to Santiago, and her ashes were to be scattered over the sea. So there would be no inscribed headstone.

But what if I could choose an epitaph? I would ask to have these words engraved:

He died while he was still alive.

That might sound like a contradiction in terms, but I knew many people who had ceased to live, even though they continued to work and eat and engage in their usual social activities. They did everything automatically, oblivious to the magic moment that each day brings with it, never stopping to think about the miracle of life, never understanding that the next minute could be their last on the face of this planet.

It was pointless trying to explain this to the nurse, largely because it was a different nurse who came to collect the supper dish. This new nurse started bombarding me with questions, possibly on the orders of some doctor. He wanted to know if I could remember my name, if I knew what year it was, the name of the President of the United States, the sort of thing they ask when they're assessing your mental state.

And all because I asked the questions that every human being should ask: have you thought about your funeral? Do you realise that sooner or later you're going to die?

That night, I went to sleep smiling. The Zahir was disappearing, and Esther was returning, and if I were to die then, despite all that had happened in my life, despite all my failures, despite the disappearance of the woman I loved, the injustices I had suffered or inflicted on others, I had remained alive until the last moment, and could, with all certainty, affirm:

'My day was good, let night fall.'

Two days later, I was back home. Marie went to prepare lunch, and I glanced through the accumulated correspondence. The entry-phone rang. It was the caretaker to say that the envelope I had expected the previous week had been delivered and should be on my desk.

I thanked him, but, contrary to all my expectations, I did not immediately rush to open it. Marie and I had lunch; I asked her how filming had gone and she asked me about my immediate plans, given that I wouldn't be able to go out much while I was wearing the orthopaedic collar. She said that she could, if necessary, come and stay.

'I'm supposed to do an appearance on some Korean TV channel, but I can always put it off or even cancel it altogether. That's, of course, if you need my company.'

'Oh, I do, and it would be lovely to have you around.'

She smiled broadly and picked up the phone to call her manager and ask her to change her engagements. I heard her say: 'Don't tell them I'm ill though. I'm superstitious, and whenever I've used that excuse in the past, I've always gone down with something really horrible. Just tell them I've got to look after the person I love.'

I had a series of urgent things to do too: interviews to be postponed, invitations that required replies, letters to be written thanking various people for the phone calls and flowers I'd received, things to read, prefaces and recommendations to write. Marie spent the whole day on the phone to my agent, reorganising my diary so that no one would be left without a response. We had supper at home every evening, talking about the interesting and the banal, just like any other couple. During one of these suppers, after a few glasses of wine, she remarked that I had changed.

'It's as if having a brush with death had somehow brought you back to life,' she said.

'That happens to everyone.'

'But I must say – and, don't worry, I don't want to start an argument and I'm not about to have an attack of jealousy – you haven't mentioned Esther once since coming home. The same thing happened when you finished *A Time to Rend and a Time to Sew*: the book acted as a kind of therapy, the effects of which, alas, didn't last very long.'

'Are you saying that the accident has affected my brain?'

My tone wasn't aggressive, but she nevertheless decided to change the subject and started telling me about a terrifying helicopter trip she'd had from Monaco to Cannes. Later, in bed, we made love – with great difficulty given my orthopaedic collar – but we made love nevertheless and felt very close.

Four days later, the vast pile of paper on my desk had disappeared. There was only a large, white envelope bearing my name and the number of my apartment. Marie went to open it, but I told her it could wait.

She didn't ask me about it, perhaps it was information about my bank accounts or some confidential correspondence, possibly from another woman. I didn't explain either; I simply removed it from the desk and placed it on a shelf amongst some books. If I kept looking at it, the Zahir would come back.

At no point had the love I felt for Esther diminished; but every day spent in hospital had brought back some intriguing memory: not of conversations we had had, but of moments we had spent together in silence. I remembered her eyes, which, whenever she set off on some new adventure, were like those of an enthusiastic young girl, or like those of a wife proud of her husband's success or of the journalist fascinated by every subject she wrote about and, later, like those of the wife who no longer seemed to have a place in my life. That look of sadness had started before she told me she wanted to be a war correspondent; it became a look of joy every time she came back from an assignment, but it was only a matter of days before the look of sadness returned.

One afternoon, the phone rang:

'It's that young man,' Marie said, passing me the phone.

At the other end I heard Mikhail's voice, first saying how sorry he was about the accident and then asking me if I had received the envelope.

'Yes, it's here with me.'

'Are you going to go and find her?'

Marie was listening to our conversation and so I thought it best to change the subject.

'We can talk about that when I see you.'

'I'm not nagging or anything, but you did promise to help me.'

'And I always keep my promises. As soon as I'm better, we'll get together.'

He left me his mobile number, and when I hung up, I looked across at Marie, who seemed a different woman.

'So nothing's changed then,' she said.

'On the contrary. Everything's changed.'

I should have expressed myself more clearly and explained that I still wanted to see Esther, that I knew where she was. When the time was right, I would take a train, taxi, plane or whatever just to be by her side. This would, of course, mean losing the woman who was there by my side at that moment, steadfastly doing all she could to prove how important I was to her.

I was, of course, being a coward. I was ashamed of myself, but that was what life was like and – in a way I couldn't really explain – I loved Marie too.

The other reason I didn't say more was because I had always believed in signs, and when I recalled the moments of silence I had shared with my wife, I knew that – with or without voices, with or without explanations – the time to find Esther had still not yet arrived. I needed to concentrate more on those shared silences than on any of our conversations, because that would give me the freedom I needed to understand the time when things had gone right between us and the moment when they had started to go wrong.

Marie was there, looking at me. Could I go on being disloyal to someone who was doing so much for me? I started to feel uncomfortable, but I couldn't tell her everything, unless ... unless I could find an indirect way of saying what I was feeling.

'Marie, let's suppose that two firemen go into a forest to put out a small fire. Afterwards, when they emerge and go over to a stream, the face of one is all smeared with black, while the other man's face is completely clean. My question is this: which of the two will wash his face?'

'That's a silly question. The one with the dirty face of course.'

'No, the one with the dirty face will look at the other man and assume that he looks like him. And, vice versa, the man with the clean face will see his colleague covered in grime and say to himself: I must be dirty too. I'd better have a wash.'

'What are you trying to say?'

'I'm saying that, during the time I spent in hospital, I came to realise that I was always looking for myself in the women I loved. I looked at their lovely, clean faces and saw myself reflected in them. They, on the other hand, looked at me and saw the dirt on my face and, however intelligent or self-confident they were, they ended up seeing themselves reflected in me and thinking that they were worse than they were. Please, don't let that happen to you.'

I would like to have added: that's what happened to Esther, and I've only just realised it, remembering now how the look in her eyes changed. I'd always absorbed her life and her energy, and that made me feel happy and confident, able to go forward. She, on the other hand, had looked at me and felt ugly, diminished, because, as the years passed, my career – the career that she had done so much to make a reality – had relegated our relationship to second place.

If I was to see her again, my face needed to be as clean as hers. Before I could find her, I must first find myself.

ARIADNE'S

THREAD

'I am born in a small village, some kilometres from a slightly larger village where they have a school and a museum dedicated to a poet who lived there many years before. My father is nearly seventy years old, my mother is twenty-five. They met only recently when he was selling carpets; he had travelled all the way from Russia, but when he met her he decided to give up everything for her sake. She could be his daughter, but she behaves more like his mother, even helping him to sleep, something he has been unable to do properly since he was seventeen and was sent to fight the Germans in Stalingrad, one of the longest and bloodiest battles of the Second World War. Out of a battalion of three thousand men, only three survived.'

Oddly, Mikhail speaks almost entirely in the present tense. He doesn't say 'I was born' but 'I am born'. It is as if everything were happening here and now.

'In Stalingrad, my father and his best friend are caught in an exchange of fire on their way back from a reconnaissance patrol. They take cover in a bomb crater and spend two days in the mud and snow, with no food and no means of keeping warm. They can hear other Russians talking in a nearby building and know that they must try to reach them, but the firing never stops, the smell of blood fills the air, the wounded lie screaming for help day and night. Suddenly, everything falls silent. My father's friend, thinking that the Germans have withdrawn, stands up. My father tugs at his legs, yelling: "Get down!" But it's too late; a bullet pierces his friend's skull.

Another two days pass, my father is alone, with his friend's corpse beside him. He can't stop yelling "Get down!" At last, someone rescues him and takes him to the nearby building. There is no food, only ammunition and cigarettes. They eat the tobacco. A week later, they start to eat the flesh of their dead, frozen companions. A third battalion arrives and shoots a way through to them; the survivors are rescued, the wounded are treated and then immediately sent back to the front. Stalingrad must not fall; the future of Russia is at stake. After four months of intense fighting, of cannibalism, of limbs being amputated because of frost bite, the Germans finally surrender – it is the beginning of the end for Hitler and his Third Reich. My father returns on foot to his village, almost a thousand kilometres from Stalingrad. He now finds it almost impossible to sleep and when he does manage to drop off, he dreams every night of the friend he could have saved.

Two years later, the war ends. He receives a medal, but cannot find employment. He takes part in services of commemoration, but has almost nothing to eat. He is considered one of the heroes of Stalingrad, but can only survive by doing odd jobs for which he is paid a pittance.

In the end, someone offers him work selling carpets. Suffering as he does from insomnia, he chooses to travel at night; he gets to know smugglers, wins their confidence, and begins to earn some money.

He is caught out by the Communist government, who accuse him of consorting with criminals and, despite being a war hero, he spends the next ten years in Siberia labelled "a traitor of the people". When he is finally released, he is an old man and the only thing he knows anything about are carpets. He manages to re-establish his old contacts, someone gives him a few carpets to sell, but no one is interested in buying – times are hard. He decides to go a long way away, begging as he goes, and ends up in Kazakhstan.

He is old and alone, but he needs to work in order to eat. He spends the days doing odd jobs and, at night, sleeps only fitfully and is woken by his own cries of "Get down!" Strangely enough, despite all that he has been through, despite the insomnia, the poor food, the frustrations, the physical wear and tear, and the cigarettes that he smokes whenever he can scrounge them, he still has an iron constitution.

In a small village, he meets a young woman. She lives with her parents; she takes him to her house, for, in that region, hospitality is paramount. They let him sleep in the living room, but are woken by his screams. The girl goes to him, says a prayer, strokes his head and, for the first time in many decades, he sleeps peacefully.

The following day, she says that, when she was a girl, she had dreamed that a very old man would give her a child. She waited for years, had various suitors, but was always disappointed. Her parents were terribly worried, for they did not want to see their only daughter end up a spinster, rejected by the community.

She asks him if he will marry her. He is taken aback; after all, she is nearly young enough to be his grand-daughter, and so he says nothing. At sunset, in the small living room, she asks if she can stroke his head before he goes to sleep. He enjoys another peaceful night.

The following day, the subject of marriage comes up again, this time in the presence of her parents, who seem to think it a good idea; they just want their daughter to find a husband and to cease being a source of family shame. They invent a story about an old man who has come from far away and who is, in fact, a wealthy trader in carpets, but has grown weary of living a life of luxury and comfort, and has given it all up in order to go in search of adventure. People are impressed, they imagine a generous dowry, huge bank accounts, and think how lucky my mother is to have finally found someone who can take her away from that village in the back of beyond. My father listens to these stories with a mixture of fascination and surprise; he thinks of all the years he has spent alone, travelling, of all he has suffered, of how he never again found his own family, and he thinks that now, for the first time in his life, he could have a home of his own. He accepts the proposal, colludes with the lies about his past, and they get married according to the Muslim tradition. Two months later, she is pregnant with me.

I live with my father until I am seven years old; he sleeps well, works in the fields, goes hunting and talks to the other villagers about his money and his lands; and he looks at my mother as if she were the only good thing that has ever happened to him. I grow up believing that I am the son of a rich man, but one night, by the fire, he tells me about his past and why he married, but begs me not to tell anyone else. Soon, he says, he will die, and four months later he does. He breathes his last in my mother's arms, smiling, as if he had never known a moment's sadness. He dies a happy man.'

Mikhail is telling his story on a very cold spring night, although it is certainly not as cold as in Stalingrad, where temperatures can plummet to -35°C. We are sitting with some beggars who are warming themselves before an improvised bonfire. I had gone there after a second phone call from Mikhail, asking me to keep my part of the promise. During our conversation, he did not once mention the envelope he had left at my apartment, as if he knew – perhaps through the 'voice' – that I had, in the end, decided to follow the signs and allow things to happen in their own time and thus free myself from the power of the Zahir.

When he asked me to meet him in one of the most dangerous parts of Paris, my first reaction was one of alarm. Normally, I would have said that I was far too busy and tried to convince him that we would be better off going to some cosy bar where we could safely discuss important matters. I was still afraid that he might have another epileptic fit in public, even though I now knew what to do, but that was preferable to the risk of being mugged when I was wearing an orthopaedic collar and had no way of defending myself.

Mikhail insisted: I had to meet the beggars; they were part of his life and part of Esther's life too. I had realised while I was in hospital that there was something wrong with my own life and that change was urgently needed. How best to achieve that change? By doing something totally different; for example, going to dangerous places and meeting social outcasts.

There is a story about a Greek hero, Theseus, who goes into a labyrinth in order to slay a monster. His beloved, Ariadne, gives him one end of a thread so that he can unroll it as he goes and thus be able to find his way out again. Sitting with those people, listening to Mikhail's story, it occurs to me that I have not experienced anything like this for a long time – the taste of the unknown, of adventure. Who knows, perhaps Ariadne's thread was waiting for me in precisely the kind of place that I would never normally visit, or only if I was convinced that I had to make an enormous effort to change my story and my life.

Mikhail continued his story, and I saw that the whole group was listening to what he was saying: the most satisfying encounters do not always happen around elegant tables in nice, warm restaurants.

'Every day, I have to walk nearly an hour to the village where I go to school. I see the women going to fetch water, the endless steppes, the Russian soldiers driving past in long convoys, the snow-capped mountains which, I am told, conceal a vast country: China. The village I walk to each day has a museum dedicated to its one poet, a mosque, a school and three or four streets. We are taught about the existence of a dream, an ideal: we must fight for the victory of Communism and for equality amongst all human beings. I do not believe in this dream, because even in this wretchedly poor village, there are marked differences: the Party representatives are above everyone else; now and again, they visit the big city, Almaty, and return bearing packages of exotic food, presents for their children, expensive clothes.

One afternoon, on my way home, I feel a strong wind blowing, see lights all around me and lose consciousness for a few moments. When I come to, I am sitting on the ground, and a very white little girl, wearing a white dress with a blue belt, is floating in the air above me. She smiles, but says nothing, then disappears.

I run home, interrupt my mother's work, and tell her what I have seen. She is terrified and asks me never to repeat what I have just told her. She explains to me – as well as one can explain such a complicated concept to an eight-year-old boy – that it was just an hallucination. I tell her that I really did see the girl, that I can describe her in every detail. I add that I wasn't afraid and came home at once because I wanted her to know what had happened.

The following day, coming back from school, I look for the girl, but she isn't there. Nothing happens for a whole week, and I begin to think that perhaps my mother was right: I must simply have dropped asleep and dreamed it all.

Then, this time very early one morning, on my way to school, I again see the girl floating in the air and surrounded by a white halo. I don't fall to the ground or see any flashing lights. We stand for a while, looking at each other; she smiles and I smile back; I ask her name, but receive no answer. At school, I ask my classmates if they have ever seen a girl floating in the air. They all laugh.

During class, I am summoned to the headmaster's office. He explains to me that I must have some mental problem – there is no such thing as "visions"; the only reality is what we see around us; religion was merely invented to fool the people. I ask about the mosque in the city; he says that only the old and superstitious go there, ignorant, idle people who lack the necessary energy to rebuild the socialist world. Then he issues a threat: if I repeat the story about the little girl, I will be expelled. Terrified, I beg him not to say anything to my mother, and he agrees, as long as I tell my classmates that I made the whole thing up.

He keeps his promise and I keep mine. My friends aren't much interested anyway and don't even ask me to show them the place where I saw the girl. However, she continues to appear to me for the whole of the following month. Sometimes I faint first, sometimes I don't. We never talk, we simply stay together for as long as she chooses to stay. My mother is beginning to grow worried because I always arrive home at a different time. One night, she forces me to explain what I do between leaving school and getting home. I again tell her about the little girl.

To my surprise, this time, instead of scolding me, she says that she will go to the place with me. The following day, we wake early and, when we arrive, the girl appears, but my mother cannot see her. My mother tells me to ask the girl something about my father. I don't understand the question, but I do as she requests, and then, for the first time, I hear the "voice". The girl does not move her lips, but I know she is talking to me: she says that my father is fine and is watching over us, and that he is being rewarded now for all his sufferings on earth. She suggests that I remind my mother about the heater. I do so, and my mother starts to cry and explains that because of his many hardships during the war, the thing my father most enjoyed was sitting next to a heater. The girl says that the next time my mother passes that way she should tie a scrap of fabric and a prayer around the small tree growing there.

The visions continue for a whole year. My mother tells some of her closest friends, who tell other friends, and soon the tree is covered in scraps of fabric. Everything is done in the greatest secrecy; the women ask about loved ones who have died; I listen to the voice's answers and pass on the messages. Usually, their loved ones are fine, and on only two occasions does the girl ask the group to go to a nearby hill at sunrise and say a wordless prayer for the souls of those people. Apparently, I sometimes go into a trance, fall to the ground, babble incomprehensibly, but I can never remember anything about it. I only know that when I am about to go into a trance, I feel a warm wind blowing and see bubbles of light all around me.

One day, when I am taking a group to meet the little girl, we are prevented from doing so by the police. The women protest and shout, but we cannot get through. I am escorted to school, where the headmaster informs me that I have just been expelled for provoking rebellion and encouraging superstition.

On the way back, I see that the tree has been cut down and the "ribbons" scattered on the ground. I sit down alone and weep, because those had been the happiest days of my life. At that moment, the girl reappears. She tells me not to worry, that this was all part of the plan, even the destruction of the tree, and that she will accompany me now for the rest of my days and will always tell me what I must do.'

'Did she never tell you her name?' asks one of the beggars.

'Never. But it doesn't matter because I always know when she's talking to me.'

'Could we find out something about our dead?'

'No. That only happened during one particular period. Now my mission is different. May I go on with my story?'

'Absolutely,' I say. 'But can I just ask one thing? There's a town in south-west France called Lourdes. A long time ago, a shepherdess saw a little girl, who seems to correspond to your vision.'

'No, you're wrong,' says one of the older beggars, who has an artificial leg. 'The shepherdess, whose name was Bernadette, saw the Virgin Mary.'

'I've written a book about her visions and I had to study the matter closely,' I say. 'I read everything that was published about it at the end of the nineteenth century; I had access to Bernadette's many statements to the police, to the Church and to scholars. At no point does she say that she saw a woman; she insists it was a girl. She repeated the same story all her life and was deeply angered by the statue that was placed in the grotto; she said it bore no resemblance to her vision, because she had seen a little girl, not a woman. Nevertheless, the Church appropriated the story, the visions and the place, and transformed the apparition into the Mother of Jesus, and the truth was forgotten. If a lie is repeated often enough, it ends up convincing everyone. The only difference is that "the little girl" – as Bernadette always referred to her – had a name.'

'What was it?' asks Mikhail.

'"I am the Immaculate Conception." Obviously that isn't a name like Beatriz or Maria or Isabelle. She describes herself as a fact, an event, a happening, which is sometimes translated as "I am birth without sex". Now, please, go on with your story.'

'Before he does, can I ask you something?' says another beggar, who must be about my age. 'You just said that you've written a book; what's the title?'

'I've written many books.'

And I tell him the title of the book in which I mention the story of Bernadette and her vision.

'So you're the husband of the journalist?'

'Are you Esther's husband?' asks a female beggar, wide-eyed; she is dressed garishly, in a green hat and a purple coat.

I don't know what to say.

'Why hasn't she been back here?' asks someone else. 'I hope she isn't dead. She was always going to such dangerous places. I often told her she shouldn't. Look what she gave me!'

PAULO COELHO

And she shows me a scrap of bloodstained fabric, part of the dead soldier's shirt.

'No, she's not dead,' I say. 'But I'm surprised to hear that she used to come here.'

'Why? Because we're different?'

'No, you misunderstand me. I'm not judging you. I'm surprised and pleased to know that she did.'

However, the vodka we have been drinking to ward off the cold is having an effect on all of us.

'Now you're being ironic,' says a burly man with long hair, who looks as if he hasn't shaved for several days. 'If you think you're in such bad company, why don't you leave.'

I have been drinking too and that gives me courage.

'Who are you? What kind of life is this? You're healthy, you could work, but instead you prefer to hang around doing nothing!'

'We choose to stay outside, outside a world that is fast collapsing, outside people who live in constant fear of losing something, who walk along the street as if everything was fine, when, in fact, everything is bad, very bad indeed! Don't you beg too? Don't you ask for alms from your boss to pay the owner of your apartment?'

'Aren't you ashamed to be wasting your life?' asks the woman in the purple coat.

'Who said I'm wasting my life? I do precisely what I want to do.'

The burly man interrupts, saying:

'And what is it you want? To live on top of the world? Who told you that the mountain is necessarily better than the plain? You think we don't know how to live, don't you? Well, your wife understood that we know *exactly* what we want from life. Do you know what we want? Peace! Freedom! And not to be obliged to follow the latest fashions – we make our own fashions here! We drink when we want to and sleep whenever we feel like it! Not one person here chose slavery and we're proud of it, even though you and people like you may think we're just a lot of pathetic freeloaders!'

The voices are beginning to grow aggressive. Mikhail steps in:

'Do you want to hear the rest of my story or shall we leave now?'

'He's criticising us!' says the man with the artificial leg. 'He came here to judge us, as if he was God!'

There are a few more rumbles of complaint, someone slaps me on the back, I offer round my cigarettes, the bottle of vodka is placed in my hand again. People gradually calm down, and I am still surprised and shocked that these people knew Esther, apparently better than I did, since she gave them – and not me – a piece of that bloodstained shirt.

Mikhail goes on with his story:

'Since I have nowhere to go and study and I'm still too young to look after horses – which are the pride of our region and of our country – I become a shepherd. During the first week, one of the sheep dies and a rumour goes around that I'm cursed, that I'm the son of a man who came from far away and promised my mother great wealth, then ended up leaving us nothing. The Communists may have told them that religion is just a way of giving false hopes to the desperate, they may all have been brought up to believe that only reality exists and that anything our eyes can't see is just the fruit of the human imagination; but the ancient traditions of the steppes remain untouched and are passed by word of mouth across the generations.

Now that the tree has been felled, I no longer see the little girl, although I still hear her voice. I ask her to help me in tending the flocks, and she tells me to be patient; there are difficult times ahead, but before I am twenty-two a woman from far away will come and carry me off to see the world. She also tells me that I have a mission to fulfil, and that mission is to spread the true energy of love throughout the world.

The owner of the sheep is worried by the increasingly wild rumours. Oddly, the people spreading these rumours and trying to destroy my life are the very people whom the little girl had helped during the whole of the previous year. One day, he decides to go to the Communist Party office in the next village, where he learns that both I and my mother are considered to be enemies of the people. I am immediately dismissed. Not that this greatly affects our life, because my mother does embroidery for a company in the largest city in the region and there no one knows that we are enemies of the people and of the working classes; all the factory owners want is for her to continue working on her embroidery from dawn to dusk.

I now have all the time in the world and so I wander the steppes with the hunters, who know my story and believe that I have magical powers, because they always find foxes when I'm around. I spend whole days at the museum of the poet, studying his possessions, reading his books, listening to the people who come there to recite his verses. Now and then, I feel the warm wind blowing, see the lights and fall to the ground, and then the voice tells me concrete facts – when the next drought will come, when the animals will fall sick, when the traders will arrive. I tell no one except my mother, who is becoming ever more anxious and concerned about me.

One day, she takes me to see a doctor who is visiting the area. After listening attentively to my story, taking notes, peering into my eyes with a strange instrument, listening to my heart and tapping my knee, he diagnoses a form of epilepsy. He says it isn't contagious and that the attacks will diminish with age.

I know it isn't an illness, but I pretend to believe him so as to reassure my mother. The director of the museum, who notices me struggling to learn, takes pity on me and becomes my teacher. With him I learn geography and literature and the one thing that will prove vital to me in the future: English. One afternoon, the voice asks me to tell the director that he will shortly be offered an important post. When I tell him this, all I hear is a timid laugh and a firm response: there isn't the remotest chance of this ever happening because not only has he never been a Party member, he is a devout Muslim.

I am fifteen years old. Two months after this conversation, I sense that something is changing in the region. The normally arrogant civil servants are suddenly much kinder and ask if I would like to go back to school. Great convoys of Russian soldiers head off to the frontier. One evening, while I am studying in the little office that once belonged to the poet, the director comes running in and looks at me with a mixture of alarm and embarrassment. He tells me that the one thing he could never imagine happening – the collapse of the Communist regime – is happening right now, and with incredible speed. The former Soviet republics are becoming independent countries; the news from Almaty is all about the formation of a new government, and he has been appointed to govern the province!

Instead of joyfully embracing me, he asks me how I knew this was going to happen. Had I overheard someone talking about it? Had I been engaged by the secret services to spy on him because he did not belong to the Party? Or – worst of all – had I, at some point in my life, made a pact with the Devil?

I remind him that he knows my story: the little girl, the voice, the attacks that allow me to hear things that other people do not know. He says this is just part of my illness; there is only one prophet, Mohammed, and everything that needed to be said has already been revealed. This, he goes on, does not mean that the Devil is not still abroad in the world, using all kinds of tricks – including a supposed ability to foresee the future – to deceive the weak and lure people away from the true faith. He had given me a job because Islam demands that we should be charitable, but now he deeply regretted it: I am clearly either a tool of the secret services or an envoy of the Devil.

He dismisses me there and then.

Life had not been easy before and it now becomes harder still. The factory for which my mother works, and which once belonged to the government, falls into private hands, and the new owners have very different ideas; they restructure the whole business and she, too, is dismissed. Two months later, we have nothing to live on and all that remains for us is to leave the village where I have spent my whole life and go in search of work.

My grandparents refuse to leave; they would rather die of hunger on the land where they were born and have spent their entire lives. My mother and I go to Almaty and I see my first big city: I am amazed at the cars, the huge buildings, the neon signs, the escalators and – above all – the lifts. My mother gets a job in a shop and I go to work at a garage as a trainee mechanic. Much of the money we earn is sent back to my grandparents, but there is enough left over for us to be able to eat and for me to see things I have never seen before: films, funfairs and football games.

When we move to the city, my attacks vanish, but so does the voice and the little girl's presence. It's better that way, I decide. I am too fascinated by Almaty and too busy earning a living to miss the invisible friend who has been my companion since I was eight years old; I realise that all it takes to become "someone" in the world is a little intelligence. Then, one Sunday night, I am sitting at our small apartment's only window, which looks out onto a small dirt alleyway. I am very worried because, the day before, I dented a car as I was manoeuvring it inside the garage and am so frightened I might get the sack that I haven't eaten all day.

Suddenly, I feel the warm wind and see the lights. According to my mother, I fell to the floor, spoke in a strange language and the trance seemed to last longer than usual. I remember that it was then that the voice reminded me of my mission. When I come to, I can feel the presence of the little girl again and, although I cannot see her, I can talk to her.

A change of home has meant a change of worlds too, and I am no longer interested in all this. Nevertheless, I ask her what my mission is: the voice tells me that it is the mission shared by all human beings – to fill the world with the energy of total love. I ask about the one thing that is really worrying me at that precise moment: the dented car and the owner's reaction. She tells me not to worry, just tell the truth and he will understand.

I work at the garage for five more years. I make friends, have my first girlfriends, discover sex, get involved in street fights; in short, I have an entirely normal adolescence. I have a few fits and, at first, my friends are surprised, but then I invent some story about being in possession of "higher powers" and this earns me their respect. They ask for my help, consult me when they have problems with their girlfriends or with their families, but I never ask the voice for advice – the traumatic experience of seeing the tree cut down all those years ago has made me realise that when you help someone you get only ingratitude in return.

If my friends probe further, I tell them I belong to a "secret society". After decades of religious repression in Kazakhstan, mysticism and the esoteric are now very fashionable in Almaty. Books are published about people with so-called higher powers, about gurus and teachers from India and China; courses of self-improvement abound. I go to a few, but realise that I have nothing to learn. The only thing I really trust is the voice, but I am too busy to pay attention to what it is saying.

One day, a woman in a four-wheel drive stops at the garage where I work and asks me to fill up the tank. She addresses me in halting, heavily accented Russian, and I respond in English. She seems relieved and asks if I know of an interpreter who could go with her into the interior of Kazakhstan.

The moment she says this, the little girl's presence fills the whole place, and I understand that this is the person I have been waiting for all my life. She is my way out, and I must not miss this opportunity. I tell her that, if she wants, I can be her interpreter. She says that I obviously have a job already and, besides, she needs someone older, more experienced, someone who is free to travel. I say that I know every path in the steppes and the mountains, and I lie, saying that the job I have is only temporary. I beg her to give me a chance; reluctantly, she arranges to meet me later in the city's most luxurious hotel.

We meet in the lounge; she tests my knowledge of English, asks a series of questions about the geography of Central Asia, wants to know who I am and where I come from. She is suspicious and will not say exactly what she does or where she wants to go. I try to play my part as best I can, but I can see she's not convinced.

And I am surprised to realise that, for no apparent reason, I am in love with her, with this woman I have only known for a matter of hours. I control my anxiety and once more place my trust in the voice. I plead for help from the invisible girl and ask her to enlighten me; I promise that, if I get this job, I will carry out the mission entrusted to me; she had told me that one day a woman would come and take me far away from there; she had been there with me when the woman stopped to fill her tank; I need a positive response.

After Esther's intense questioning, I sense that I am beginning to win her confidence; she warns me that what she wants to do is completely illegal. She explains that she is a journalist and wants to write an article about the American bases being built in a neighbouring country in preparation for a war that is about to begin. Her application for a visa has been turned down and so we will have to travel on foot, crossing the border at points where there are no guards. Her contacts have given her a map and shown her where it is safe to cross, but she says she will reveal none of this until we are far from Almaty. If I want to go with her, I must be at the hotel in two days' time at eleven o'clock in the morning. She promises me only a week's wages, unaware that I have a permanent job, earn enough to help out my mother and my grandparents, and that my boss trusts me despite having been witness to several of the convulsive attacks – what he calls my 'epileptic fits' – that always accompany my contacts with the unknown world.

Before saying goodbye, the woman tells me her name – Esther – and warns me that if I go to the police to report her, she will be arrested and deported. She also says that there are moments in life when we need to trust blindly in intuition, which is what she is doing now. I tell her not to worry. I feel tempted to say something about the voice and the presence, but decide against it. I go home, talk to my mother and tell her I've found a new job as an interpreter, which is better paid, but will involve me going away for a while. She doesn't seem in the least concerned; everything around me is developing as if it had long been planned and we were all just waiting for the right moment.

I sleep badly and the following day I arrive earlier than usual at the garage. I tell my boss that I'm sorry, but I've found a new job. He says that, sooner or later, they'll find out about my illness, that it's very risky giving up steady employment for something less certain, but, just as happened with my mother, he makes no real fuss about letting me go, as if the voice were manipulating the minds of all the people I have to talk to that day, facilitating things, helping me take the first step.

When Esther and I meet at the hotel, I tell her: "If we're caught, you'll just be deported but I'll get put in prison, possibly for many years. Since I'm running the greater risk, you really ought to trust me." She seems to understand what I'm saying. We walk for two days; a group of men are waiting for her on the other side of the frontier; she goes off with them and returns shortly afterwards, frustrated and angry. The war is about to start, all the roads are being guarded, and it's impossible to go any further without being arrested as a spy.

We start the journey back. The usually self-confident Esther seems suddenly sad and confused. To distract her, I recite some lines written by the poet who used to live close to my village, at the same time thinking that in forty-eight hours this whole experience will be over. However, I prefer to trust in the voice. I must do everything I can to prevent Esther leaving as suddenly as she came; perhaps I should show her that I have always been waiting for her, that she is important to me.

That night, after rolling out our sleeping bags near some rocks, I reach out and touch her hand. She gently pulls back, saying that she's married. I realise that I have made a foolish blunder; then, since I now have nothing to lose, I tell her about the visions I had as a child, about my mission to spread love throughout the world, about the doctor's diagnosis of epilepsy.

To my surprise, she understands exactly what I'm talking about. She tells me a little about her life. She says that she loves her husband and that he loves her, but that, with the passing of time, something important has been lost, and she prefers now to be far away from him, rather than watch her marriage slowly disintegrate. She had everything in life, and yet she was unhappy; although she could easily go through the rest of her life pretending that this unhappiness didn't exist, she was terrified of falling into a depression from which she might never emerge.

That is why she decided to give up everything and go in search of adventure, in search of things that leave her no time to think about a love that is dying. However, the more she looked, the more confused she became, the more alone she felt. She feels she has completely lost her way, and the experience we have just had seems to be telling her that she is on the wrong track and should go back to her daily routine.

I suggest trying a less closely guarded trail, say that I know smugglers in Almaty who could help us, but she seems to have no energy, no will to go on.

At that moment, the voice tells me to bless Esther and

to dedicate her to the earth. Without really knowing what I am doing, I get up, open my rucksack, dip my fingers in the small bottle of oil we have taken with us for cooking, place my hand on her head and pray in silence, asking, at the end, that she continue her search, because it is important for all of us. The voice is telling me – and I repeat the words out loud to her – that if just one person changes, the whole human race is changed. She puts her arms around me, and I can feel the earth blessing her, and we stay like that together for several hours.

Afterwards, I ask if she believes what I told her about the voice. She says that she both does and doesn't. She believes that we all have a power that we never use and that I have clearly come into contact with that power through my epileptic fits, but this is something we can find out about together. She has been thinking of interviewing a nomad who lives to the north of Almaty and who is said by everyone to have magical powers. I am welcome to accompany her. When she tells me the man's name, I realise that I know his grandson and that this could greatly facilitate matters.

We drive through Almaty, stopping only to fill the tank with petrol and buy some food, then we drive on in the direction of a tiny village near an artificial lake constructed by the Soviet regime. I find out where the nomad is staying, but despite telling one of his assistants that I know the man's grandson, we still have to wait many hours, for there is a large crowd wanting the advice of this man they consider to be a saint.

At last, we are ushered in. By acting as interpreter at that interview and by reading and re-reading Esther's article when it was published, I learn several things I needed to know.

Esther asks why people are sad.

"That's simple," says the old man. "They are the prisoners of their personal history. Everyone believes that the main aim in life is to follow a plan. They never ask if that plan is theirs or if it was created by another person. They accumulate experiences, memories, things, other people's ideas, and it is more than they can possibly cope with. And that is why they forget their dreams."

Esther remarks that many people say to her: "You're lucky, you know what you want from life, whereas I don't even know what I want to do."

"Of course they know," replies the nomad. "How many people do you know who say: I've never done what I wanted, but then, that's life. If they say they haven't done what they wanted, then, at some point, they must have known what it was that they did want. As for life, it's just a story that other people tell us about the world and about how we should behave in the world."

"Even worse are those people who say: I'm happy because I'm sacrificing my life for those I love."

"And do you think that the people who love us want to see us suffering for their sakes? Do you think that love is a source of suffering?"

"To be honest, yes."

"Well, it shouldn't be."

"If I forget the story other people have told me, I'll also forget a lot of very important things life has taught me. What was the point of struggling to learn so much? What was the point of struggling to gain experience, so as to be able to deal with my career, my husband, my various crises?"

"Accumulated knowledge is useful when it comes to cooking or living within your means or wrapping up warm in winter or respecting certain limits or knowing where particular bus and train lines go. Do you believe that your past loves have taught you to love better?"

"They've taught me to know what I want."

"I didn't ask that. Have your past loves taught you to love your husband better?"

"No, on the contrary. In order to surrender myself to him, I had to forget all the scars left by other men. Is that what you mean?"

"In order for the true energy of love to penetrate your soul, your soul must be as if you had just been born. Why are people unhappy? Because they want to imprison that energy, which is impossible. Forgetting your personal history means leaving that channel clear, allowing that energy to manifest itself each day in whatever way it chooses, allowing yourself to be guided by it."

"That's all very romantic, but very difficult too, because that energy gets blocked by all kinds of things: commitments, children, your social situation ..."

" ... and, after a while, by despair, fear, loneliness and your attempts to control the uncontrollable. According to the tradition of the steppes – which is known as the Tengri – in order to live fully, it is necessary to be in constant movement; only then can each day be different from the last. When they passed through cities, the nomads would think: The poor people who live here, for them everything is always the same. The people in the cities probably looked at the nomads and thought: Poor things, they have nowhere to live. The nomads had no past, only the present, and that is why they were always happy, until the Communist governors made them stop travelling and forced them to live on collective farms. From then on, little by little, they came to believe that the story society told them was true. Consequently, they have lost all their strength."

"No one nowadays can spend their whole life travelling."

"Not physically, no, but they can on a spiritual plane. Going farther and farther, distancing yourself from your personal history, from what you were forced to become."

"How does one go about abandoning the story one was told?"

"By repeating it out loud in meticulous detail. And as we tell our story, we say goodbye to what we were and, as you'll see if you try, we create space for a new, unknown world. We repeat the old story over and over until it is no longer important to us."

"Is that all?"

"There is just one other thing: as those spaces grow, it is important to fill them up quickly, even if only provisionally, so as not to be left with a feeling of emptiness."

"How?"

"With different stories, with experiences we never dared to have or didn't want to have. That is how we change. That is how love grows. And when love grows, we grow with it."

"Does that mean we might lose things that are important?"

"Never. The important things always stay; what we lose are the things we thought were important but which are, in fact, useless, like the false power we use to control the energy of love."

The old man tells her that her time is up and that he has other people to see. Despite my pleas he proves inflexible, but tells Esther that if she ever comes back, he will teach her more.

Esther is only staying in Almaty for another week, but promises to return. During that time, I tell her my story over and over and she tells me hers, and we see that the old man is right: something is leaving us, we are lighter, although we could not really say that we are any happier.

The old man had given us another piece of advice: fill that space up quickly. Before she leaves, she asks if I would like to go to France so that we can continue this process of forgetting. She has no one with whom she can share all this; she can't talk to her husband; she doesn't trust the people she works with; she needs someone from outside, from far away, who has, up until then, had nothing to do with her personal history.

I say that I would like to do that and only then mention what the voice had prophesied. I also tell her that I don't know French and that my only work experience so far has been tending sheep and working in a garage.

At the airport, she asks me to take an intensive course in French. I ask her why she wants me to go to France. She repeats what she has said and admits she's afraid of the space opening up around her as she erases

209

her personal history; she's afraid that everything will rush back in more intensely than before, and then there will be no way of freeing herself from her past. She tells me not to worry about buying a ticket or getting a visa; she will take care of everything. Before going through passport control, she looks at me, smiles, and says that, although she may not have known it, she had been waiting for me as well. The days we had spent together had been the happiest she had known in the last three years.

I start working at night, as a bouncer at a striptease joint, and during the day I devote myself to learning French. Oddly enough, the attacks diminish, but the presence also goes away. I tell my mother that I've been invited to go abroad, and she tells me not to be so naive, I'll never hear from the woman again.

A year later, Esther returns to Almaty. The expected war has begun, and someone else has written an article about the secret American bases, but Esther's interview with the old man had been a great success and now she has been asked to write a long article on the disappearance of the nomads. "Apart from that," she said, "it's been ages since I told my story to anyone and I'm starting to get depressed."

I help put her in touch with the few tribes who still travel, with the Tengri tradition, and with local shamans. I am now fluent in French, and over supper she gives me various forms from the consulate to fill in, gets me a visa, buys me a ticket, and I come to Paris. We both notice that, as we empty our minds of old stories, a new space opens up, a mysterious feeling of joy slips in, our intuitions grow sharper, we become braver, take more risks, do things which might be right or which might be wrong, we can't be sure, but we do them anyway. The days seem longer and more intense.

When I arrive in Paris, I ask where I'm going to work, but she has already made plans: she has persuaded the owner of a bar to allow me to appear there once a week, telling him that I specialise in an exotic kind of performance art from Kazakhstan which consists in encouraging people to talk about their lives and to empty their minds.

At first, it is very difficult to get the sparse audience to join in, but the drunks enjoy it and word spreads. "Come and tell your old story and discover a new one," says the small handwritten notice in the window, and people, thirsty for novelty, start to come.

One night, I experience something strange: it is not me on the small improvised stage in one corner of the bar, it is the presence. And instead of telling stories from my own country and then moving on to suggest that they tell their stories, I merely say what the voice tells me to. Afterwards, one of the spectators is crying and speaks about his marriage in intimate detail to the other strangers there.

The same thing happens the following week – the voice speaks for me, asking people to tell stories not about love, but about the lack of love, and the energy in the air is so different that the normally discreet French begin discussing their personal lives in public. I am also managing to control my attacks better; if, when I'm on stage, I start to see the lights or feel that warm wind, I immediately go into a trance, lose consciousness, and no one notices. I only have "epileptic fits" at moments when I am under great nervous strain.

Other people join the group. Three young men the same age as me, who had nothing to do but travel the world – the nomads of the Western world; and a couple of musicians from Kazakhstan, who have heard about their fellow countryman's "success", ask if they can join the show, since they are unable to find work elsewhere. We include percussion instruments in the performance. The bar is becoming too small, and we find a room in the restaurant where we currently appear; but now we are starting to outgrow that space too, because when people tell their stories, they feel braver; when they dance, they are touched by the energy and begin to change radically; love – which, in theory, should be threatened by all these changes – becomes stronger, and they recommend our meetings to their friends.

Esther continues travelling in order to write her articles, but always comes to the meetings when she is in Paris. One night, she tells me that our work at the restaurant is no longer enough; it only reaches those people who have the money to go there. We need to work with the young. Where will we find them, I ask? They drift, travel, abandon everything and dress as beggars or characters out of sci-fi movies.

She says that beggars have no personal history, so why don't we go to them and see what we can learn. And that is how I came to meet all of you.

These are the things I have experienced. You have never asked me who I am or what I do, because you're not interested. But today, because we have a famous writer in our midst, I decided to tell you.'

'But you're talking about your past,' said the woman in the clashing hat and coat. 'Even though the old nomad ...'

'What's a nomad?' someone asks.

'People like us,' she responds, proud to know the meaning of the word. 'People who are free and manage to live with only what they can carry.'

I correct her:

'That's not quite true. They're not poor.'

'What do you know about poverty?' The tall, aggressive man, who now has even more vodka in his veins, looks straight at me. 'Do you really think that poverty has to do with having no money? Do you think we're miserable wretches just because we go around begging money from rich writers and guilt-ridden couples, from tourists who think how terribly squalid Paris has become or from idealistic young people who think they can save the world? You're the one who's poor – you have no control over your time, you can't do what you want, you're forced to follow rules you didn't invent and which you don't understand ...'

Mikhail again interrupted the conversation and asked the woman:

'What did you actually want to know?'

'I wanted to know why you're telling us your story when the old nomad said you should forget it.'

'It's not my story any more: whenever I speak about the past now, I feel as if I were talking about something that has nothing to do with me. All that remains in the present are the voice, the presence, and the importance of fulfilling my mission. I don't regret the difficulties I experienced; I think they helped me to become the person I am today. I feel the way a warrior must feel after years of training: he doesn't remember the details of everything he learned, but he knows how to strike when the time is right.'

'And why did you and that journalist keep coming to visit us?'

'To take nourishment. As the old nomad from the steppes said, the world we know today is merely a story someone has told to us, but it is not the true story. The other story includes special gifts and powers and the ability to go beyond what we know. I have lived with the presence ever since I was a child and, for a time, was even capable of seeing her, but Esther showed me that I was not alone. She introduced me to other people with special gifts, people who could bend forks by sheer force of will, or carry out surgery using rusty penknives and without anaesthetic, so that the patient could get up after the operation and leave.

I am still learning to develop my unknown potential, but I need allies, people like you who have no personal history.'

I felt like telling my story to these strangers too, in order to begin the process of freeing myself from the past, but it was late and I had to get up early the next day to see the doctor and have him remove the orthopaedic collar.

I asked Mikhail if he wanted a lift, but he said no, he needed to walk a little, because he felt Esther's absence particularly acutely that night. We left the group and headed for a street where I would be able to find a taxi.

'I think that woman was right,' I said. 'If you tell a story, then that means you're still not really free of it.'

'I am free, but, as I'm sure you'll understand, therein lies the secret; there are always some stories that are "interrupted", and they are the stories that remain nearest to the surface and so still occupy the present; only when we close that story or chapter can we begin the next one.'

I remembered reading something similar on the Internet; it was attributed to me, although I didn't write it:

That is why it is so important to let certain things go. To release them. To cut loose. People need to understand that no one is playing with marked cards; sometimes we win and sometimes we lose. Don't expect to get anything back, don't expect recognition for your efforts, don't expect your genius to be discovered or your love to be understood. Complete the circle. Not out of pride, inability or arrogance, but simply because whatever it is no longer fits in your life. Close the door, change the record, clean the house, get rid of the dust. Stop being who you were and become who you are.

But I had better find out what Mikhail means.

'What are "interrupted stories"?'

'Esther isn't here. She reached a point where she could go no further in the process of emptying herself of unhappiness and allowing joy to flow in. Why? Because her story, like that of millions of other people, is bound up with the energy of love. It can't evolve on its own: she must either stop loving or wait until her beloved comes to her.

In failed marriages, when one person stops walking, the other is forced to do the same. And while he or she is waiting, other lovers appear, or there is charitable work to get involved in, there are the children to worry about, there are long hours at the office, etc. It would be much easier to talk openly about things, to insist, to yell: "Let's move on, we're dying of tedium, anxiety, fear."'

'Are you telling me that Esther can't continue with the process of freeing herself from sadness because of me?'

'No, that's not what I meant. I don't believe that one person can blame another, under any circumstances. All I said was that she has a choice between stopping loving you or making you come to her.'

'That's what she's doing.'

'I know, but, if it were up to me, we would only go to her when the voice allows us to.'

'Right, this should be the last you see of the orthopaedic collar, I certainly hope so anyway. But, please, avoid making any sudden movements. Your muscles need to get used to working on their own again. By the way, what happened to the girl who made those predictions?'

'What girl? What predictions?'

'Didn't you tell me at the hospital that someone had claimed to hear a voice warning that something was going to happen to you?'

'Oh, it wasn't a girl. And you said you were going to find out about epilepsy for me.'

'Yes, I got in touch with a specialist and asked him if he knew of any such cases. His answer surprised me a bit, but let me just remind you that medicine has its mysteries. Do you remember the story I told you about the boy who goes out to buy five apples and returns with two?'

'Yes, and how he might have lost them or given them away, or else they might have turned out to be more expensive than expected, etc. Don't worry, I know there are no absolute answers. But, first, did Joan of Arc suffer from epilepsy?'

'Oddly enough, my friend mentioned her during our conversation. Joan of Arc started hearing voices when she

PAULO COELHO

was thirteen. Her statements reveal that she saw lights, which is one of the symptoms of an attack. According to the neurologist, Dr Lydia Bayne, the warrior-saint's ecstatic experiences were caused by what we now call musicogenic epilepsy, which is provoked by hearing a particular kind of sound or music: in Joan's case, it was the sound of bells. Were you there when the boy had a fit?'

'Yes.'

'Was there any music playing?'

'I can't remember. But even if there was, the clatter of cutlery and the buzz of conversation would have drowned it out.'

'Did he seem tense?'

'Yes, very.'

'That's another thing that can provoke an attack. Epilepsy has been around for longer than you might think. In Mesopotamia, there are remarkably accurate descriptions of what they called "the falling sickness", which was followed by convulsions. Ancient people believed that it was caused by demons invading a person's body; only much later on did the Greek Hippocrates relate these convulsions to some dysfunction of the brain. Even so, epileptics are still the victims of prejudice.'

'I'm sure. I was absolutely terrified when it happened.'

'You mentioned the word prophecy, and so I asked my friend to concentrate his researches in that area. According to him, most scientists agree that, although a lot of famous people have suffered from epilepsy, the disease itself does not confer greater or lesser powers on anyone. Nevertheless, the more famous epileptics did succeed in persuading other people to see their fits as having a "mystical aura".'

'Give me an example of some famous epileptics.'

'Napoleon, Alexander the Great, Dante ... I didn't make a full list, since what you were interested in was the boy's prophecy. What's his name, by the way?'

'You don't know him, and since you've nearly always got another appointment to go to, perhaps you'd better just finish your explanation.'

'All right. Medical scientists who study the Bible are sure that the Apostle Paul was an epileptic. They base this on the fact that, on the road to Damascus, he saw a brilliant light near him which caused him to fall to the ground, leaving him temporarily blind and unable to eat or drink for some days. In medical terms, this is known as "temporal lobe epilepsy".'

'I don't think the Church would agree.'

'I'm not even sure that I agree, but that's what the medical literature says. Other epileptics develop their self-destructive side, as was the case with van Gogh. He described his convulsions as "the storm within". In Saint-Rémy, where he was a patient, one of the nurses saw him having a convulsive seizure.'

'At least he managed in his paintings to transform his self-destruction into a reconstruction of the world.'

'Some people suspect that Lewis Carroll wrote *Alice in Wonderland* in order to describe his own experiences of epilepsy. The story at the beginning of the book, when Alice falls down a black hole, is an experience familiar to most epileptics. During her journey through Wonderland,

Alice often sees things flying and she herself feels very light – another very precise description of the effects of an epileptic attack.'

'So it would seem epileptics have a propensity for art.'

'Not at all, it's just that because artists tend to become famous, art and epilepsy become linked in people's minds. Literature is full of examples of writers with a suspected or confirmed diagnosis of epilepsy: Molière, Edgar Allen Poe, Flaubert ... Dostoevsky had his first attack when he was nine years old, and said that it brought him moments when he felt utterly at peace with the world as well as moments of terrible depression. Don't take all of this too seriously, and don't go thinking that you might develop epilepsy because of your accident. I haven't come across a single case of epilepsy being caused by colliding with a motorbike.'

'As I said, this is someone I actually know.'

'Does the boy with the predictions really exist or did you invent all this simply because you think you might have passed out when you stepped off the pavement?'

'On the contrary, I hate knowing about illnesses. Whenever I read a medical book, I immediately start to get all the symptoms.'

'Let me tell you something, but please don't take it the wrong way. I think this accident did you a lot of good. You seem calmer, less obsessed. A brush with death always helps us to live our lives better; that's what your wife told me when she gave me a bit of bloodstained fabric, which I always carry with me, even though, as a doctor, I see death, close to, every day.'

'Did she say why she gave you the cloth?'

'She was very generous in her description of my work. She said that I was capable of combining technique with intuition, discipline with love. She told me that a soldier, before he died, had asked her to take his blood-soaked shirt, cut it into pieces and share those pieces out amongst people who were genuinely trying to reveal the world as it is. I imagine you, with all your books, must also have a bit of this shirt.'

'No, I haven't.'

'Do you know why?'

'I do, or, rather, I'm beginning to find out.'

'And since I'm not only your doctor, but your friend, may I give you some advice? If this epileptic boy did tell you that he can foresee the future, then he knows nothing about medicine.'

Zagreb, Croatia.
6.30 a.m.

Marie and I are sitting by a frozen fountain. It appears that, this year, spring has decided not to happen; indeed, it looks as if we will jump straight from winter into summer. In the middle of the fountain stands a column with a statue on top.

I have spent the entire afternoon giving interviews and cannot bear to say another word about my new book. The journalists all ask the usual questions: has my wife read the book (I don't know); do I feel I've been unfairly treated by the critics (what?); has *A Time to Rend and a Time to Sew* shocked my readers at all, given that I reveal a great deal about my personal life (a writer can only write about his own life); will the book be made into a film (I repeat for the nth time that the film happens in the reader's mind and that I have forbidden the sale of film rights on any of my books); what do I think about love; why did I choose to write about love; how can one be happy in love, love, love, love …

Once the interviews are over, there's the publisher's supper – it's part of the ritual. The table is packed with local worthies who keep interrupting me just as I'm about to put my fork in my mouth, and usually ask the same thing: 'Where do you find your inspiration?' I try to eat, but I must also be pleasant, I must chat, fulfil my role as celebrity, tell a few interesting stories, make a good impression. I know that the publisher is a real hero, because he can never tell whether a book will sell or not; he could be selling bananas or soap instead; it would certainly be easier: they're not vain, they don't have inflated egos, they don't complain if they don't like the publicity campaign or if their book doesn't appear in a particular bookshop.

After supper, it's the usual routine: they want to show me their city's monuments, historic places, fashionable bars. There is always a guide who knows absolutely everything and fills my head with information, and I have to look as if I'm really listening and ask the occasional question just to show interest. I know nearly all the monuments, museums and historic places of all the many cities I have visited to promote my work – and I can't remember any of them. What I do remember are the unexpected things, the meetings with readers, the bars, perhaps a street I happened to walk down, where I turned a corner and came upon something wonderful.

One day, I'm going to write a travel guide containing only maps, addresses of hotels, and with the rest of the pages blank. That way people will have to make their own itinerary, to discover for themselves restaurants, monuments, and all the magnificent things that every city has, but which are never mentioned because 'the history we have been taught' does not include them under the heading 'Things you must see'.

I've been to Zagreb before. And this fountain doesn't appear in any of the local tourist guides, but it is far more important to me than anything else I saw here – because it is pretty, because I discovered it by chance, and because it is linked to a story in my life. Many years ago, when I was a young man travelling the world in search of adventure, I sat in this very spot with a Croatian painter who had travelled with me for much of the journey. I was heading off into Turkey and he was going home. We said goodbye here, drank two bottles of wine between us, and talked about everything that had happened while we had been together, about religion, women, music, the price of hotels, drugs. We talked about everything except love, because although there were people we loved, there was no need to talk about it.

After the painter had returned to his house, I met a young woman and we spent three days together and loved each other with great intensity because we both knew that it would not last very long. She helped me to understand the soul of those people and I never forgot her, just as I never forgot the fountain or saying goodbye to my travelling companion.

This was why – after the interviews, the autographs, the supper, the visits to monuments and historic places – I pestered my publishers into bringing me to this fountain. They asked me where it was, and I had no idea, just as I had no idea that Zagreb had so many fountains. After nearly an hour of searching, we finally managed to locate it. I asked for a bottle of wine, we said goodbye to everyone, and Marie and I sat down together in silence, our arms about each other, drinking wine and waiting for the sun to come up.

'You seem to get happier and happier by the day,' she says, resting her head on my shoulder.

'That's because I'm trying to forget who I am. Or rather, I don't need to carry the weight of my whole history on my shoulders.'

I tell her about Mikhail's conversation with the nomad.

'It's rather like that with actors,' she says. 'With each new role, we have to stop being who we are in order to become the character. We tend to end up confused and neurotic. Is it such a good idea to abandon your personal history, do you think?'

'Didn't you say I seemed better?'

'Less egotistical, yes. Although it amused me the way you wouldn't let us rest until you found this fountain, but that goes against what you've just said, since the fountain is part of your past.'

'For me, it's a symbol. But I don't carry this fountain around with me, I don't think about it all the time, I don't take photos of it to show my friends, I don't long for the painter or for the young woman I fell in love with. It's really good to come back here again, but if I hadn't come back, it wouldn't make any difference to that initial experience.'

'I see what you're saying.'

'I'm glad.'

'And I'm sad, because it makes me think that you're about to leave. I've known you would ever since we first met, but it's still difficult, because I've got used to being with you.'

'That's the problem, we do get used to things.'

'It's human too.'

'That's why the woman I married became the Zahir. Until I had that accident, I had convinced myself that I could only be happy with her, not because I loved her more than anything and anyone in the world, but because I thought only she could understand me; she knew my likes, my eccentricities, my way of seeing the world. I was grateful for what she had done for me, and I thought she should be grateful for what I had done for her. I was used to seeing the world through her eyes. Do you remember that story about the two firemen who emerge from the fire and one has his face all blackened by smoke?'

She sat up straight. I noticed that her eyes were full of tears.

'Well, that is what the world was like for me,' I went on. 'A reflection of Esther's beauty. Is that love? Or is that dependency?'

'I don't know. I think love and dependency go hand in hand.'

'Possibly. But let's suppose that instead of writing *A Time to Rend and a Time to Sew*, which is really just a letter to a woman who is far away, I had chosen a different plot, for example, a husband and wife who have been together for ten years. They used to make love every day, now they only make love once a week, but that doesn't really matter because there is also solidarity, mutual support, companionship. He feels sad when he has to have supper alone because she is working late. She hates it when he has to go away, but accepts that it is part of his job. They feel that something is missing, but they are both grown-ups, they are both mature people, and they know how important it is to keep their relationship stable, even if only for the children's sake. They devote more and more time to work and to the children, they think less and less about their marriage. Everything appears to be going really well, and there's certainly no other man or woman in their lives.

Yet they sense that something is wrong. They can't quite put their finger on the problem. As time passes, they grow more and more dependent on each other; they are getting older; any opportunities to make a new life are vanishing fast. They try to keep busy doing reading or embroidery, watching television, seeing friends, but there is always the conversation over supper or after supper. He is easily irritated, she is more silent than usual. They can see that they are growing farther and farther apart, but cannot understand why. They reach the conclusion that this is what marriage is like, but won't talk to their friends about it; they are the image of the happy couple who support each other and share the same interests. She takes a lover, so does he, but it's never anything serious, of course. What is important, necessary, essential, is to act as if nothing was happening, because it's too late to change.'

'I know that story, although I've never experienced it myself. And I think we spend our lives being trained to put up with situations like that.'

I take off my coat and climb onto the edge of the fountain. She asks me what I'm doing.

'I'm going to walk over to that column in the middle of the fountain.'

'You're mad. It's spring now, the ice will be getting really thin.'

'I need to walk over to the column.'

I place one foot on the surface, the whole sheet of ice moves, but does not crack. With one eye on the rising sun, I make a kind of wager with God: if I manage to reach the column and come back without the ice cracking, that will be a sign that I am on the right path, and that His hand is showing me where I should go.

'You'll fall in the water.'

'So? The worst that can happen is that I'll get a bit cold, but the hotel isn't far away and I won't have to suffer for long.'

I put my other foot on the ice: I am now in the fountain. The ice breaks away from the edges and a little water laps onto the surface of the ice, but the ice does not break. I set off towards the column. It's only about four metres there and back, and all I risk is getting a very cold bath. However, I mustn't think about what might happen: I've taken the first step and I must continue to the end.

I reach the column, touch it with my hand, hear everything around me creaking, but I'm still on the ice. My first instinct is to run back, but something tells me that if I do that, my steps will become heavier, firmer and I'll fall into the water. I must walk back slowly, at the same pace.

The sun is rising ahead of me; it dazzles me slightly. I can see only Marie's silhouette and the shapes of the buildings and the trees. The sheet of ice keeps shifting, water spills over onto the surface, but I know – with absolute certainty – that I will reach the edge. I am in communion with the day, with my choices. I know the limits of the frozen water; I know how to deal with it, how to ask for its help, to keep me from falling. I begin to enter a kind of trance, a euphoric state; I am a child again, doing something that is wrong, forbidden, but which gives me enormous pleasure. Wonderful! Crazy pacts with God, along the lines of 'If I manage to do this, then so and so will happen', signs provoked not by anything that comes from outside, but by instinct, by my capacity to forget the old rules and create new situations.

I am grateful for having met Mikhail, the epileptic who thinks he can hear voices. I went to his 'meeting' at the restaurant in search of my wife and discovered that I was turning into a pale reflection of myself. Is Esther still important? I think so, for it was her love that changed my life once and which is transforming me now. My history had grown old and was becoming ever heavier to carry, and far too serious for me ever to take risks like walking on ice, making a wager with God, forcing a sign to appear. I had forgotten that one has to continue walking the road to Santiago, to discard any unnecessary baggage, to keep only what you need in order to live each day, and to allow the energy of love to flow freely, from the outside in and from the inside out.

Another cracking sound, and a fault line appears across the surface, but I know I will make it, because I am light, so light that I could even walk on a cloud and not fall to earth. I am not carrying with me the weight of fame, of stories I have told, of itineraries to follow. I am so transparent that the sun's rays can penetrate my body and illumine my soul. I see that there are still many dark areas inside me, but with perseverance and courage they will gradually be washed away.

Another step, and I remember the envelope on my desk at home. Soon I will open it and, instead of walking on ice, I will set off along the path that leads me to Esther. I will do so not because I want her by my side, for she is free to remain where she is. It is not because I dream day and night of the Zahir; that loving, destructive obsession seems to have vanished. It is not because I am used to my past as it was and passionately want to go back to it.

Another step, more sounds of cracking, but safety and the edge of the fountain are close.

I will open the envelope and go and find her because – as Mikhail, the epileptic, the seer, the guru of the Armenian restaurant, says – this story needs to reach its end. When everything has been told and retold countless times, when the places I have visited, the things I have experienced, the steps I have taken because of her are all transformed into distant memories, nothing will remain but pure love. I won't feel as if I 'owe' anything, I won't feel that I need her because only she can understand me, because I'm used to her, because she knows my vices and my virtues, knows that I like to have a slice of toast before I go to bed and to watch the international news when I wake up, that I have to go for a walk every morning, or that she knows about my collection of books on archery, about the hours spent in front of the computer screen, writing, about how annoyed I get when the maid keeps calling me to tell me the food is on the table.

All that will disappear. What remains will be the love that moves the heavens, the stars, people, flowers, insects, the love that obliges us all to walk across the ice despite the danger, that fills us with joy and with fear, and gives meaning to everything.

I touch the edge of the fountain, a hand reaches out to me, I grab hold of it, and Marie helps to steady me as I step down.

'I'm proud of you. I would never do anything like that.'

'Not so long ago, I wouldn't have either; it seems so childish, irresponsible, unnecessary, pointless. But I am being reborn and I need to take new risks.'

'The morning light is obviously good for you; you're talking like a wise man.'

'No wise man would do what I've just done.'

I have to write an important article for a magazine that is one of my major creditors in the Favour Bank. I have hundreds, thousands of ideas in my head, but I don't know which of them merits my effort, my concentration, my blood.

It is not the first time this has happened, but I feel as if I have said everything of importance that I need to say, I feel as if I'm losing my memory and forgetting who I am.

I go over to the window and look out at the street. I try to convince myself that I am professionally fulfilled and have nothing more to prove, that I can justifiably withdraw to a house in the mountains and spend the rest of my life reading, walking and talking about food and the weather. I tell myself over and over that I have achieved what almost no other writer has achieved – my books have been translated into nearly every written language in the world. Why worry about a mere magazine article, however important the magazine itself might be? Because of the Favour Bank. So I really do need to write something, but what have I got to say to people? Should I tell them that they need to forget all the stories that have been told to them and take more risks?

They'll all say: 'I'm an independent being, thank you very much. I'll do as I please.'

Should I tell them that they must allow the energy of love to flow more freely?

They'll say: 'I feel love already. In fact, I feel more and more love', as if love could be measured the way we measure the distance between two railway tracks, the height of buildings, or the amount of yeast needed to make a loaf of bread.

I return to my desk. The envelope Mikhail left for me is open. I now know where Esther is; I just need to know how to get there. I phone him and tell him about my walk across the ice. He is impressed. I ask him what he's doing tonight, and he says he's going out with his girlfriend, Lucrecia. I suggest taking them both to supper. No, not tonight, but, if I like, I could go out with him and his friends next week.

I tell him that next week I'm giving a talk in America. There's no hurry, he says, we can wait two weeks.

'You must have heard a voice telling you to walk on the ice,' he says.

'No, I heard no voice.'

'So why did you do it?'

'Because I felt it needed to be done.'

'That's just another way of hearing the voice.'

'I made a bet. If I could cross the ice, that meant I was ready. And I think I am.'

'Then the voice gave you the sign you needed.'

'Did the voice say anything to you about it?'

'No, it didn't have to. When we were on the banks of

234

the Seine and I said that the voice would tell us when the time had come, I knew that it would also tell you.'

'As I said, I didn't hear a voice.'

'That's what you think. That's what everyone thinks. And yet, judging by what the presence tells me, everyone hears voices all the time. They are what help us to know when we are face to face with a sign, you see.'

I decide not to argue. I just need some practical details: where to hire a car, how long the journey takes, how to find the house, because otherwise all I have, apart from the map, are a series of vague indications – follow the lake shore, look for a company sign, turn right, etc. Perhaps he knows someone who can help me.

We arrange our next meeting. Mikhail asks me to dress as discreetly as possible – the 'tribe' is going walkabout in Paris.

I ask him who this tribe is. 'They're the people who work with me at the restaurant,' he replies, without going into detail. I ask him if he wants me to bring him anything from America, and he asks for a particular remedy for heartburn. There are, I think, more interesting things I could bring, but I make a note of his request.

And the article?

I go back to the desk, think about what I'm going to write, look again at the open envelope, and conclude that I was not surprised by what I found inside. After a few meetings with Mikhail, it was pretty much what I had expected.

Esther is living in the steppes, in a small village in Central Asia; more precisely, in a village in Kazakhstan.

I am no longer in a hurry. I continue reviewing my own story, which I tell to Marie in obsessive detail; she has decided to do the same, and I am surprised by some of the things she tells me, but the process seems to be working; she is more confident, less anxious.

I don't know why I so want to find Esther, now that my love for her has illumined my life, taught me new things, which is quite enough really. But I remember what Mikhail said: 'The story needs to reach its end', and I decide to go on. I know that I will discover the moment when the ice of our marriage cracked, and how we carried on walking through the chill water, as if nothing had happened. I know that I will discover this before I reach that village, in order to close the circle or make it larger still.

The article! Has Esther become the Zahir again, thus preventing me from concentrating on anything else?

No, when I need to do something urgent, something that requires creative energy, this is my working method: I get into a state of near hysteria, decide to abandon the task altogether, and then the article appears. I've tried doing things differently, preparing everything carefully, but my imagination only works when it's under enormous pressure. I must respect the Favour Bank, I must write three pages about – guess what! – the problems of male–female relationships. Me, of all people! But the editors believe that the man who wrote *A Time to Rend and a Time to Sew* must know the human soul well.

I try to log on to the Internet, but it's not working. It's never been the same since I destroyed the connection. I called various technicians, but, when they finally turned up, they could find nothing wrong with the computer. They asked me what I was complaining about, spent half an hour doing tests, changed the configuration, and assured me that the problem lay not with me but with the server. I allowed myself to be convinced that everything was, in fact, fine, and I felt ridiculous for having asked for help. Two or three hours later, the computer and the connection would both crash. Now, after months of physical and psychological wear and tear, I simply accept that technology is stronger and more powerful than me: it works when it wants to, and when it doesn't, it's best to sit down and read the paper or go for a walk, and just wait until the cables and the telephone links are in a better mood and the computer decides to work again. I am not, I have discovered, my computer's master: it has a life of its own.

I try a few more times, but I know from experience that it's best just to give up. The Internet, the biggest library in the world, has closed its doors to me for the moment. What about reading a few magazines in search of inspiration? I pick up one that has just arrived in the post and read a strange interview with a woman who has recently published a book about – guess what? – love? The subject seems to be pursuing me everywhere.

The journalist asks if the only way a human being can find happiness is by finding his or her beloved. The woman says 'No'.

The idea that love leads to happiness is a modern invention, dating from the end of the seventeenth century. Ever since then, people have been taught to believe that love should last for ever and that marriage is the best place in which to exercise that love. In the past, there was less optimism about the longevity of passion. Romeo and Juliet isn't a happy story, it's a tragedy. In the last few decades, expectations about marriage as the road to personal fulfilment have grown considerably, as have disappointment and dissatisfaction.

It's quite a brave thing to say, but no good for my article, mainly because I don't agree with her at all. I search my shelves for a book that has nothing to do with male–female relationships: *Magical Practices in North Mexico*. Since obsession will not help me to write my article, I need to refresh my mind, to relax.

I start leafing through it and suddenly I read something that surprises me:

The acomodador *or giving-up point: there is always an event in our lives that is responsible for us failing to progress: a trauma, a particularly bitter defeat, a disappointment in love, even a victory that we did not quite understand, can make cowards of us and prevent us from moving on. As part of the process of increasing his hidden powers, the shaman must first free himself from that giving-up point and, to do so, he must review his whole life and find out where it occurred.*

The *acomodador*. This fitted in with my experience of learning archery – the only sport I enjoyed – for the teacher of archery says that no shot can ever be repeated, and there is no point trying to learn from good or bad shots. What matters is repeating it hundreds and thousands of times, until we have freed ourselves from the idea of hitting the target and have ourselves become the arrow, the bow, the target. At that moment, the energy of the 'thing' (my teacher of *kyudo* – the form of Japanese archery I practised – never used the word 'God') guides our movements and then we begin to release the arrow not when we want to, but when the 'thing' believes that the moment has come.

The *acomodador*. Another part of my personal history resurfaces. If only Marie were here! I need to talk about myself, about my childhood, to tell her how, when I was little, I was always fighting and beating up the other children because I was the oldest in the class. One day, my cousin gave me a thrashing, and I was convinced from then on that I would never ever win another fight, and since then I have avoided any physical confrontation, even though this has often meant me behaving like a coward and being humiliated in front of girlfriends and friends alike.

The *acomodador*. For two years, I tried to learn how to play the guitar. To begin with, I made rapid progress, but then reached a point where I could progress no further, because I discovered that other people were learning faster than I was, which made me feel mediocre; and so as not to have to feel ashamed, I decided that I was no longer interested in learning. The same thing happened with snooker, football, bicycle racing. I learned enough to do everything reasonably well, but there was always a point where I got stuck.

Why?

Because according to the story we are told, there always comes a moment in our lives when we reach 'our

239

limit'. I often recalled my struggle to deny my destiny as a writer and how Esther had always refused to allow the *acomodador* to lay down rules for my dream. The paragraph I had just read fitted in with the idea of forgetting one's personal history and being left only with the instinct that develops out of the various difficulties and tragedies one has experienced. This is what the shamans of Mexico did and what the nomads on the steppes of Central Asia preached.

The *acomodador*: 'there is always an event in our lives that is responsible for us failing to progress'.

It described exactly what happens in marriages in general and what had happened in my relationship with Esther in particular.

I could now write my article for that magazine. I went over to the computer and within half an hour I had written a first draft and was happy with the result. I wrote a story in the form of a dialogue, as if it were fiction, but which was, in fact, a conversation I had had in a hotel room in Amsterdam, after a day spent promoting my books and after the usual publishers' supper and the statutory tour of the sights, etc.

In my article, the names of the characters and the situation in which they find themselves are omitted. In real life, Esther is in her nightdress and is looking out at the canal outside our window. She has not yet become a war correspondent, her eyes are still bright with joy, she loves her work, travels with me whenever she can, and life is still one big adventure. I am lying on the bed in silence; my mind is far away, worrying about the next day's appointments.

'Last week, I interviewed a man who's an expert in police interrogations. He told me that they get most of their information by using a technique they call "cold/hot". They always start with a very aggressive policeman who says he has no intention of sticking to the rules, who shouts and thumps the table. When he has scared the prisoner nearly witless, the "good policeman" comes in and tells his colleague to stop, offers the prisoner a cigarette, pretends to be his friend and gets the information he wants.'

'Yes, I've heard about that.'

'Then he told me about something else that really frightened me. In 1971, a group of researchers at Stanford University, in California, decided to create a simulated prison in order to study the psychology of interrogations. They selected twenty-four student volunteers and divided them into "guards" and "criminals".

After just one week, they had to stop the experiment. The "guards" – girls and boys with normal decent values, from nice families – had become real monsters. The use of torture had become routine and the sexual abuse of "prisoners" was seen as normal. The students who took part in the project, both "guards" and "criminals", suffered major traumas and needed long-term medical help, and the experiment was never repeated.'

'Interesting.'

'What do you mean "interesting"? I'm talking about something of real importance: man's capacity to do evil whenever he's given the chance. I'm talking about my work, about the things I've learned!'

'That's what I found interesting. Why are you getting so angry?'

'Angry? How could I possibly get angry with someone who isn't paying the slightest bit of attention to what I'm saying? How can I possibly be angry with someone who isn't even provoking me, who's just lying there, staring into space?'

'How much did you have to drink tonight?'

'You don't even know the answer to that, do you? I've been by your side all evening, and you've no idea whether I've had anything to drink or not! You only spoke to me when you wanted me to confirm something you had said or when you needed me to tell some flattering story about you!'

'Look, I've been working all day and I'm exhausted. Why don't you come to bed and sleep? We can talk in the morning.'

'Because I've been doing this for weeks and months, for the last two years in fact! I try to have a conversation, but you're always tired, so we say, all right, we'll go to sleep and talk tomorrow. But tomorrow there are always other things to do, another day of work and publisher's suppers, so we say, all right, we'll go to sleep and talk tomorrow. That's how

I'm spending my life, waiting for the day when I can have you by my side again, until I've had my fill; that's all I ask, to create a world where I can always find refuge if I need it: not so far away that I can't be seen to be having an independent life, and not so close that it looks as if I'm invading your universe.'

'What do you want me to do? Stop working? Give up everything we've struggled so hard to achieve and go off on a cruise to the Caribbean? Don't you understand that I enjoy what I'm doing and haven't the slightest intention of changing my life?'

'In your books, you talk about the importance of love, the need for adventure, the joy of fighting for your dreams. And who do I have before me now? Someone who doesn't read what he writes. Someone who confuses love with convenience, adventure with taking unnecessary risks, joy with obligation. Where is the man I married, who used to listen to what I was saying?'

'Where is the woman I married?'

'You mean the one who always gave you support, encouragement and affection? Her body is here, looking out at the Singel canal in Amsterdam, and she will, I believe, stay with you for the rest of her life. But that woman's soul is standing at the door ready to leave.'

'But why?'

'Because of those three wretched words: "we'll talk tomorrow". Isn't that enough? If not, just consider that the woman you married was excited about life, full of ideas and joy and desires, and is now rapidly turning into a housewife.'

'That's ridiculous.'

'Of course it is! It's nonsense! A trifle, especially considering that we have everything we could possibly want. We're very fortunate, we have money, we never discuss any little flings we might have, we never have jealous rages. Besides, there are millions of children in the world starving to death, there are wars, diseases, hurricanes, tragedies happening every second. So what can I possibly have to complain about?'

'Do you think we should have a baby?'

'That's how all the couples I know resolve their problems – by having a baby! You're the one who has always prized your freedom and put off having children for later on. Have you really changed your mind?'

'I think the time is right.'

'Well, in my opinion, you couldn't be more wrong! I don't want your child. I want a child by the man I knew, who had dreams, who was always by my side! If I ever do become pregnant it will be by someone who understands me, keeps me company, listens to me, who truly desires me!'

'You *have* been drinking. Look, I promise, we'll talk tomorrow, but, please, come to bed now, I'm tired.'

'All right, we'll talk tomorrow. And if my soul, which is standing at the door, does decide to leave, I doubt it will affect our lives very much.'

'Your soul won't leave.'

'You used to know my soul very well, but you haven't spoken to it for years, you don't know how much it has changed, how *desperately* it's begging you to listen. Even to banal topics of conversation, like experiments at American universities.'

'If your soul has changed so much, how come you're the same?'

'Out of cowardice. Because I genuinely think that tomorrow we *will* talk. Because of everything we've built together and which I don't want to see destroyed. Or for that worst of all possible reasons, because I've simply given up.'

'That's just what you've been accusing me of doing.'

'You're right. I looked at you, thinking it was you I was looking at, but the truth is I was looking at myself. Tonight I'm going to pray with all my might and all my faith and ask God not to let me spend the rest of my days like this.'

I hear the applause, the theatre is packed. I'm about to do the one thing that always gives me sleepless nights, I'm about to give a lecture.

The master of ceremonies begins by saying that there's no need to introduce me, which is a bit much really, since that's what he's there for and he isn't taking into account the possibility that there might be lots of people in the audience who have simply been invited along by friends. Despite what he says, however, he ends up giving a few biographical details and talking about my qualities as a writer, the prizes I've won, and the millions of books I've sold. He thanks the sponsors, turns to me and the floor is mine.

I thank him too. I tell the audience that the most important things I have to say are in my books, but that I feel I have an obligation to my public to reveal the man who lies behind those words and paragraphs. I explain that our human condition makes us tend to share only the best of ourselves, because we are always searching for love and approval. My books, however, will only ever be the mountain top visible amongst the clouds, or an island in the ocean: the light falls on it, everything seems to be in its place, but beneath the surface lies the unknown, the darkness, the incessant search for self.

I describe how difficult it was to write *A Time to Rend and a Time to Sew*, and that there are many parts of the book which I myself am only beginning to understand now, as I re-read it, as if the created thing were always greater and more generous than its creator.

I say that there is nothing more boring than reading interviews or going to lectures by authors who insist on explaining the characters in their books: if a book isn't self-explanatory, then the book isn't worth reading. When a writer appears in public, he should attempt to show the audience his universe, not try to explain his books; and in this spirit, I begin talking about something more personal.

'Some time ago, I was in Geneva for a series of interviews. At the end of a day's work, and because a woman friend I was supposed to have supper with cancelled at the last minute, I set off for a stroll around the city. It was a particularly lovely night, the streets were deserted, the bars and restaurants still full of life, and everything seemed utterly calm, orderly, pretty, and yet suddenly ... suddenly I realised that I was utterly alone.

Needless to say, I had been alone on other occasions during the year. Needless to say, my girlfriend was only two hours away by plane. Needless to say, after a busy day, what could be better than a stroll through the narrow streets and lanes of the old city, without having to talk to anyone, simply enjoying the beauty around me. And yet the feeling that surfaced was one of oppressive, distressing loneliness – not having someone with whom I could share the city, the walk, the things I'd like to say.

I got out my mobile phone; after all, I had a reasonable number of friends in the city, but it was too late to phone anyone. I considered going into one of the bars and ordering a drink; someone was bound to recognise me and invite me to join them. But I resisted the temptation and tried to get through that moment, discovering, in the process, that there is nothing worse than the feeling that no one cares whether we exist or not, that no one is interested in what we have to say about life, and that the world can continue turning without our awkward presence.

I began to imagine how many millions of people were, at that moment, feeling utterly useless and wretched – however rich, charming and delightful they might be – because they were alone that night, as they were yesterday, and as they might well be tomorrow. Students with no one to go out with, older people sitting in front of the TV as if it were their sole salvation, businessmen in their hotel rooms, wondering if what they were doing made any sense, women who spent the afternoon carefully applying their makeup and doing their hair in order to go to a bar only to pretend that they're not looking for company; all they want is confirmation that they're still attractive; the men ogle them and chat them up, but the women reject them all disdainfully, because they feel inferior and are afraid the men will find out that they're single mothers or lowly clerks with nothing to say about what's going on in the world because they work from dawn to dusk to scrape a living and have no time to read the newspapers. People who look at themselves in the mirror and think themselves ugly, believing that being beautiful is what really matters, and spend their time reading magazines in which everyone is pretty, rich, and famous. Husbands and wives who wish they could talk over supper as they used to, but there are always other things demanding their attention, more important things, and the conversation can always wait for a tomorrow that never comes.

That day, I had lunch with a friend who had just got divorced and she said to me: 'Now I can enjoy the freedom I've always dreamed of having.' But that's a lie. No one wants that kind of freedom: we all want commitment, we all want someone to be beside us to enjoy the beauties of Geneva, to discuss books, interviews, films, or even to share a sandwich with because there isn't enough money to buy one each. Better to eat half a sandwich than a whole one. Better to be interrupted by the man who wants to get straight back home because there's a big game on TV tonight or by the woman who stops outside a shop window and interrupts what we were saying about the cathedral tower, far better that than to have the whole of Geneva to yourself with all the time and quiet in the world to visit it.

Better to go hungry than to be alone. Because when you're alone – and I'm talking here about an enforced solitude not of our choosing – it's as if you were no longer part of the human race.

A lovely hotel awaited me on the other side of the river, with its luxurious rooms, its attentive employees, its five-star service. And that only made me feel worse, because I should have felt contented, satisfied with all I had achieved.

On the way back, I passed other people in the same situation and noticed that they fell into two categories: those who looked arrogant, because they wanted to pretend they had chosen to be alone on that lovely night, and those who looked sad and ashamed of their solitary state.

I'm telling you all this because the other day I remembered being in a hotel room in Amsterdam with a woman who was talking to me about her life. I'm telling you all this because, although in Ecclesiastes it says there is a time to rend and a time to sew, sometimes the time to rend leaves deep scars. Being with someone else and making that person feel as if they were of no importance in our life is far worse than feeling alone and miserable in the streets of Geneva.'

There was a long moment of silence before the applause.

I arrived in a gloomy part of Paris, which was nevertheless said to have the most vibrant cultural life of the whole city. It took me a while to recognise the scruffy group of people before me as the same ones who appeared on Thursdays in the Armenian restaurant immaculately dressed in white.

'Why are you all wearing fancy dress? Is this some kind of tribute to a movie?'

'It's not fancy dress,' replied Mikhail. 'Don't you change your clothes to go to a gala supper? Would you wear a jacket and tie to play golf?'

'All right, let me put the question another way: why have you decided to dress like young homeless people?'

'Because, at this moment, we are young homeless people, or, rather, four young homeless people and two homeless adults.'

'Let me put the question a third way, then: why are you dressed like that?'

'In the restaurant, we feed our body and talk about the Energy to people with something to lose. Amongst the beggars, we feed our soul and talk to those who have nothing to lose. Now, we come to the most important part of our work: meeting the members of the invisible

253

movement that is renewing the world, people who live each day as if it were their last, while the old live each day as if it were their first.'

He was talking about something I had already noticed and which seemed to be growing by the day: this was how young people dressed, in grubby, but highly imaginative outfits, based on military uniforms or sci-fi movies. They all went in for body-piercing too and sported highly individual haircuts. Often, the groups were accompanied by a threatening-looking Alsatian dog. I once asked a friend why these people always had a dog with them and he told me – although I don't know if it's true – that the police couldn't arrest the owners because they had nowhere to put the dog.

A bottle of vodka began doing the rounds; we had drunk vodka when we were with the beggars and I wondered if this was to do with Mikhail's origins. I took a sip, imagining what people would say if they saw me there.

I decided they would say: 'He's probably doing research for his next book,' and felt more relaxed.

'I'm ready now to go and find Esther, but I need some more information, because I know nothing about your country.'

'I'll go with you.'

'What?'

That wasn't in my plans at all. My journey was a return to everything I had lost in myself, and would end somewhere in the Central Asian steppes. It was something intimate and personal, something that did not require witnesses.

'As long as you pay for my ticket, of course. I need to go back to Kazakhstan. I miss my country.'

'I thought you had work to do here. Haven't you got to be at the restaurant on Thursdays for the performances.'

'You keep calling it a performance. I've told you before, it's a meeting, a way of reviving what we have lost, the tradition of conversation. But don't worry. Anastásia here', and he pointed to a girl wearing a nose stud, 'is already developing her gift. She can take care of everything while I'm away.'

'He's jealous,' said Alma, the woman who played the instrument that looked like a cymbal and who told stories at the end of each 'meeting'.

'Understandable really,' said another boy, who was dressed in a leather outfit adorned with metal studs, safety pins and buckles made to look like razor blades. 'Mikhail is younger, better-looking and more in touch with the Energy.'

'He's also less famous, less rich and less in touch with those in power,' said Anastásia. 'From the female point of view, things are pretty evenly balanced, so I reckon they're both in with a chance.'

Everyone laughed and the bottle went the rounds again. I was the only one who didn't see the joke. I was surprising myself, though; it had been many years since I had sat on a pavement in Paris, and this pleased me.

'The tribe is bigger than you think. They're everywhere, from the Eiffel Tower down as far as the town of Tarbes where I was staying recently. But I can't honestly say I understand what it's all about.'

'They can be found farther south than Tarbes, and they follow routes every bit as interesting as the Road to Santiago. They set off from somewhere in France or somewhere else in Europe, swearing that they're going to be part of a society that exists outside of society. They're afraid of going back home and getting a job and getting married – they'll fight against all that for as long as they can. There are rich and poor amongst them, but they're not that interested in money. They look completely different, and yet when people walk past them, they usually pretend not to see them because they're afraid.'

'Do they have to look so aggressive?'

'Yes, because the passion to destroy is a creative passion. If they weren't aggressive, the boutiques would immediately fill up with clothes like these; publishers would soon be producing magazines about the new movement "sweeping the world with its revolutionary attitudes"; TV programmes would have a strand devoted to the tribe; sociologists would write learned articles; psychiatrists would counsel the families of tribe members, and it would lose all its impact. So the less they know about us, the better: our attack is really a defence.'

'Actually, I only came tonight so that I could ask you for some information, but, who knows, perhaps spending the night with you will turn out to be just the kind of rich and novel experience to move me on from a personal history that no longer allows for new experiences. As for the journey to Kazakhstan, I've no intention of taking anyone with me. If I can't get help from you, the Favour Bank will provide me with all the necessary contacts. I'm going away in two days' time and I'm a guest at an important supper tomorrow night, but after that, I'm free for two weeks.'

Mikhail appeared to hesitate.

'It's up to you. You've got the map, the name of the village, and it shouldn't be hard to find the house where she's staying. I'm sure the Favour Bank can help get you as far as Almaty, but I doubt it will get you much further than that, because the rules of the steppes are different. Besides, I reckon I've made a few deposits in your account at the Favour Bank too. It's time to reclaim them. I miss my mother.'

He was right.

'We've got to start work,' said Alma's husband.

'Why do you want to go with me, Mikhail? Is it really just because you miss your mother?'

He didn't reply. The man started playing the drum and Alma was clanging the cymbal, while the others begged for money from passersby. Why did he want to go with me? And how would I be able to draw on the Favour Bank in the steppes, if I knew absolutely no one? I could get a visa from the Kazakhstan embassy, hire a car and a guide from the French consulate in Almaty – what else did I need?

I stood there observing the group, not knowing quite what to do. It wasn't the right moment to discuss the trip, and I had work to do and a girlfriend waiting for me at home: why didn't I just leave now?

I didn't leave because I was feeling free, doing things I hadn't done for years, opening up a space in my soul for new experiences, driving the *acomodador* out of my life, experiencing things that might not interest me very much, but which were at least different.

The vodka ran out and was replaced by rum. I hate rum, but since that was all there was, it was best to adapt to the circumstances. The two musicians continued to play and whenever anyone was brave enough to come near, one of the girls would hold out her hand and ask if they had any spare change. The person approached would normally quicken their pace, but would always receive a 'Thanks, have a nice evening'. One person, seeing that he had been offered thanks rather than abuse, turned back and gave us some money.

After watching this scene for more than ten minutes, without anyone in the group addressing a single word to me, I went into a bar, bought two bottles of vodka, came back and poured the rum into the gutter. Anastásia seemed pleased by my gesture and so I tried to start a conversation.

'Can you explain why you all use body-piercing?'

'Why do other people wear jewels or high heels or low-cut dresses even in winter?'

'That's not an answer.'

'We use body-piercing because we're the new barbarians sacking Rome. We don't wear uniforms and so we need something to identify us as one of the invading tribes.'

She made it sound as if they were part of an important historical movement, but for the people going home, they were just a group of unemployed young people with nowhere to sleep, cluttering up the streets of Paris, bothering the tourists who were so good for the local economy, and driving to despair the mothers and fathers who had brought them into the world and now had no control over them.

I had been like that once, when the hippie movement was at its height – the huge rock concerts, the big hair, the garish clothes, the Viking symbol, the peace sign. As Mikhail said, the whole hippie thing had turned into just another consumer product and had vanished, destroying its icons.

A man came down the street. The boy in leather and safety pins went over to him with his hand outstretched. He asked for money. However, instead of hurrying on or muttering something like 'I haven't any change', the man stopped and looked at us and said very loudly:

'I wake up every morning with a debt of approximately 100,000 euros, because of my house, because of the economic situation in Europe, because of my wife's expensive tastes. In other words, I'm worse off than you are and with far more on my mind! How about you giving *me* a bit of change to help me decrease my debt just a little?'

Lucrecia – whom Mikhail claimed was his girlfriend – produced a fifty-euro note and gave it to the man.

'Buy yourself some caviar. You need a bit of joy in your miserable life.'

The man thanked her and walked off, as if it were the most natural thing in the world to be given fifty euros by a beggar. The Italian girl had had a fifty-euro note in her bag and here we were begging in the street!

'Let's go somewhere else,' said the boy in leather.

'Where?' asked Mikhail.

'We could see if we can find the others. North or South?'

Anastásia chose West. After all, she was, according to Mikhail, developing her gift.

We passed by the Tour de Saint-Jacques where, centuries before, pilgrims heading for Santiago de Compostela used to gather. We passed Notre Dame, where there were a few more 'new barbarians'. The vodka had run out and so I went to buy two more bottles, even though I wasn't sure that everyone in the group was over eighteen. No one thanked me; they seemed to think it was perfectly normal.

I started to feel a little drunk and began eyeing up one of the girls who had just joined us. Everyone talked very loudly, kicked a few litter bins – strange metal objects with a plastic bag dangling from them – and said absolutely nothing of any interest.

We crossed the Seine and were suddenly brought to a halt by one of those orange-and-white tapes that are used to mark off an area under construction. It prevented people from walking along the pavement, forcing them to step off the kerb into the road and then rejoin the pavement five metres further on.

'It's still here,' said one of the new arrivals.

'What's still here?' I asked.

'Who's he?'

'A friend of ours,' replied Lucrecia. 'In fact, you've probably read one of his books.'

The newcomer recognised me, but showed neither surprise nor reverence; on the contrary, he asked if I could give him some money, a request I instantly refused.

'If you want to know why the tape is there, you'll have to give me a euro. Everything in life has its price, as you know better than anyone. And information is one of the most expensive products in the world.'

No one in the group came to my aid, and so I had to pay him a euro for his answer.

'The tape is here because we put it there. As you can see, there are no repairs going on at all, just a stupid orange-and-white tape blocking the stupid pavement. But no one asks what it's doing there; they step off the pavement, walk along the road at the risk of being knocked down and get back on further up. By the way, I read somewhere that you'd had an accident. Is that true?'

'Yes, I did, and all because I stepped off the pavement.'

'Don't worry, when people step off the pavement here, they're always extra careful. It was one of the reasons we put the tape up, to make people more aware of what was going on around them.'

'No, it wasn't,' said the girl I was attracted to. 'It's just a joke, so that we can laugh at the people who obey without even thinking about what they're obeying. There's no reason, it's not important, and no one will get knocked down.'

More people joined the group. Now there were eleven of us and two Alsatian dogs. We were no longer begging, because no one dared go near this band of savages who seemed to enjoy the fear they aroused. The drink had run out again and they all looked at me and asked me to buy another bottle, as if I had a duty to keep them drunk. I realised that this was my 'passport' to the pilgrimage and so set off in search of a shop.

The girl I was interested in – and who was young enough to be my daughter – seemed to notice me looking at her and started talking to me. I knew it was simply a way of provoking me, but I joined in. She didn't tell me anything about her personal life, she just asked me how many cats and how many lamp-posts there were on the back of a ten-dollar bill.

'Cats and lamp-posts?'

'You don't know, do you? You don't give any real value to money at all. Well, for your information, there are four cats and eleven lamp-posts.'

Four cats and eleven lamp-posts. I promised myself that I would check this out the next time I saw a ten-dollar bill.

'Do any of you take drugs?'

'Some, but mainly it's just alcohol. Not much at all, in fact, it's not our style. Drugs are more for people of your generation, aren't they? My mother, for example, drugs herself on cooking for the family, compulsively tidying the house, and suffering over me. When something goes wrong with my dad's business, she suffers. Can you believe that? She suffers over me, my father, my brothers and sisters, everything. I was wasting so much energy pretending to be happy all the time, I thought it was best just to leave home.'

Another personal history.

'Like your wife,' said a young man with fair hair and an eyebrow ring. 'She left home too, didn't she? Was that because she had to pretend to be happy all the time?'

So she had been here too. Had she given some of these young people a piece of that bloodstained shirt?

'She suffered too,' laughed Lucrecia. 'But as far as we know, she's not suffering any more. That's what I call courage!'

'What was my wife doing here?'

'She came with the Mongolian guy, the one with all the strange ideas about love that we're only just beginning to understand. And she used to ask questions and tell us her story. One day, she stopped doing both. She said she was tired of complaining. We suggested that she give up everything and come with us, because we were planning a trip to North Africa. She thanked us, but said she had other plans and would be heading off in the opposite direction.'

'Didn't you read his latest book?' asked Anastásia.

'No, I didn't fancy it, people told me it was too romantic. Now when are we going to get some more booze?'

People made way for us as if we were samurai riding into a village, bandits arriving in a frontier town, barbarians entering Rome. The tribe didn't make any aggressive gestures, the aggression was all in the clothes, the body-piercing, the loud conversations, the sheer oddness. We finally found a minimart: to my great discomfort and alarm, they all went in and started rummaging around on the shelves.

I didn't know any of them, apart from Mikhail, and even then I didn't know if what he had told me about himself was true. What if they stole something? What if one of them was armed? As the oldest member of the group, was I responsible for their actions?

The man on the till kept glancing up at the security mirror suspended from the ceiling in the tiny shop. The group, knowing that he was worried, spread out, gesturing to each other, and the tension grew. To cut things short, I picked up three bottles of vodka and walked quickly over to the till.

A woman buying cigarettes said that, in her day, Paris had been full of bohemians and artists, not threatening bands of homeless people. She suggested that the cashier call the police.

'I've got a feeling something bad is going to happen any minute now,' she muttered.

The cashier was terrified by this invasion of his little world, the fruit of years of work and many loans, where perhaps his son worked in the morning, his wife in the afternoon and he at night. He nodded to the woman, and I realised that he had already called the police.

I hate getting involved in things that are none of my business, but I also hate being a coward. Every time it happens, I lose all self-respect for a week.

'Don't worry ...' I began.

It was too late.

Two policemen came in and the owner beckoned them over, but the young people disguised as extraterrestrials paid no attention – it was all part of standing up to representatives of the established order. It must have happened to them many times before. They knew they hadn't committed any crime (apart from crimes against fashion, but that could all change with next season's haute couture). They must have been afraid, but they didn't show it and continued talking loudly.

'I saw a comedian the other day. He said that stupid people should have "stupid" written on their identity card,' said Anastásia to no one in particular, 'that way, we'd know who we were talking to.'

'Yeah, stupid people are a real danger to society,' said the girl with the angelic face and vampire clothing, who, shortly before, had been talking to me about the number of lamp-posts and cats to be found on the back of a ten-dollar bill. 'They should be tested once a year and have a licence for walking the streets, like drivers do to drive.'

The policemen, who couldn't have been very much older than the 'tribe', said nothing.

'Do you know what I'd like to do,' it was Mikhail's voice, but I couldn't see him because he was concealed behind a shelf. 'I'd like to change the labels on everything in this shop. People would be completely lost. They wouldn't know whether things should be eaten hot or cold, boiled or fried. If they don't read the instructions, they don't know how to prepare a meal. They've lost all their culinary instincts.'

Everyone who had spoken up until then had done so in perfect Parisian French. Only Mikhail had a foreign accent.

'May I see your passport,' said one of the policemen.

'He's with me.'

The words emerged naturally, even though I knew what it could mean – another scandal. The policeman looked at me.

'I wasn't talking to you, but since you're obviously with this lot, I hope you've got some kind of document to prove who you are, and a good reason for being surrounded by people half your age and buying vodka.'

I could refuse to show my papers. I wasn't legally obliged to have them with me. But I was thinking about Mikhail. One of the policemen was standing next to him now. Did he really have permission to stay in France? What did I know about him apart from the stories he had told me about his visions and his epilepsy? What if the tension of the moment provoked an attack?

I stuck my hand in my pocket and took out my driver's licence.

'So you're …'

'I am.'

'I thought it was you. I've read one of your books. But that doesn't put you above the law.'

The fact that he had read one of my books threw me completely. There was this shaven-headed young man in a uniform, albeit a very different one from that worn by the 'tribes' in order to tell each other apart. Perhaps he too had once dreamed of having the freedom to be different, of subtly challenging authority, although never disrespectfully enough to end up in jail. He probably had a father who had never offered him any alternative, a family who needed his financial support, or perhaps he was just afraid of going beyond his own familiar world.

I said gently:

'No, I'm not above the law. In fact, no one here has broken the law. Unless the gentleman at the till or the lady buying cigarettes would like to make some specific complaint.'

When I turned round, the woman who had mentioned the artists and bohemians 'of her day', that prophet of imminent doom, the embodiment of truth and good manners, had disappeared. She would doubtless tell her neighbours the next day that, thanks to her, an attempted robbery had been averted.

'I've no complaints,' said the man behind the till, 'I got worried because they were talking so loudly, but it looks like they weren't actually doing any harm.'

'Is the vodka for you, sir?'

I nodded. They knew that everyone there was drunk, but they didn't want to make a big deal out of a harmless situation.

'A world without stupid people would be complete chaos!' said the boy wearing leather and metal studs. 'Instead of all the unemployed people we have today, there would be too many jobs and no one to do the work!'

'Shut up!'

My voice sounded authoritative, decisive.

'Just stop talking, all of you!'

To my surprise, silence fell. My heart was beating furiously, but I continued talking to the policemen as if I were the calmest person in the world.

'If they were really dangerous, they wouldn't be talking like that.'

The policeman turned to the cashier:

'If you need us, we'll be around.'

And before going out, he said to his colleague, so that his voice echoed round the whole shop.

'I love stupid people. If it wasn't for them, we might be having to tackle some real criminals.'

'You're right,' said the other policeman. 'Stupid people are a nice safe distraction.'

They gave their usual salute and left.

The only thing it occurred to me to do when we left the shop, was to smash the bottles of vodka. I saved one of them, though, and it was passed rapidly from mouth to mouth. By the way they were drinking, I could see they were frightened, as frightened as I was. The only difference was that they had gone on the offensive when threatened.

'I don't feel good,' said Mikhail to one of them. 'Let's go.' I didn't know what he meant by 'Let's go': each to his own house or town or bridge? No one asked me if I wanted to go with them, so I simply followed after. Mikhail's remark 'I don't feel good' unsettled me; that meant we wouldn't have another chance that night to talk about the trip to Central Asia. Should I just leave? Or should I stick it out and see what 'let's go' meant? I discovered that I was enjoying myself and that I'd like to try seducing the girl in the vampire outfit.

Onward, then.

I could always leave at the first sign of danger.

As we headed off – where, I didn't know – I was thinking about this whole experience. A tribe. A symbolic return to a time when men travelled in protective groups and required very little to survive. A tribe in the midst of another hostile tribe called society, crossing society's lands and using aggression as a defence against rejection. A group of people who had joined together to form an ideal society, about which I knew nothing beyond the body-piercing and the clothes that they wore. What were their values? What did they think about life? How did they earn their money? Did they have dreams or was it enough just to wander the world? All this was much more interesting than the supper I had to go to the following evening, where I knew exactly what would happen. I was convinced that it must be the effect of the vodka, but I was feeling free, my personal history was growing ever more remote, there was only the present moment, instinct; the Zahir had disappeared ...

The Zahir?

Yes, it had disappeared, but now I realised that the Zahir was more than a man obsessed with an object, with a vein in the marble of one of the twelve hundred columns in the mosque in Córdoba, as Borges puts it, or, as in my own painful case for the last two years, with a woman in Central Asia. The Zahir was a fixation on everything that had been passed from generation to generation; it left no question unanswered, it took up all the space; it never allowed us even to consider the possibility that things could change.

The all-powerful Zahir seemed to be born with every human being and to gain full strength in childhood, imposing rules that would thereafter always be respected:

People who are different are dangerous; they belong to another tribe; they want our lands and our women.

We must marry, have children, reproduce the species.

Love is only a small thing, enough for one person, and any suggestion that the heart might be larger than this is considered perverse.

When we marry, we are authorised to take possession of the other person, body and soul.

We must do jobs we detest because we are part of an organised society, and if everyone did what they wanted to do, the world would come to a standstill.

We must buy jewellery; it identifies us with our tribe, just as body-piercing identifies those of a different tribe.

We must be amusing at all times and sneer at those who express their real feelings; it's dangerous for a tribe to allow its members to show their feelings.

We must at all costs avoid saying 'No' because people prefer those who always say 'Yes', and this allows us to survive in hostile territory.

What other people think is more important than what we feel.

Never make a fuss, it might attract the attention of an enemy tribe.

If you behave differently, you will be expelled from the tribe because you could infect others and destroy something that was extremely difficult to organise in the first place.

We must always consider the look of our new cave, and if we don't have a clear idea of our own, then we must call in a decorator who will do his best to show others what good taste we have.

We must eat three meals a day, even if we're not hungry, and when we fail to fit the current ideal of beauty we must fast, even if we're starving.

We must dress according to the dictates of fashion, make love whether we feel like it or not, kill in the name of our country's frontiers, wish time away so that retirement comes more quickly, elect politicians, complain about the cost of living, change our hairstyle, criticise anyone who is different, go to a religious service on Sunday, Saturday or Friday, depending on our religion, and there beg forgiveness for our sins and puff ourselves up with pride because we know the truth and despise the other tribe, who worship a false god.

Our children must follow in our footsteps; after all, we are older and know about the world.

We must have a university degree even if we never get a job in the area of knowledge we were forced to study.

We must study things that we will never use, but which someone told us was important to know: algebra, trigonometry, the code of Hammurabi.

We must never make our parents sad, even if this means giving up everything that makes us happy.

We must play music quietly, talk quietly, weep in private, because I am the all-powerful Zahir, who lays down the rules and determines the distance between railway tracks, the meaning of success, the best way to love, the importance of rewards.

We stop outside a relatively chic building in an expensive area. One of the group taps in the code at the front door and we all go up to the third floor. I thought we would find one of those understanding families who put up with their son's friends in order to keep him close to home and to keep an eye on him. But when Lucrecia opened the door, everything was in darkness. As my eyes grew accustomed to the light from the street filtering in through the windows, I saw a large empty living room. The only decoration was a fireplace that probably hadn't been used for years.

A fair-haired boy, who was nearly six feet tall and wore a long rain cape and a Sioux Indian haircut, went into the kitchen and returned with some lighted candles. We all sat round in a circle on the floor and, for the first time that night, I felt afraid: it was like being in a horror movie in which a satanic ritual is about to begin, and where the victim will be the stranger who was unwise enough to tag along.

Mikhail was looking pale and his eyes kept darting about, unable to fix on any one place, and that only increased my feeling of unease. He was on the point of having an epileptic fit. Would the people there know what to do in that situation? Wouldn't it be better just to leave now and not get involved in a potential tragedy?

That would perhaps be the most prudent thing to do, in keeping with a life in which I was a famous author who writes about spirituality and should therefore be setting an example. Yes, if I was being sensible, I would say to Lucrecia that, in case of an attack, she should place something in her boyfriend's mouth to stop his tongue rolling back and prevent him choking to death. She must know this already, but in the world of the followers of the social Zahir, we leave nothing to chance, we need to be at peace with our conscience.

That is how I would have acted before my accident, but now my personal history had become unimportant. It had stopped being history and was once more becoming a legend, a search, an adventure, a journey into and away from myself. I was once more in a time in which the things around me were changing and that is how I wanted it to be for the rest of my days (I remembered one of my ideas for an epitaph: He died while he was still alive). I was carrying with me the experiences of my past, which allowed me to react with speed and precision, but I wasn't bothered about the lessons I had learned. Imagine a warrior, in the middle of a fight, pausing to decide which move to make next? He would be dead in an instant.

And the warrior in me, using intuition and technique, decided that I needed to stay, to continue the night's experiences, even if it was late and I was tired and drunk and afraid that a worried or angry Marie might be waiting up for me. I sat down next to Mikhail so that I could act quickly should he have a fit.

I noticed that he seemed to be in control of his epileptic attack. He gradually grew calmer, and his eyes took on the same intensity as when he was the young man in white standing on the stage at the Armenian restaurant.

'We will start with the usual prayer,' he said.

And the young people, who, up until then, had been aggressive, drunken misfits, closed their eyes and held hands in a large circle. Even the two Alsatian dogs sitting in one corner of the room seemed calmer.

'Dear Lady, when I look at the cars, the shop windows, the people oblivious to everyone else, when I look at all the buildings and the monuments, I see in them Your absence. Make us capable of bringing You back.'

The group continued as one:

'Dear Lady, we recognise Your presence in the difficulties we are experiencing. Help us not to give up. Help us to think of You with tranquillity and determination, even when it is hard to accept that we love You.'

I noticed that everyone there was wearing the same symbol somewhere on their clothing. Sometimes it was in the form of a brooch, or a metal badge, or a piece of embroidery, or was even drawn on the fabric with a pen.

'I would like to dedicate tonight to the man sitting on my right. He sat down beside me because he wanted to protect me.'

How did he know that?

'He's a good man. He knows that love transforms and he allows himself to be transformed by love. He still carries much of his personal history in his soul, but he is continually trying to free himself from it, which is why he stayed with us tonight. He is the husband of the woman we all know, the woman who left me a relic as proof of her friendship and as a talisman.'

Mikhail took out the piece of bloodstained cloth and put it down in front of him.

'This is part of the unknown soldier's shirt. Before he died, he said to the woman: "Cut up my clothes and distribute the pieces amongst those who believe in death and who, for that reason, are capable of living as if today were their last day on earth. Tell those people that I have just seen the face of God; tell them not to be afraid, but not to grow complacent either. Seek the one truth, which is love. Live in accordance with its laws."'

They all gazed reverently at the piece of cloth.

'We were born into a time of revolt. We pour all our enthusiasm into it, we risk our lives and our youth, and suddenly, we feel afraid, and that initial joy gives way to the real challenges: weariness, monotony, doubts about our own abilities. We notice that some of our friends have already given up. We are obliged to confront loneliness, to cope with sharp bends in the road, to suffer a few falls with no one near to help us, and we end up asking ourselves if it's worth all that effort.'

Mikhail paused.

'It is. And we will carry on, knowing that our soul, even though it is eternal, is, at this moment, caught in the web of time, with all its opportunities and limitations. We will, as far as possible, free ourselves from this web. When this proves impossible and we return to the story we were told, we will, nevertheless, remember our battles and be ready to resume the struggle as soon as the conditions are right. Amen.'

'Amen,' echoed the others.

'I need to talk to the Lady,' said the fair young man with the Sioux Indian haircut.

'Not tonight. I'm tired.'

There was a general murmur of disappointment. Unlike those people at the Armenian restaurant, they knew Mikhail's story and knew about the 'presence' he felt by his side. He got up and went into the kitchen to get a glass of water. I went with him.

I asked how they had come by that apartment, and he explained that in French law anyone can legally move into a building that is not being used by its owner. It was, in short, a squat.

I began to be troubled by the thought that Marie would be waiting up for me. Mikhail took my arm.

'You said today that you were going to the steppes. I'll say this one more time: please, take me with you. I need to go back to my country, even if only for a short time, but I haven't any money. I miss my people, my mother, my friends. I could say "the voice tells me that you will need me", but that wouldn't be true: you could find Esther easily enough and without any help at all. But I need an infusion of energy from my homeland.'

'I can give you the money for a return ticket.'

'I know you can, but I'd like to be there with you, to go with you to the village where she's living, to feel the wind on my face, to help you along the road that will lead you back to the woman you love. She was – and still is – very important to me. I learned so much from the changes she went through, from her determination, and I want to go on learning. Do you remember me talking once about "interrupted stories"? I would like to be by your side right up until the moment we reach her house. That way, I will have lived through to the end this period of your – and my – life. When we reach her house, I will leave you alone.'

I didn't know what to say. I tried to talk about something else and asked about the people in the living room.

'They're people who are afraid of ending up like your generation, a generation that dreamed it could revolutionise the world, but ended up giving in to "reality". We pretend to be strong because we're weak. There are still only a few of us, very few, but I think that's only a passing phase; people can't go on deceiving themselves for ever. Now what's your answer to my question?'

'Mikhail, you know how much I want to free myself from my personal history. If you had asked me a while ago, I would have found it much more comfortable, more convenient even, to travel with you, since you know the country, the customs and the possible dangers. Now, though, I feel that I should roll up Ariadne's thread into a ball and escape from the labyrinth I got myself into and that I should do this alone. My life has changed; I feel as if I were ten or even twenty years younger, and that in itself is enough for me to want to set off in search of adventure.'

'When will you leave?'

'As soon as I get my visa. In two or three days' time.'

'May the Lady go with you. The voice is saying that it is the right moment. If you change your mind, let me know.'

I walked past the group of people lying on the floor, ready to go to sleep. On the way home, it occurred to me that life was a much more joyful thing than I had thought it would be at my age: it's always possible to go back to being young and crazy again. I was so focused on the present moment that I was surprised when I saw that people didn't recoil from me as I passed, didn't fearfully lower their eyes. No one even noticed me, but I liked the idea; the city was once again the city of which Henry IV – when accused of betraying his Protestant religion by marrying a Catholic – had said: 'Paris is well worth a mass.'

It was worth much more than that. I could see again the religious massacres, the blood-lettings, the kings, the queens, the museums, the castles, the tortured artists, the drunken writers, the philosophers who took their own lives, the soldiers who plotted to conquer the world, the traitors who, with a gesture, brought down a whole dynasty, the stories that had once been forgotten and were now remembered and retold.

For the first time in ages, I arrived home and did not immediately go over to the computer to find out if anyone had e-mailed me, if there was some pressing matter requiring urgent action: nothing was that urgent. I didn't go into the bedroom to see if Marie was asleep either, because I knew she would only be pretending to sleep.

I didn't turn on the TV to watch the late-night news, because the news was exactly the same news I used to listen to as a child: one country was threatening another country, someone had betrayed someone else, the economy was going badly, some grand passion had come to an end, Israel and Palestine had failed, after fifty long years, to reach an agreement, another bomb had exploded, a hurricane had left thousands of people homeless.

I remembered that the major networks that morning, having no terrorist attacks to report, had all chosen as their main item a rebellion in Haiti. What did I care about Haiti? What difference would that make to my life or to that of my wife, to the price of bread in Paris, to Mikhail's tribe? How could I have spent five minutes of my precious life listening to someone talking about the rebels and the president, watching the usual scenes of street protests being repeated over and over, and being reported as if it were a great event in the history of humanity – a rebellion in Haiti! And I had swallowed it whole! I had watched until the end! Stupid people really should be issued with their own special identity cards because they are the ones who feed the collective stupidity.

I opened the window and let in the icy night air; I took off my clothes and told myself that I could withstand the cold. I stood there, not thinking anything, just aware of my feet on the floor, my eyes fixed on the Eiffel Tower, my ears hearing dogs barking, police sirens and conversations I couldn't quite understand.

I was not I, I was nothing – and that seemed to me quite marvellous.

'You seem strange.'

'What do you mean "strange"?'

'You seem sad.'

'I'm not sad. I'm happy.'

'You see? Even your tone of voice is false: you're sad about me, but you don't dare say anything.'

'Why should I be sad?'

'Because I came home late last night and I was drunk. You haven't even asked me where I went.'

'I'm not interested.'

'Why aren't you interested? I told you I was going out with Mikhail, didn't I?'

'Didn't you go out with him, then?'

'Yes. I did.'

'So what's there to ask?'

'Don't you think that when your boyfriend, whom you claim you love, comes home late, you should at least try to find out what happened?'

'All right, then, what happened?'

'Nothing. I went out with Mikhail and some of his friends.'

'Fine.'

'Do you believe me?'

'Of course I do.'

'I don't think you love me any more. You're not jealous. You don't care. Do I normally get back home at two in the morning?'

'Didn't you say you were a free man?'

'And I am.'

'In that case, it's normal that you should get back home at two in the morning and do whatever you want to do. If I was your mother, I'd be worried, but you're a grown-up, aren't you? You men should stop behaving as if you wanted the women in your life to treat you like children.'

'I don't mean that kind of worried. I'm talking about jealousy.'

'Would you prefer it if I made a scene right now, over breakfast?'

'No, don't do that, the neighbours will hear.'

'I don't care about the neighbours. I won't make a scene because I don't feel like it. It's been hard for me, but I've finally accepted what you told me in Zagreb and I'm trying to get used to the idea. Meanwhile, if it makes you happy, I can always pretend to be jealous, angry, crazy or whatever.'

'Like I said, you seem strange. I'm beginning to think I'm not important in your life any more.'

'And I'm beginning to think you've forgotten there's a journalist waiting for you in the sitting room, and who is quite possibly listening to our conversation.'

Ah, the journalist. I go onto automatic pilot, because I know what questions he will ask. I know how the interview will begin ('Let's talk about your new novel. What's the main message'), and I know how I will respond ('If I wanted to put across a message, I'd write a single sentence, not a book').

I know he'll ask me what I feel about the critics, who are usually very hard on my work. I know that he will end by asking: 'And have you already started writing a new book? What projects are you working on now?' To which I will respond: 'That's a secret.'

The interview begins as expected:

'Let's talk about your new book. What's the main message?'

'If I wanted to put across a message, I'd write a single sentence, not a book.'

'And why do you write?'

'Because that's my way of sharing my feelings with others.'

This phrase is also part of my automatic pilot script, but I stop and correct myself:

'Although that particular story could be told in a different way.'

'In a different way? Do you mean you're not happy with *A Time to Rend and a Time to Sew*?'

'No, on the contrary, I'm very pleased with the book, but I'm not so pleased with the answer I've just given you. Why do I write? The real answer is this: I write because I want to be loved.'

The journalist eyed me suspiciously: what kind of confession was this?

'I write because when I was an adolescent, I was useless at football, I didn't have a car or much of an allowance, and I was pretty much of a weed.'

I was making a huge effort to keep talking. The conversation with Marie had reminded me of a past that no longer made any sense; I needed to talk about my real personal history, in order to become free of it. I went on:

'I didn't wear trendy clothes either. That's all the girls in my class were interested in, and so they just ignored me. At night, when my friends were out with their girlfriends, I spent my free time creating a world in which I could be happy: my companions were writers and their books. One day, I wrote a poem for one of the girls in the street where I lived. A friend found the poem in my room and stole it, and when we were all together, he showed it to the entire class. Everyone laughed. They thought it was ridiculous – I was in love!

The only one who didn't laugh was the girl I wrote the poem for. The following evening, when we went to the theatre, she managed to fix things so that she sat next to me, and she held my hand. We left the theatre hand-in-hand; there was ugly, puny, untrendy me strolling along with the girl all the boys in the class fancied.'

I paused. It was as if I were going back into the past, to the moment when her hand touched mine and changed my life.

'And all because of a poem,' I went on. 'A poem showed me that by writing and revealing my invisible world, I could compete on equal terms with the visible world of my classmates: physical strength, fashionable clothes, cars, being good at sport.'

The journalist was slightly surprised, and I was even more surprised. He managed to compose himself, though, and asked:

'Why do you think the critics are so hard on your work?'

My automatic pilot would normally reply: 'You just have to read the biography of any writer from the past who is now considered a classic – not that I'm comparing myself with them, you understand – to see how implacable their critics were then. The reason is simple: critics are extremely insecure, they don't really know what's going on, they're democrats when it comes to politics, but fascists when it comes to culture. They believe that people are perfectly capable of choosing who governs them, but have no idea when it comes to choosing films, books, music.'

I had abandoned my automatic pilot again, knowing full well that the journalist was unlikely to publish my response.

'Have you ever heard of the Law of Jante?'

'No, I haven't,' he said.

'Well, it's been in existence since the beginning of civilisation, but it was only officially set down in 1933 by a Danish writer. In the small town of Jante, the powers-that-be came up with ten commandments telling people how they should behave, and it seems to exist not only in Jante, but everywhere else too. If I had to sum it up in one sentence, I'd say: "Mediocrity and anonymity are the safest choice. If you opt for them, you'll never face any major problems in life. But if you try to be different … "'

'I'd like to know what these Jante commandments are,' said the journalist, who seemed genuinely interested.

'I don't have them here, but I can summarise if you like.'

I went over to my computer and printed out a condensed and edited version.

'You are nobody, never even dare to think that you know more than we do. You are of no importance, you can do nothing right, your work is of no significance, but as long as you never challenge us, you will live a happy life. Always take what we say seriously and never laugh at our opinions.'

The journalist folded up the piece of paper and put it in his pocket.

'You're right. If you're a nobody, if your work has no impact, then it deserves to be praised. If, however, you climb out of that state of mediocrity and are a success, then you're defying the law and deserve to be punished.'

I was so pleased that he had reached this conclusion on his own.

'And it isn't only the critics who say that,' I added. 'More people, far more people than you might think, say exactly the same thing.'

Later that afternoon, I rang Mikhail's mobile number:

'Let's travel to Kazakhstan together.'

He didn't seem in the least surprised; he merely thanked me and asked what had made me change my mind.

'For two years, my life has consisted of nothing but the Zahir. Since I met you, I've been following a long-forgotten path, an abandoned railway track with grass growing between the rails, but which can still be used by trains. I haven't yet reached the final station, so I have no way of stopping along the way.'

He asked me if I had managed to get a visa. I explained that the Favour Bank had once again come to my aid: a Russian friend had phoned his girlfriend, who was the director of a major newspaper company in Kazakhstan. She had phoned the ambassador in Paris, and the visa would be ready that afternoon.

'When do we leave?'

'Tomorrow. In order to buy the tickets, I just need to know your real name; the travel agent is on the other line now.'

'Before you hang up, I'd just like to say one thing: I really liked what you said about the distance between the tracks and what you said just now about the abandoned railway line, but I don't think that's why you're asking me to come with you. I think it's because of something you wrote once, and which I know by heart; your wife was always quoting these lines, and what they say is far more romantic than that business about the Favour Bank:

A warrior of light knows that he has much to be grateful for.

He was helped in his struggle by the angels; celestial forces placed each thing in its place, thus allowing him to give of his best. That is why, at sunset, he kneels and gives thanks for the Protective Cloak surrounding him.

His companions say: 'He's so lucky!' But he knows that 'luck' is knowing to look around him and to see where his friends are, because it was through their words that the angels were able to make themselves heard.

'I don't always remember what I wrote, but thank you for that. Now I just need your name to give to the travel agent.'

It takes twenty minutes for the taxi company to answer the phone. A tetchy voice tells me I'll have to wait another half an hour. Marie seems happy in her exuberantly sexy black dress, and I think of the Armenian restaurant and the man who admitted to feeling aroused by the thought that his wife was desired by other men. I know that all the women at the gala supper will be wearing outfits designed to make their breasts and curves the centre of attention, and that their husbands or boyfriends, knowing that their wives or girlfriends are desired by other men, will think: 'All right, have a good look, but keep your distance, because she's with me, she's mine. I'm better than you are, because I have something you'd all like to have.'

I'm not going to be doing any business, I'm not going to be signing contracts or giving interviews; I am merely attending a ceremony, to repay a deposit made into my account at the Favour Bank. I will sit next to someone boring at supper, someone who will ask me where I find the inspiration for my books. Next to me, on the other side, a pair of breasts will perhaps be on show, possibly belonging to the wife of a friend, and I will constantly have to stop myself glancing down because, if I do, even for a second, she will tell her husband that I was coming on to her. While we wait for the taxi, I draw up a list of possible topics of conversation:

a) Comments about people's appearance: 'You're looking very elegant', 'What a beautiful dress', 'Your skin's looking fabulous.' When they go back home, they'll say how badly dressed everyone was and how ill they looked.

b) Recent holidays: 'You must visit Aruba, it's fantastic', 'There's nothing like a summer night in Cancun, sipping a Martini by the seashore.' In fact, no one enjoys themselves very much on these holidays, they just experience a sense of freedom for a few days and feel obliged to enjoy themselves because they spent all that money.

c) More holidays, this time to places which they feel free to criticise: 'I was in Rio de Janeiro recently - such a violent city', 'The poverty in the streets of Calcutta is really shocking.' They only went to these places in order to feel powerful while they were there and privileged when they came back to the mean reality of their little lives, where at least there is no poverty or violence.

d) New therapies: 'Just one week of drinking wheatgrass juice really improves the texture of your hair', 'I spent two days at a spa in Biarritz; the water there opens the pores and eliminates toxins.' The following week, they will discover that wheatgrass has absolutely no special properties and that any old hot water will open the pores and eliminate toxins.

e) Other people: 'I haven't seen so-and-so for ages, what's he up to?' 'I understand that what's-her-name is in difficulties financially and has had to sell her apartment.' They can talk about the people who weren't invited to the party in question, they can criticise all they like, as long as they end by saying, with an innocent, pitying air: 'Still, he/she's a wonderful person.'

f) A few little complaints about life, just to add savour to the evening: 'I wish something new would happen in my life', 'I'm so worried about my children, they never listen to proper music or read proper literature.' They wait for comments from other people with the same problem and then feel less alone and leave the party happy.

g) At intellectual gatherings, like the one this evening, we will discuss the Middle East conflict, the problem of Islamism, the latest exhibition, the latest philosophy guru, the fantastic book that no one has heard of, the fact that music isn't what it used to be; we will offer our intelligent, sensible opinions, which run completely counter to our real feelings – because we all know how much we hate having to go to those exhibitions, read those unbearable books, or see those dreary films, just so that we will have something to talk about on nights like tonight.

The taxi arrives, and while we are being driven to the venue I add another very personal item to my list: I complain to Marie about how much I loathe these suppers. She reminds me – and it's true – that I always enjoy myself in the end and have a really good time.

We enter one of Paris's most elegant restaurants and head for a room reserved for the event – a presentation of a literary prize for which I was one of the judges. Everyone is standing around talking; some people say hello and others merely look at me and make some comment to each other; the organiser of the prize comes over to me and introduces me to the people who are there, always with the same irritating words: 'You know who this gentleman is, of course.' Some people give a smile of recognition, others merely smile and don't recognise me at all, but pretend to know who I am, because to admit otherwise would be to accept that the world they're living in doesn't exist, and that they are failing to keep up with the things that matter.

I remember the 'tribe' of the previous night and think: stupid people should all be marooned on a ship on the high seas and forced to attend parties night after night, being endlessly introduced to people for several months, until they finally manage to remember who is who.

I draw up a catalogue of the kind of people who attend events like this. Ten per cent are 'Members', the decision-makers, who came out tonight because of some debt they owe to the Favour Bank, but who always have an eye open for anything that might be of benefit to their work – how to make money, where to invest. They can soon tell whether or not an event is going to prove profitable or not, and they are always the first to leave the party; they never waste their time.

Two per cent are the 'Talents', who really do have a promising future; they have already managed to ford a few rivers, have just become aware of the existence of the

Favour Bank and are all potential customers; they have important services to offer, but are not as yet in a position to make decisions. They are nice to everyone because they don't know who exactly they are talking to, and they are more open-minded than the Members, because, for them, any road might lead somewhere.

Three per cent are what I call the 'Tupamaros' – in homage to the former Uruguayan guerrilla group. They have managed to infiltrate this party and are mad for any kind of contact; they're not sure whether to stay or to go on to another party that is taking place at the same time; they are anxious; they want to show how talented they are, but they weren't invited, they haven't scaled the first mountains, and as soon as the other guests suss this out, they immediately withdraw any attention they have been paying them.

The last 85 per cent are the 'Trays'. I call them this because, just as no party can exist without that particular utensil, so no event can exist without these guests. The Trays don't really know what is going on, but they know it's important to be there; they are on the guest list drawn up by the promoters because the success of something like this also depends on the number of people who come. They are all ex-something-or-other-important – ex-bankers, ex-directors, the ex-husband of some famous woman, the ex-wife of some man now in a position of power. They are Counts in a country where the monarchy no longer exists, Princesses and Marchionesses who live by renting out their castles. They go from one party to the next, from one supper to the next – don't they ever get sick of it, I wonder?

When I commented on this recently to Marie, she said that just as some people are addicted to work, so others are addicted to fun. Both groups are equally unhappy, convinced that they are missing something, but unable to give up their particular vice.

A pretty young blonde comes over while I'm talking to one of the organisers of a conference on cinema and literature and tells me how much she enjoyed *A Time to Rend and a Time to Sew*. She's from one of the Baltic countries, she says, and works in film. She is immediately identified by the group as a Tupamaro, because while appearing to be interested in one thing (me), she is, in fact, interested in something else (the organisers of the conference). Despite having made this almost unforgivable gaffe, there is still a chance that she might be an inexperienced Talent. The organiser of the conference asks what she means by 'working in film'. The young woman explains that she writes film reviews for a newspaper and has published a book (about cinema? No, about her life, her short, dull life, I imagine).

She then commits the cardinal sin of jumping the gun and asking if she could be invited to this year's event. The organiser explains that the woman who publishes my books in that same Baltic country, an influential and hardworking woman (and very pretty too, I think to myself), has already been invited. They continue talking to me; the Tupamaro lingers for a few more minutes, not knowing what to say, then moves off.

Given that it's a literary prize, most of the guests tonight – Tupamaros, Talents and Trays – belong to the world of the arts. The Members, on the other hand, are either sponsors or people connected with foundations that support museums, classical music concerts, and promising young artists. After various conversations about which of the candidates for the prize that night had applied most pressure in order to win, the master of ceremonies mounts the stage, asks everyone to take their places at the tables (we all sit down), makes a few jokes (it's part of the ritual, and we all laugh), and says that the winners will be announced between the entrée and the first course.

I am on the top table; this allows me to keep the Trays at a safe distance, and also means that I don't have to bother with any enthusiastic and self-interested Talents. I am seated between the female director of a car-manufacturing firm, which is sponsoring the party, and an heiress who has decided to invest in art – to my surprise, neither of them is wearing a dress with a provocative décolletage. The other guests at our table are the director of a perfumery; an Arab prince (who was doubtless passing through Paris and was pounced on by one of the promoters to add lustre to the event); an Israeli banker who collects fourteenth-century manuscripts; the main organiser of tonight's event; the French Consul to Monaco; and a blonde woman whose presence here I can't quite fathom, although I suspect she might be the organiser's next mistress.

I have to keep putting on my glasses and sur-reptitiously reading the names of the people on either side of me (I ought to be marooned on that imaginary ship and invited to this same party dozens of times until I have memorised the names of all the guests). Marie, as protocol demands, has been placed on another table;

someone, at some point in history, decided that at formal suppers, couples should always be seated separately, thus leaving it open to doubt whether the person beside us is married, single, or married but available. Or perhaps he or she thought that if a couple were seated together, they would simply talk to each other; but, in that case, why go out, why take a taxi and go to the supper in the first place?

As foreseen in my list of possible conversational topics, we begin with cultural small talk – isn't that a marvellous exhibition, wasn't that an intelligent review … I would like to concentrate on the entrée – caviar with salmon and egg – but I am constantly interrupted by the usual questions about how my new book is doing, where I find my inspiration, whether I'm working on a new project. Everyone seems very cultured, everyone manages to mention – as if by chance, of course – some famous person who also happens to be a close friend. Everyone can speak cogently about the current state of politics or about the problems facing culture.

'Why don't we talk about something else?'

The question slips out inadvertently. Everyone at the table goes quiet. After all, it is extremely rude to interrupt other people and worse still to draw attention to oneself. It seems, however, that last night's tour of the streets of Paris in the guise of a beggar has caused some irreparable damage, which means that I can no longer stand such conversations.

'We could talk about the *acomodador*: the moment in our lives when we decide to abandon our desires and make do, instead, with what we have.'

No one seems very interested. I decide to change the subject.

'We could talk about the importance of forgetting the story we've been told and trying to live an entirely different story. Try doing something different every day – like talking to the person on the next table to you in a restaurant, visiting a hospital, putting your foot in a puddle, listening to what another person has to say, allowing the energy of love to flow freely, instead of putting it in a jug and standing it in a corner.'

'Are you talking about adultery?' asks the director of the perfumery.

'No, I mean allowing yourself to be the instrument of love, not its master, being with someone because you really want to be, not because convention obliges you to be.'

With great delicacy, and just a touch of irony, the French Consul to Monaco assures me that all the people round our table are, of course, exercising that right and freedom. Everyone agrees, although no one believes that it's true.

'Sex!' cries the blonde woman whose role that evening no one has quite identified. 'Why don't we talk about sex? It's much more interesting and much less complicated!'

At least her remark is spontaneous. One of the women sitting next to me gives a wry laugh, but I applaud.

'Sex is certainly more interesting, but I'm not sure it's a different topic of conversation. Besides, it's no longer forbidden to talk about sex.'

'It's also in extremely bad taste,' says one of my neighbours.

'May we know what *is* forbidden?' asks the organiser, who is starting to feel uncomfortable.

'Well, money, for example. All of us around this table have money, or pretend that we do. We assume we've been invited here because we're rich, famous and influential. But have any of us ever thought of using this kind of event to find out what everyone actually earns? Since we're all so sure of ourselves, so important, why don't we look at our world as it is and not as we imagine it to be?'

'What are you getting at?' asks the director of the car-manufacturing firm.

'It's a long story. I could start by talking about Hans and Fritz sitting in a bar in Tokyo and go on to mention a Mongolian nomad who says we need to forget who we think we are in order to become who we really are.'

'You've lost me.'

'That's my fault. I didn't really explain. But let's get down to the nitty-gritty: I'd like to know how much everyone here earns, what it means, in money terms, to be sitting at the top table.'

There is a momentary silence – my gamble is not paying off. The other people round the table are looking at me with startled eyes: asking about someone's financial situation is a bigger taboo than sex, more frowned upon than asking about betrayals, corruption or parliamentary intrigues.

However, the Arab prince – perhaps because he's bored by all these receptions and banquets with their empty chatter, perhaps because that very day he has been told by his doctor that he is going to die, or perhaps for some other reason – decides to answer my question:

'I earn about 20,000 euros a month, depending on the amount approved by the parliament in my country. That bears no relation to what I spend, though, because I have an unlimited so-called "entertainment" allowance. In other words, I am here courtesy of the embassy's car and chauffeur, the clothes I'm wearing belong to the government, and tomorrow I will be travelling to another European country in a private jet, with the cost of pilot, fuel and airport taxes deducted from that allowance.'

And he concludes:

'Apparent reality is not an exact science.'

If the prince can speak so frankly, and given that he is, hierarchically, the most important person at the table, the others cannot possibly embarrass him by remaining silent. They are going to have to participate in the game, the question and the embarrassment.

'I don't know exactly how much I earn,' says the organiser, one of the Favour Bank's classic representatives, known to some as a 'lobbyist'. 'Somewhere in the region of 10,000 euros a month, but I, too, have an entertainment allowance from the various organisations I head. I can deduct everything – suppers, lunches, hotels, air tickets, sometimes even clothes, although I don't have a private jet.'

The wine has run out; he signals to a waiter and our glasses are refilled. Now it was the turn of the director of the car-manufacturing firm, who, initially, had hated the idea of talking about money, but who now seems to be rather enjoying herself.

'I reckon I earn about the same, and have the same unlimited entertainment allowance.'

One by one, everyone confessed how much they earned. The banker was the richest of them all, with ten million euros a year, as well as shares in his bank that were constantly increasing in value.

When it came to the turn of the young blonde woman who had not been introduced to anyone, she refused to answer:

'That's part of my secret garden. It's nobody's business but mine.'

'Of course it isn't, but we're just playing a game,' said the organiser.

The woman refused to join in, and by doing so, placed herself on a higher level than everyone else: after all, she was the only one in the group who had secrets. However, by placing herself on a higher level, she only succeeded in earning everyone else's scorn. Afraid of feeling humiliated by her miserable salary, she had, by acting all mysterious, managed to humiliate everyone else, not realising that most of the people there lived permanently poised on the edge of the abyss, utterly dependent on those entertainment allowances that could vanish overnight.

The question inevitably came round to me.

'It depends. In a year when I publish a new book, I could earn five million dollars. If I don't publish a book, then I earn about two million from royalties on existing titles.'

'You only asked the question so that you could say how much you earned,' said the young woman with the 'secret garden'. 'No one's impressed.'

She had realised that she had made a wrong move

earlier on and was now trying to correct the situation by going onto the attack.

'On the contrary,' said the prince. 'I would have expected a leading author like yourself to be far wealthier.'

A point to me. The blonde woman would not open her mouth again all night.

The conversation about money broke a series of taboos, given that how much people earn was the biggest of them all. The waiter began to appear more frequently, the bottles of wine began to be emptied with incredible speed, the compère-cum-organiser rather tipsily mounted the stage, announced the winner, presented the prize and immediately rejoined the conversation, which had carried on even though politeness demands that we keep quiet when someone else is talking. We discussed what we did with our money (this consisted mostly of buying 'free time', travelling or practising a sport).

I thought of changing tack and asking them what kind of funeral they would like – death was as big a taboo as money – but the atmosphere was so jolly and everyone was so full of talk that I decided to say nothing.

'You're all talking about money, but you don't know what money is,' said the banker. 'Why do people think that a bit of coloured paper, a plastic card or a coin made out of fifth-rate metal has any value? Worse still, did you know that your money, your millions of dollars are nothing but electronic impulses?'

Of course we did.

'Once, wealth was what these ladies are wearing,' he went on. 'Ornaments made from rare materials that were

301

easy to transport, count and share out. Pearls, nuggets of gold, precious stones. We all carried our wealth in a visible place. Such things were, in turn, exchanged for cattle or grain, because no one walks down the street carrying cattle or sacks of grain. The funny thing is that we still behave like some primitive tribe – we wear our ornaments to show how rich we are, even though we often have more ornaments than money.'

'It's the tribal code,' I said. 'In my day, young people wore their hair long, whereas nowadays they all go in for body-piercing. It helps them identify like-minded people, even though it can't buy anything.'

'Can our electronic impulses buy one extra hour of life? No. Can they buy back those loved ones who have departed? No. Can they buy love?'

'They can certainly buy love,' said the director of the car-manufacturing firm in a jokey tone of voice.

Her eyes, however, betrayed a terrible sadness. I thought of Esther and of what I had said to the journalist in the interview I had given that morning. We rich, powerful, intelligent people knew that, deep down, we had acquired all these ornaments and credit cards only in order to find love and affection and to be with someone who loved us.

'Not always,' said the director of the perfumery, turning to look at me.

'No, you're right, not always. After all, my wife left me, and I'm a wealthy man. But almost always. By the way, does anyone round this table know how many cats and how many lamp-posts there are on the back of a ten-dollar bill?'

No one knew and no one was interested. The comment about love had completely spoiled the jolly atmosphere, and we went back to talking about literary prizes, exhibitions, the latest film, and the play that was proving to be such an unexpected success.

'How was it on your table?'

'Oh, the usual.'

'Well, I managed to spark an interesting discussion about money, but, alas, it ended in tragedy.'

'When do you leave?'

'I have to leave here at half past seven in the morning. Since you're flying to Berlin, we could share a taxi.'

'Where are you going?'

'You know where I'm going. You haven't asked me, but you know.'

'Yes, I know.'

'Just as you know that we're saying goodbye at this very moment.'

'We could go back to the time when we first met: a man in emotional tatters over someone who had left him, and a woman madly in love with her neighbour. I could repeat what I said to you once: "I'm going to fight to the bitter end." Well, I fought and I lost, now I'll just have to lick my wounds and leave.'

'I fought and lost as well. I'm not trying to sew up what was rent. Like you, I want to fight to the bitter end.'

'I suffer every day, did you know that? I've been suffering for months now, trying to show you how much

I love you, how things are only important when you're by my side. But now, whether I suffer or not, I've decided that enough is enough. It's over. I'm tired. After that night in Zagreb, I lowered my guard and said to myself: if the blow comes, it comes. It can lay me out on the canvas, it can knock me out cold, but one day I'll recover.'

'You'll find someone else.'

'Of course I will: I'm young, pretty, intelligent, desirable, but will I experience all the things I experienced with you?'

'You'll experience different emotions and, you know, although you may not believe it, I loved you while we were together.'

'I'm sure you did, but that doesn't make it any the less painful. We'll leave in separate taxis tomorrow. I hate goodbyes, especially at airports or train stations.'

THE RETURN

TO ITHACA

'We'll sleep here tonight and, tomorrow, we'll continue on horseback. My car can't cope with the sand of the steppes.'

We were in a kind of bunker, which looked like a relic from the Second World War. A man, with his wife and his granddaughter, welcomed us and showed us a simple, but spotlessly clean room.

Dos went on:

'And don't forget to choose a name.'

'I don't think that's necessary,' said Mikhail.

'Of course it is,' insisted Dos. 'I was with his wife recently. I know how she thinks, I know what she has learned, I know what she expects.'

Dos's voice was simultaneously firm and gentle. Yes, I would choose a name, I would do exactly as he suggested; I would continue to discard my personal history and, instead, embark on my personal legend – even if only out of sheer tiredness.

I was exhausted. The previous night I had slept for two hours at most: my body had still not adjusted to the enormous time difference. I had arrived in Almaty at about eleven o'clock at night – local time – when in France it was only six o'clock in the evening. Mikhail had left me at the hotel and I had dozed for a bit, then woken

up in the small hours. I had looked out at the lights
below and thought how in Paris it would just be time to
go out to supper. I was hungry and asked room service if
they could send me up something to eat: 'Of course we
can, sir, but you really must try to sleep; if you don't,
your body will stay stuck on its European timetable.'

For me, the worst possible torture is not being able to
sleep. I ate a sandwich and decided to go for a walk. I
asked the receptionist my usual question: 'Is it dangerous
to go walking at this hour?' He told me it wasn't, and so
I set off down the empty streets, narrow alleyways, broad
avenues; it was a city like any other, with its neon signs,
the occasional passing police car, a beggar here, a
prostitute there. I had to keep repeating out loud: 'I'm in
Kazakhstan!' If I didn't, I would end up thinking I was
merely in some unfamiliar quarter of Paris.

'I'm in Kazakhstan!' I said to the deserted city, and a
voice replied:

'Of course you are.'

I jumped. A man was sitting close by, on a bench in a
square at dead of night, with his rucksack by his side. He
got up and introduced himself as Jan, from Holland,
adding:

'And I know why you're here.'

Was he a friend of Mikhail's? Or was I being followed
by the secret police?

'Why am I here, then?'

'Like me, you've travelled from Istanbul, following the
Silk Road.'

I gave a sigh of relief, and decided to continue the
conversation:

'On foot? As I understand it, that means crossing the whole of Asia.'

'It's something I needed to do. I was dissatisfied with my life. I've got money, a wife, children, I own a hosiery factory in Rotterdam. For a time, I knew what I was fighting for – my family's stability. Now I'm not so sure. Everything that once made me happy just bores me, leaves me cold. For the sake of my marriage, the love of my children, and my enthusiasm for my work, I decided to take two months out just for myself, and to take a long look at my life. And it's working.'

'I've been doing the same thing these last few months. Are there a lot of pilgrims like you?'

'Lots of them. Loads. It can be dangerous, because the political situation in some of these countries is very dodgy indeed, and they hate Westerners. But we get by. I think that, as a pilgrim, you'll always be treated with respect, as long as you can prove you're not a spy. But I gather from what you say that you have different reasons for being here. What brings you to Almaty?'

'The same thing as you. I came to reach the end of a particular road. Couldn't you sleep either?'

'I've just woken up. The earlier I set out, the more chance I have of getting to the next town; if not, I'll have to spend the night in the freezing cold steppes, with that constant wind blowing.'

'Have a good journey, then.'

'No, stay a while. I need to talk, to share my experiences. Most of the other pilgrims don't speak English.'

And he started telling me about his life, while I tried to remember what I knew about the Silk Road, the old commercial route that connected Europe with the countries of the East. The traditional route started in Beirut, passed through Antioch and went all the way to the shores of the Yangtse in China; but in Central Asia it became a kind of web, with roads heading off in all directions, which allowed for the establishment of trading posts, which, in time, became towns, which were later destroyed in battles between rival tribes, rebuilt by the inhabitants, destroyed, and rebuilt yet again. Although almost everything passed along that route – gold, strange animals, ivory, seeds, political ideas, refugees from civil wars, armed bandits, private armies to protect the caravans – silk was the rarest and most coveted item. It was thanks to one of these branch roads that Buddhism travelled from China to India.

'I left Antioch with about two hundred dollars in my pocket,' said the Dutchman, having described mountains, landscapes, exotic tribes and endless problems in various countries with police patrols. 'I needed to find out if I was capable of becoming myself again. Do you know what I mean?'

'Yes, I do.'

'I was forced to beg, to ask for money. To my surprise, people are much more generous than I had imagined.'

Beg? I studied his rucksack and his clothes to see if I could spot the symbol of the 'tribe' – Mikhail's tribe – but I couldn't find it.

'Have you ever been to an Armenian restaurant in Paris?'

'I've been to lots of Armenian restaurants, but never in Paris.'

'Do you know someone called Mikhail?'

'It's a pretty common name in these parts. If I did know a Mikhail, I can't remember, so I'm afraid I can't help you.'

'No, I don't need your help. I'm just surprised by certain coincidences. It seems there are a lot of people, all over the world, who are becoming aware of the same thing and acting in a very similar way.'

'The first thing you feel, when you set out on a journey like this, is that you'll never arrive. Then you feel insecure, abandoned, and spend all your time thinking about giving up. But if you can last a week, then you'll make it to the end.'

'I've been wandering like a pilgrim through the streets of one city, and yesterday I arrived in a different one. May I bless you?'

He gave me a strange look.

'I'm not travelling for religious reasons. Are you a priest?'

'No, I'm not a priest, but I feel that I should bless you. Some things aren't logical, as you know.'

The Dutchman called Jan, whom I would never see again, bowed his head and closed his eyes. I placed my hands on his shoulders and, in my native tongue – which he wouldn't understand – I prayed that he would reach his destination safely and leave behind him on the Silk Road both his sadness and his sense that life was meaningless; I prayed, too, that he would return to his family with shining eyes and with his soul washed clean.

He thanked me, took up his rucksack, and headed off in the direction of China. I went back to the hotel thinking that I had never, in my whole life, blessed anyone before. But I had responded to an impulse, and the impulse was right; my prayer would be answered.

The following day, Mikhail turned up with his friend, Dos, who would accompany us. Dos had a car, knew my wife and knew the steppes, and he, too, wanted to be there when I reached the village where Esther was living.

I considered remonstrating with them – first, it was Mikhail, now it was his friend, and by the time we finally reached the village, there would be a huge crowd following me, applauding and weeping, waiting to see what would happen. But I was too tired to say anything. The next day, I would remind Mikhail of the promise he had made, not to allow any witnesses to that moment.

We got into the car and, for some time, followed the Silk Road. They asked me if I knew what it was and I told them that I had met a Silk Road pilgrim the previous night, and they said that such journeys were becoming more and more commonplace and could soon bring benefits to the country's tourist industry.

Two hours later, we left the main road and continued along a minor road as far as the 'bunker' where we are now, eating fish and listening to the soft wind that blows across the steppes.

'Esther was very important for me,' Dos explains, showing me a photo of one of his paintings, which

315

includes one of those pieces of bloodstained cloth. 'I used to dream of leaving here, like Oleg ...'

'You'd better call me Mikhail, otherwise he'll get confused.'

'I used to dream of leaving here, like lots of people my age. Then one day, Oleg – or, rather, Mikhail – phoned me. He said that his benefactress had decided to come and live in the steppes for a while and he wanted me to help her. I agreed, thinking that here was my chance and that perhaps I could extract the same favours from her: a visa, a plane ticket and a job in France. She asked me to go with her to some remote village that she knew from an earlier visit.

I didn't ask her why, I simply did as she requested. On the way, she insisted on going to the house of a nomad she had visited years before. To my surprise, it was my grandfather she wanted to see! She was received with the hospitality that is typical of the people who live in this infinite space. My grandfather told her that, although she thought she was sad, her soul was, in fact, happy and free, and love's energy had begun to flow again. He assured her that this would have an effect upon the whole world, including her husband. My grandfather taught her many things about the culture of the steppes, and asked me to teach her the rest. In the end, he decided that she could keep her name, even though this was contrary to tradition.

And while she learned from my grandfather, I learned from her, and realised that I didn't need to go far away, as Mikhail had done: my mission was to be in this empty space – the steppes – and to understand its colours and transform them into paintings.'

'I don't quite understand what you mean about teaching my wife. I thought your grandfather said that we should forget everything.'

'I'll show you tomorrow,' said Dos.

And the following day, he did show me and there was no need for words. I saw the endless steppes, which, although they appeared to be nothing but desert, were, in fact, full of life, full of creatures hidden in the low scrub. I saw the flat horizon, the vast empty space, heard the sound of horses' hooves, the quiet wind, and then, all around us, nothing, absolutely nothing. It was as if the world had chosen this place to display, at once, its vastness, simplicity and complexity. It was as if we could – and should – become like the steppes, empty, infinite and, at the same time, full of life.

I looked up at the blue sky, took off my dark glasses, and allowed myself to be filled by that light, by the feeling of being simultaneously nowhere and everywhere. We rode on in silence, stopping now and then to let the horses drink from streams that only someone who knew the place would have been able to find. Occasionally, we would see other horsemen in the distance or shepherds with their flocks, framed by the plain and by the sky.

Where was I going? I hadn't the slightest idea and I didn't care. The woman I was looking for was somewhere in that infinite space. I could touch her soul, hear the song she was singing as she wove her carpets. Now I understood why she had chosen this place: there was nothing, absolutely nothing to distract her attention; it was the emptiness she had so yearned for. The wind would gradually blow her pain away. Could she ever have imagined that one day I would be here, on horseback, riding to meet her?

A sense of Paradise descends from the skies. And I am aware that I am living through an unforgettable moment in my life; it is the kind of awareness we often have precisely when the magic moment has passed. I am entirely here, without past, without future, entirely focused on the morning, on the music of the horses' hooves, on the gentleness of the wind caressing my body, on the unexpected grace of contemplating sky, earth, men. I feel a sense of adoration and ecstasy. I am thankful for being alive. I pray quietly, listening to the voice of nature, and understanding that the invisible world always manifests itself in the visible world.

I ask the sky some questions, the same questions I used to ask my mother when I was a child:

Why do we love certain people and hate others?
Where do we go after we die?
Why are we born if, in the end, we die?
What does God mean?

The steppes respond with the constant sound of the wind. And that is enough: knowing that the fundamental questions of life will never be answered, and that we can, nevertheless, still go forward.

Mountains loomed on the horizon, and Dos asked us to stop. I saw that there was a stream nearby.

'We'll camp here.'

We removed the saddlebags from the horses and put up the tent. Mikhail started digging a hole in the ground.

'This is how the nomads used to do it; we dig a hole, fill the bottom with stones, put more stones all around the edge, and that way we have a place to light a fire without the wind bothering us.'

To the south, between the mountains and us, a cloud of dust appeared, which I realised at once was caused by galloping horses. I pointed this out to my two friends, who jumped to their feet. I could see that they were tense. Then they exchanged a few words in Russian and relaxed. Dos went back to putting up the tent and Mikhail set about lighting the fire.

'Would you mind telling me what's going on?' I said.

'It may look as if we're surrounded by empty space, but it can't have escaped your notice that we've already seen all kinds of things: shepherds, rivers, tortoises, foxes and horsemen. It feels as if we had a clear view all around us, so where do these people come from? Where are their houses? Where do they keep their flocks?

That sense of emptiness is an illusion: we are constantly watching and being watched. To a stranger who cannot read the signs of the steppes, everything is under control and the only things he can see are the horses and the riders. To those of us who were brought up here, we can also see the yurts, the circular houses that blend in with the landscape. We know how to read what's going on by observing how horsemen are moving and in which direction they're heading. In the olden days, the survival of the tribe depended on that ability, because there were enemies, invaders, smugglers.

And now the bad news: they've found out that we're riding towards the village at the foot of those mountains and are sending people to kill the shaman who sees visions of children as well as the man who has come to disturb the peace of the foreign woman.'

He gave a loud laugh.

'Just wait a moment and you'll understand.'

The riders were approaching, and I was soon able to see what was going on.

'It looks very odd to me – a woman being pursued by a man.'

'It is odd, but it's also part of our lives.'

The woman rode past us, wielding a long whip, and, by way of a greeting, gave a shout and a smile directed at Dos, then started galloping round and round the place where we were setting up camp. The smiling, sweating man pursuing her gave us a brief greeting too, all the while trying to keep up with the woman.

'Nina shouldn't be so cruel,' said Mikhail. 'There's no need for all this.'

'It's precisely because there's no need for it that she can afford to be cruel,' replied Dos. 'She just has to be beautiful and have a good horse.'

'But she does this to everyone.'

'I unseated her once,' said Dos proudly.

'The fact that you're speaking English means that you want me to understand.'

The woman was laughing and riding ever faster; her laughter filled the steppes with joy.

'It's a form of flirtation. It's called Kyz Kuu or "Bring

the girl down". And we've all taken part in it at some time in our childhood or youth.'

The man pursuing her was getting closer and closer, but we could see that his horse couldn't take much more.

'Later on, we'll talk a bit about Tengri, the culture of the steppes,' Dos went on. 'But now that you're seeing this, let me just explain something very important. Here, in this land, the woman is in charge. She comes first. In the event of a divorce, she receives half the dowry back even if she's the one who wants the divorce. Whenever a man sees a woman wearing a white turban, that means she's a mother and we, as men, must place our hand on our heart and bow our head as a sign of respect.'

'But what's that got to do with "Bring the girl down"?'

'In the village at the foot of the mountains, a group of men on horseback would have gathered around this girl; her name is Nina and she's the most desirable girl in the area. They would have begun playing the game of Kyz Kuu, which was thought up in ancient times, when the women of the steppes, known as amazons, were also warriors.

At the time, no one would have dreamt of consulting the family if they wanted to get married: the suitors and the girl would simply get together in a particular place, all on horseback. She would ride round the men, laughing, provoking them, whipping them. Then the bravest of the men would start chasing her. If the girl was able to keep out of his grasp for a set period of time, then the man would have to call on the earth to cover him for ever, because he would be considered a bad horseman – the warrior's greatest shame.

If he got close, despite her whip, and pulled her to the ground, then he was a real man and was allowed to kiss her and to marry her. Obviously, then just as now, the girls knew who they should escape from and who they should let themselves be caught by.'

Nina was clearly just having a bit of fun. She had got ahead of the man again and was riding back to the village.

'She only came to show off. She knows we're on our way and will take the news back to the village.'

'I have two questions. The first might seem stupid: do you still choose your brides like that?'

Dos said that, nowadays, it was just a game. In the West, people got all dressed up and went to bars or fashionable clubs, whereas in the steppes, Kyz Kuu was the favoured game of seduction. Nina had already humiliated quite a number of young men, and had allowed herself to be unseated by a few as well – exactly as happens in all the best discotheques.

'The second question will seem even more idiotic: is the village at the foot of the mountains where my wife is living?'

Dos nodded.

'If we're only two hours away, why don't we sleep there? It'll be a while yet before it gets dark.'

'You're right, we are only two hours away, and there are two reasons why we're stopping here for the night. First, even if Nina hadn't come out here, someone would already have seen us and would have gone to tell Esther that we were coming. This way, she can decide whether or not she wants to see us, or if she would prefer to go to another village for a few days. If she did that, we wouldn't follow her.'

My heart contracted.

'Even after all I've been through to get here?'

'If that's how you feel, then you have understood nothing. What makes you think that your efforts should be rewarded with the submission, gratitude, and recognition of the person you love? You came here because this was the road you must follow, not in order to buy your wife's love.'

However unfair his words might seem, he was right. I asked him about the second reason.

'You still haven't chosen your name.'

'That doesn't matter,' Mikhail said again. 'He doesn't understand our culture, and he's not part of it.'

'It's important to me,' said Dos. 'My grandfather said that I must protect and help the foreign woman, just as she protected and helped me. I owe Esther the peace of my eyes, and I want her eyes to be at peace too.

He will have to choose a name. He will have to forget for ever his history of pain and suffering, and accept that he is a new person who has just been reborn and that, from now on, he will be reborn every day. If he doesn't do that, and if they ever do live together again, he will expect her to pay him back for all the pain she once caused him.'

'I chose a name last night,' I said.

'Wait until this evening to tell me.'

As soon as the sun began to sink low on the horizon, we went to an area on the steppes that was full of vast sand dunes. I became aware of a different sound, a kind of resonance, an intense vibration. Mikhail said that it was one of the few places in the world where the dunes sang.

'When I was in Paris and I talked to people about this, they only believed me because an American said that he had experienced the same thing in North Africa; there are only thirty places like it in the world. Nowadays, of course, scientists can explain everything. It seems that because of the place's unique formation, the wind penetrates the actual grains of sand and creates this sound. For the ancients, though, this was one of the magical places in the steppes, and it is a great honour that Dos should have chosen it for your name-changing.'

We started climbing one of the dunes, and as we proceeded the noise grew more intense and the wind stronger. When we reached the top, we could see the mountains standing out clearly to the south and the gigantic plain stretching out all around us.

'Turn towards the west and take off your clothes,' Dos said.

I did as he ordered, without asking why. I started to feel cold, but they seemed unconcerned about my well-being. Mikhail knelt down and appeared to be praying. Dos looked up at the sky, at the earth, at me, then placed his hands on my shoulders, just as I had done to the Dutchman, though without knowing why.

'In the name of the Lady, I dedicate you. I dedicate you to the earth, which belongs to the Lady. In the name of the horse, I dedicate you. I dedicate you to the world, and pray that the world helps you on your journey. In the name of the steppes, which are infinite, I dedicate you. I dedicate you to the infinite Wisdom, and pray that your horizon may always be wider than you can see. You have chosen your name and will speak it now for the first time.'

'In the name of the infinite steppes, I choose a name,' I replied, without asking if I was doing as the ritual demanded, merely allowing myself to be guided by the noise of the wind in the dunes. 'Many centuries ago, a poet described the wanderings of a man called Ulysses on his way back to an island called Ithaca, where his beloved awaits him. He confronts many perils, from storms to the temptations of comfort. At one point, in a cave, he encounters a monster with only one eye.

The monster asks him his name. "Nobody," says Ulysses. They fight and he manages to pierce the monster's one eye with his sword and then seals the mouth of the cave with a rock. The monster's companions hear his cries and rush to help him. Seeing that there is a rock covering the mouth of the cave, they ask who is with him. "Nobody! Nobody!" replies the monster. His companions leave, since there is clearly no threat to the community, and Ulysses can then continue on his journey back to the woman who waits for him.'

'So your name is Ulysses?'

'My name is Nobody.'

I am trembling all over, as if my skin were being pierced by hundreds of needles.

'Focus on the cold, until you stop trembling. Let the cold fill your every thought, until there is no space for anything else, until it becomes your companion and your friend. Do not try to control it. Do not think about the sun, that will only make it worse, because you will know then that something else – heat – exists and then the cold will feel that it is not loved or desired.'

My muscles were furiously stretching and contracting in order to produce energy and keep my organism alive. However, I did as Dos ordered, because I trusted him, trusted in his calm, his tenderness and his authority. I let the needles pierce my skin, allowed my muscles to struggle, my teeth to chatter, all the while repeating to myself: 'Don't fight; the cold is your friend.' My muscles refused to obey, and I remained like that for almost fifteen minutes, until my muscles eventually gave in and stopped shaking, and I entered a state of torpor. I tried to sit down, but Mikhail grabbed hold of me and held me up, while Dos spoke to me. His words seemed to come from a long way off, from a place where the steppes meet the sky:

'Welcome, nomad who crosses the steppes. Welcome to the place where we always say that the sky is blue even when it is grey, because we know that the colour is still there above the clouds. Welcome to the land of the Tengri. Welcome to me, for I am here to receive you and to honour you for your search.'

Mikhail sat down on the ground and asked me to drink something that immediately warmed my blood. Dos helped me to get dressed, and we made our way back down the dunes that continued to talk amongst themselves; we made our way back to our improvised camp site. Before Dos and Mikhail had even started cooking, I had fallen into a deep sleep.

'What's happening? Isn't it light yet?'

'It's been light for ages. It's just a sandstorm, don't worry. Put your dark glasses on to protect your eyes.'

'Where's Dos?'

'He's gone back to Almaty, but he was very moved by the ceremony yesterday evening. He didn't really need to do that. It was a bit of a waste of time for you really and a great opportunity to catch pneumonia. I hope you realise that it was just his way of showing you how welcome you are. Here, take the oil.'

'I overslept.'

'It's only a two-hour ride to the village. We'll be there before the sun is at its highest point.'

'I need a bath. I need to change my clothes.'

'That's impossible. You're in the middle of the steppes. Put the oil in the pan, but first offer it up to the Lady. Apart from salt, it's our most valuable commodity.'

'What is Tengri?'

'The word means "sky worship"; it's a kind of religion without religion. Everyone has passed through here – Buddhists, Hindus, Catholics, Muslims, different sects with their beliefs and superstitions. The nomads became converts to avoid being killed, but they continued and continue to profess the idea that the Divinity is everywhere all the time. You can't take the Divinity out of nature and put it in a book or between four walls. I've felt so much better since coming back to the steppes, as if I had been in real need of nourishment. Thank you for letting me come with you.'

'Thank you for introducing me to Dos. Yesterday, during that dedication ceremony, I sensed that he was someone special.'

'He learned from his grandfather, who learned from his father, who learned from his father, and so on. The nomadic way of life, and the absence of a written language until the end of the nineteenth century, meant that they had to develop the tradition of the *akyn*, the person who must remember everything and pass on the stories. Dos is an *akyn*. When I say "learn", though, I hope you don't take that to mean "accumulate knowledge". The stories have nothing to do with dates and names and facts. They are legends about heroes and heroines, animals and battles, about the symbols of man's essential self, not just his deeds. They're not stories about the vanquishers or the vanquished, but about people who travel the world, contemplate the steppes, and allow themselves to be filled by the energy of love. Pour the oil in more slowly, otherwise it will spit.'

'I felt blessed.'

'I'd like to feel that too. Yesterday, I went to visit my mother in Almaty. She asked if I was well and if I was earning money. I lied and said I was fine, that I was putting on a successful theatre production in Paris. I'm going back to my own people today, and it's as if I had left yesterday, and as if during all the time I've spent abroad, I had done nothing of any importance. I talk to beggars, wander the streets with the "tribe", organise the meetings at the restaurant, and what have I achieved? Nothing. I'm not like Dos, who learned from his grandfather. I only have the presence to guide me and sometimes I think that perhaps it *is* just a hallucination; perhaps my visions really are just epileptic fits, and nothing more.'

'A minute ago you were thanking me for bringing you with me, and now it seems to have brought you nothing but sadness. Make up your mind what you're feeling.'

'I feel both things at once, I don't have to choose. I can travel back and forth between the oppositions inside me, between my contradictions.'

'I want to tell you something, Mikhail. I too have travelled back and forth between many contradictions since I first met you. I began by hating you, then I accepted you, and as I've followed in your footsteps, that acceptance has become respect. You're still young, and the powerlessness you feel is perfectly normal. I don't know how many people your work has touched so far, but I can tell you one thing: you changed my life.'

'You were only interested in finding your wife.'

'I still am, but that didn't just make me travel across the Kazakhstan steppes: it made me travel through the whole of my past life. I saw where I went wrong, I saw where I stopped, I saw the moment when I lost Esther, the moment that the Mexican Indians call the *acomodador* – "the giving-up point". I experienced things I never imagined I would experience at my age. And all because you were by my side, guiding me, even though you might not have been aware that you were. And do you know something else? I believe that you do hear voices and that you did have visions when you were a child. I have always believed in many things, and now I believe even more.'

'You're not the same man I first met.'

'No, I'm not. I hope Esther will be pleased.'

'Are you?'

'Of course.'

'Then that's all that matters. Let's have something to eat, wait until the storm eases, and then set off.'

'Let's face the storm.'

'No, it's all right. Well, we can if you want, but the storm isn't a sign, it's just one of the consequences of the destruction of the Aral Sea.'

The furious wind is abating, and the horses seem to be galloping faster. We enter a kind of valley, and the landscape changes completely. The infinite horizon is replaced by tall, bare cliffs. I look to the right and see a bush full of ribbons.

'It was here! It was here that you saw … '

'No, my tree was destroyed.'

'So what's this, then?'

'A place where something very important must have happened.'

He dismounts, opens his saddlebag, takes out a knife, and cuts a strip off the sleeve of his shirt, then ties this to one of the branches. His eyes change; he may be feeling the presence beside him, but I prefer not to ask.

I follow his example. I ask for protection and help. I, too, feel a presence by my side: my dream, my long journey back to the woman I love.

We remount. He doesn't tell me what he asked for, and nor do I. Five minutes later, we see a small village of white houses. A man is waiting for us; he comes over to Mikhail and speaks to him in Russian. They talk for a while, then the man goes away.

'What did he want?'

'He wanted me to go to his house to cure his daughter. Nina must have told him I was arriving today, and the older people still remember my visions.'

He seems uncertain. There is no one else around; it must be a time when everyone is working, or perhaps eating. We were crossing the main road, which seemed to lead to a white building surrounded by a garden.

'Remember what I told you this morning, Mikhail. You might well just be an epileptic who refuses to accept the diagnosis and who has allowed his unconscious to build a whole story around it, but it could also be that you have a mission in the world: to teach people to forget their personal history and to be more open to love as pure, divine energy.'

'I don't understand you. All the months we've known each other, you've talked of nothing but this moment – finding Esther. And suddenly, ever since this morning, you seem more concerned about me than anything else. Perhaps Dos's ritual last night had some effect.'

'Oh, I'm sure it did.'

What I meant to say was: I'm terrified. I want to think about anything except what is about to happen in the next few minutes. Today, I am the most generous person on the face of this earth, because I am close to my objective and afraid of what awaits me. My reaction is to try and help others, to show God that I'm a good person and that I deserve this blessing that I have pursued so long and hard.

Mikhail dismounted and asked me to do the same.

'I'm going to the house of the man whose daughter is ill. I'll take care of your horse while you talk to Esther.'

He pointed to the small white building in the middle of the trees.

'Over there.'

I struggled to keep control of myself.

'What does she do?'

'As I told you before, she's learning to make carpets and, in exchange, she teaches French. By the way, although the carpets may look simple, they are, in fact, very complicated – just like the steppes. The dyes come from plants that have to be picked at precisely the right time, otherwise the colour won't be right. Then the wool is spread out on the ground, mixed with hot water, and the threads are made while the wool is still wet; and then, after many days, when the sun has dried them, the work of weaving begins. The final details are done by children. Adult hands are too big for the smallest, most delicate bits of embroidery.'

He paused.

'And no jokes about it being child's play. It's a tradition that deserves respect.'

'How is she?'

'I don't know. I haven't spoken to her for about six months.'

'Mikhail, these carpets are another sign.'

'The carpets?'

'Do you remember yesterday, when Dos asked me to choose my name, I told you the story of a warrior who returns to an island in search of his beloved? The island is called Ithaca and the woman is called Penelope. What do you think Penelope has been doing since Ulysses left? Weaving! She has been weaving a shroud for her father-in-law, Laertes, as a way of putting off her suitors. Only when she finishes the shroud will she remarry. While she waits for Ulysses to return, she unpicks her work every night and begins again the following day.

Her suitors want her to choose one of them, but she dreams of the return of the man she loves. Finally, when she has grown weary of waiting, Ulysses returns.'

'Except that the name of this village isn't Ithaca and Esther's name isn't Penelope.'

Mikhail had clearly not understood the story, and I didn't feel like explaining that it was just an example.

I handed him the reins of my horse and then walked the hundred metres that separated me from the woman who had been my wife, had then become the Zahir, and who was once more the beloved whom all men dream of finding when they return from war or from work.

I am filthy. My clothes and my face are caked with sand, my body drenched in sweat, even though it's very cold.

I worry about my appearance, the most superficial thing in the world, as if I had made this long journey to my personal Ithaca merely in order to show off my new clothes. As I walk the remaining one hundred metres, I must make an effort to think of all the important things that have happened during her – or was it my? – absence.

What should I say when we meet? I have often pondered this and come up with such phrases as: 'I've waited a long time for this moment' or 'I know now that I was wrong', or 'I came here to tell you that I love you', or even 'You're lovelier than ever.'

I decide just to say 'Hello'. As if she had never left. As if only a day had passed, not two years, nine months, eleven days and eleven hours.

And she needs to understand that I have changed as I've travelled through the same places she travelled through, places about which I knew nothing or in which I had simply never been interested. I had seen the scrap of bloodstained cloth in the hand of a beggar, in the hands of young people and adults in a Paris restaurant, in the hand of a painter, a doctor and a young man who claimed to see visions and hear voices. While I was following in her footsteps, I had got to know the woman I had married and had rediscovered, too, the meaning of my own life, which had been through so many changes and was now about to change again.

Despite being married all those years, I had never really known my wife. I had created a 'love story' like the ones I'd seen in the movies, read about in books and magazines, watched on TV. In my story, love was something that grew until it reached a certain size and, from then on, it was just a matter of keeping it alive, like a plant, watering it now and again and removing any dead leaves. 'Love' was also a synonym for tenderness, security, prestige, comfort, success. 'Love' could be translated into smiles, into words like 'I love you' or 'I feel so happy when you come home.'

But things were more complicated than I thought. I could be madly in love with Esther while I was crossing the road, and yet, by the time I had reached the other side, I could be feeling trapped and wretched at having committed myself to someone, and longing to be able to set off once more in search of adventure. And then I would think: 'I don't love her any more.' And when love returned with the same intensity as before, I would doubt it and say to myself: 'I must have just got used to it.'

Perhaps Esther had had the same thoughts and had said to herself: 'Don't be silly, we're happy, we can spend the rest of our lives like this.' After all, she had read the same stories, seen the same films, watched the same TV series, and although none of them said that love was anything more than a happy ending, why give herself a hard time about it? If she repeated every morning that she was happy with her life, then she would doubtless end up believing it herself and making everyone around us believe it too.

However, she thought differently and acted differently. She tried to show me, but I couldn't see. I had to lose her in order to understand that the taste of things recovered is the sweetest honey we will ever know. Now I was there, walking down a street in a tiny, cold, sleepy village, once again following a road because of her. The first and most important thread that bound me – 'all love stories are the same' – had broken when I was knocked down by that motorbike.

In hospital, love had spoken to me: 'I am everything and I am nothing. I am the wind, and I cannot enter windows and doors that are shut.'

And I said to love: 'But I *am* open to you.'

And love said to me: 'The wind is made of air. There is air inside your house, but everything is shut up. The furniture will get covered in dust, the damp will ruin the paintings and stain the walls. You will continue to breathe, you will know a small part of me, but I am not a part, I am Everything, and you will never know that.'

I saw that the furniture was covered in dust, that the paintings were being corroded by damp, and I had no alternative but to open the windows and doors. When I did that, the wind swept everything away. I wanted to cling on to my memories, to protect what I thought I had worked hard to achieve, but everything had disappeared and I was as empty as the steppes.

As empty as the steppes: I understood now why Esther had decided to come here. It was precisely because everything was empty that the wind brought with it new things, noises I had never heard, people with whom I had never spoken. I recovered my old enthusiasm, because I had freed myself from my personal history; I had destroyed the *acomodador* and discovered that I was a man capable of blessing others, just as the nomads and shamans of the steppes blessed their fellows. I had discovered that I was much better and much more capable than I myself had thought; age only slows down those who never had the courage to walk at their own pace.

One day, because of a woman, I made a long pilgrimage in order to find my dream. Many years later, the same woman had made me set off again, this time to find the man who had got lost along the way.

Now I am thinking about everything except important things: I am mentally humming a tune, I wonder why there aren't any cars parked here, I notice that my shoe is rubbing, and that my wristwatch is still on European time.

And all because a woman, my wife, my guide and the love of my life, is now only a few steps away; anything to fend off the reality I have so longed for and which I am so afraid to face.

I sit down on the front steps of the house and smoke a cigarette. I think about going back to France. I've reached my goal, why go on?

I get up. My legs are trembling. Instead of setting off on the return journey, I clean off as much sand from my clothes and my face as I can, grasp the door handle and go in.

Although I know that I may have lost for ever the woman I love, I must try to enjoy all the graces that God has given me today. Grace cannot be hoarded. There are no banks where it can be deposited to be used when I feel more at peace with myself. If I do not make full use of these blessings, I will lose them for ever.

God knows that we are all artists of life. One day, he gives us a hammer with which to make sculptures, another day he gives us brushes and paints with which to make a picture, or paper and a pencil to write with. But you cannot make a painting with a hammer, or a sculpture with a paintbrush. Therefore, however difficult it may be, I must accept today's small blessings, even if they seem like curses because I am suffering and it's a beautiful day, the sun is shining, and the children are singing in the street. This is the only way I will manage to leave my pain behind and rebuild my life.

The room was flooded with light. She looked up when I came in and smiled, then continued reading *A Time to Rend and a Time to Sew* to the women and children sitting on the floor, with colourful fabrics all around them. Whenever Esther paused, they would repeat the words, keeping their eyes on their work.

I felt a lump in my throat, I struggled not to cry, and then I felt nothing. I just stood studying the scene, hearing my words on her lips, surrounded by colours and light and by people entirely focused on what they were doing.

In the words of a Persian sage: Love is a disease no one wants to get rid of. Those who catch it never try to get better, and those who suffer do not wish to be cured.

Esther closed the book. The women and children looked up and saw me.

'I'm going for a stroll with a friend of mine who has just arrived,' she told the group. 'Class is over for today.'

They all laughed and bowed. She came over and kissed my cheek, linked arms with me, and we went outside.

'Hello,' I said.

'I've been waiting for you,' she said.

I embraced her, rested my head on her shoulder, and began to cry. She stroked my hair, and by the way she touched me I began to understand what I did not want to understand, I began to accept what I did not want to accept.

'I've waited for you in so many ways,' she said, when she saw that my tears were abating. 'Like a desperate wife who knows that her husband has never understood her life, and that he will never come to her, and so she has no option but to get on a plane and go back, only to leave again after the next crisis, then go back and leave and go back … '

The wind had dropped; the trees were listening to what she was saying.

'I waited as Penelope waited for Ulysses, as Romeo waited for Juliet, as Beatrice waited for Dante. The empty steppes were full of memories of you, of the times we had spent together, of the countries we had visited, of our joys and our battles. Then I looked back at the trail left by my footprints and I couldn't see you.

I suffered greatly. I realised that I had set off on a path of no return and that when one does that, one can only go forward. I went to the nomad I had met before and asked him to teach me to forget my personal history, to open me up to the love that is present everywhere. With him I began to learn about the Tengri tradition. One day, I glanced to one side and saw that same love reflected in someone else's eyes, in the eyes of a painter called Dos.'

I said nothing.

'I was still very bruised. I couldn't believe it was possible to love again. He didn't say much; he taught me to speak Russian and told me that in the steppes they use the word "blue" to describe the sky even when it's grey, because they know that, above the clouds, the sky is always blue. He took me by the hand and helped me to go through those clouds. He taught me to love myself rather than to love him. He showed me that my heart was at the service of myself and of God, and not at the service of others.

He said that my past would always go with me, but that the more I freed myself from facts and concentrated on emotions, the more I would come to realise that in the present there is always a space as vast as the steppes waiting to be filled up with more love and with more of life's joy.

Finally, he explained to me that suffering occurs when we want other people to love us in the way we imagine we want to be loved, and not in the way that love should manifest itself – free and untrammelled, guiding us with its force and driving us on.'

I looked up at her.

'And do you love him?'

'I did.'

'Do you still love him?'

'What do you think? If I did love another man and was told that you were about to arrive, do you think I would still be here?'

'No, I don't. I think you've been waiting all morning for the door to open.'

'Why ask silly questions, then?'

Out of insecurity, I thought. But it was wonderful that she had tried to find love again.

'I'm pregnant.'

For a second, it was as if the world had fallen in on me.

'By Dos?'

'No. It was someone who stayed for a while and then left again.'

I laughed, even though my heart was breaking.

'Well, I suppose there's not much else to do here in this one-horse town,' I said.

'Hardly a one-horse town,' she replied, laughing too.

'But perhaps it's time you came back to Paris. Your newspaper phoned me asking if I knew where to find you. They wanted you to report on a NATO patrol in Afghanistan, but you'll have to say "no".'

'Why?'

'Because you're pregnant! You don't want the baby being exposed to all the negative energy of a war, surely.'

'The baby? You don't think a baby's going to stop me working, do you? Besides, why should you worry? You didn't do anything to contribute.'

'Didn't contribute? It's thanks to me that you came here in the first place. Or doesn't that count?'

She took a piece of bloodstained cloth from the pocket of her white dress and gave it to me, her eyes full of tears.

'This is for you. I've missed our arguments.'

And then, after a pause, she added:

'Ask Mikhail to get another horse.'

I placed my hands on her shoulders and blessed her just as I had been blessed.

Author's Note

I wrote *The Zahir* between January and June 2004, while I was making my own pilgrimage through this world. Parts of the book were written in Paris and St Martin in France, in Madrid and Barcelona in Spain, in Amsterdam, on a road in Belgium, in Almaty and on the Kazakhstan steppes.

I would like to thank my French publishers, Anne and Alain Carrière, who undertook to check all the information about French law mentioned in the book.

I first read about the Favour Bank in *The Bonfire of the Vanities* by Tom Wolfe. The story that Esther tells about Fritz and Hans is based on a story in *Ishmael* by Daniel Quinn. The mystic quoted by Marie on the importance of remaining vigilant is Kenan Rifai. Most of what the 'tribe' in Paris say was told to me by young people who belong to such groups. Some of them post their ideas on the Internet, but it's impossible to pinpoint an author.

The lines that the main character learned as a child and remembers when he is in hospital ('When the Unwanted Guest arrives ... ') are from the poem 'Consoada' by the Brazilian poet Manuel Bandeira. Some of Marie's remarks following the chapter when the main character goes to the station to meet the American actor are based on a conversation with the Swedish actress Agneta Sjodin. The concept of forgetting one's personal history, which is part of many initiation traditions, is clearly set out in *Journey to Ixtlan* by Carlos Castaneda. The Law of Jante was developed by the Danish writer Aksel Sandemose in his novel *A Fugitive Crossing His Tracks*.

Two people who do me the great honour of being my friends, Dmitry Voskoboynikov and Evgenia Dotsuk, made my visit to Kazakhstan possible.

In Almaty, I met Imangali Tasmagambetov, author of the book *The Centaurs of the Great Steppe* and an expert on Kazakh culture, who provided me with much important information about the political and cultural situation in Kazakhstan, both past and present. I would also like to thank the President of the Republic, Nursultan Nazarbaev for making me so welcome, and I would like to take this opportunity to congratulate him for putting a stop to nuclear tests in his country, even though all the necessary technology is there, and for deciding instead to destroy Kazakhstan's entire nuclear arsenal.

Lastly, I owe many of my magical experiences on the steppes to my three very patient companions: Kaisar Alimkulov, Dos (Dosbol Kasymov), an extremely talented painter, on whom I based the character of the same name who appears at the end of the book, and Marie Nimirovskaya, who, initially, was just my interpreter but soon became my friend.

Life is a
journey

Make sure you don't miss a thing.
Live it with Paulo Coelho.

Could you be tempted into evil?

The inhabitants of a small town are challenged by a mysterious stranger to choose between good and evil.

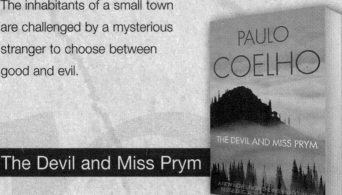

The Devil and Miss Prym

Can faith triumph over suffering?

Paulo Coelho's brilliant telling of the story of Elijah, who was forced to choose between love and duty.

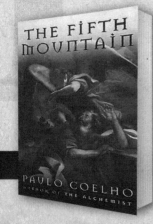

The Fifth Mountain